Broken Wings

By

Alexandrea Weis

World Castle Publishing
http://www.worldcastlelpublishing.com

ALEXANDREA WEIS

This is a work of fiction. Names, characters, places, and incidents are products of the author's imagination or are used fictitiously and are not to be construed as real. Any resemblance to actual events, locations, organizations, or person, living or dead, is entirely coincidental.

World Castle Publishing
Pensacola, Florida

Copyright © Alexandrea Weis 2012
ISBN: 9781937593360
First Edition World Castle Publishing February 14, 2012
http://www.worldcastlepublishing.com

Licensing Notes
All rights reserved. No part of this book may be used or reproduced in any manner whatsoever without written permission, except in the case of brief quotations embodied in articles and reviews.

Cover put together by: Karen Fuller
Photographer is John Snell
Editor: Maxine Bringenberg
A special thanks to John Snell for allowing us to use his photo.

DEDICATION

For all the wildlife I have rescued, rehabbed, fretted over, stayed up all night with, cried into their fur, and lost. Thank you to all of my wonderful wild babies. You have made my life complete.

ALEXANDREA WEIS

CHAPTER 1

Drab gray clouds covered the expansive horizon, obliterating the warmth of the sun. Like the delicate flora of nature covered by endless miles of sidewalks in some sprawling super city, the heavens above were suppressed behind a wall of lifeless color.

Pamela Wells stood in her back door and surveyed the sulking skies above. "It's an early spring sky," she mumbled.

Spring; thoughts of the season brought to mind frolicking bunnies and brightly colored birds preparing nests for much anticipated hatchlings. Everywhere animals would be shaking off their thick winter coats and embracing the start of a new reproductive cycle. But for Pamela, the warming breezes of the change in seasons were not always a welcomed event. She sighed as she turned her eyes to the expanse of land around her and contemplated the work that lay ahead. With the coming spring, Pamela knew all of her aches would return from their winter respite. But her pains were not limited to the constant throbbing in the various joints of her body; dark days brought an ache to her heart, as well. It was on such a day that she had met Robert, Bob to his friends. The memory of Robert Patrick dressed in his expensive tailored suit and designer Italian custom made shoes made Pamela laugh.

She had been lying in her hospital bed, days after a bad car accident, when Bob walked into her room. He was fresh out of law school and in desperate need of clients. After reading about her accident in the newspaper, Bob hunted Pamela down and signed her on as his first client. One year later, they married in a lavish ceremony inside St. Louis Cathedral in New Orleans.

Pamela shook her head. "Eight years after that, Bob turned into an asshole," she said as she gazed out at the barn behind her blue and white Acadian cottage. "Well, at least I got this place in the divorce," she whispered.

Meant as a get away from the urban overload of New Orleans, Bob bought the two-bedroom cottage on fifteen acres for Pamela as a wedding present. The wilds of St. Tammany Parish became her refuge when life as the wife of a prominent personal injury attorney had been too much for her. She moved into the cottage permanently almost six years ago when Bob unexpectedly announced that their marriage was over.

Out of nowhere, a wide raccoon with a slow, sauntering gait and a glint of childlike mischief in his masked eyes wandered up to Pamela. The raccoon stopped just below the three steps to Pamela's back porch and stood on his hind haunches. He looked at her and warbled in the way a raccoon baby calls to his mother.

"Good morning, Rodney," Pamela said to the raccoon as she walked down the steps to greet the animal. "How are you today?" She bent over and rubbed behind the raccoon's silver-tipped ears. Rodney fell on his back like a lump of whale blubber and proceeded to grab at the woman's hands and direct them to the spots on his belly that needed immediate scratching.

Pamela laughed and rubbed the animal's wide stomach as Rodney wiggled with delight. The sudden screech of an owl from a nearby tree frightened the raccoon. He jumped to a standing position and eyed a tree close to the house, snorting loudly.

Pamela patted the raccoon on his round bottom. "Relax, Rodney. You know Lester won't hurt you." She spied the owl up in the tree next to her bedroom window. "Lester, did you have a good night?"

The owl screeched again, opened his large brown and white checked wings and flapped vigorously upon his tree branch.

"Yes, I know you're hungry, Lester," Pamela said, nodding at the raptor. "But I have got baby squirrels to feed, and then there are cages to clean before you can have your ham and eggs."

The sound of a car driving down the gravel road toward the cottage made Pamela divert her attention away from the impatient owl. She turned and faced the road, just as Rodney came up beside her and wrapped his child-like arms around her lower leg.

A blue open-top Jeep Wrangler with wide off-road tires appeared from out of the brush at the end of her drive. Pamela observed the car with a feeling of trepidation sweeping through her. Strangers coming down the gravel road to her sanctuary were either delivering orphaned or injured wildlife to her care, or coming to deliver food and supplies to her wildlife sanctuary. But no one was ever unexpected at her facility, and uninvited strangers were never welcome. A cacophony of barking broke out from the direction of the front porch steps. The assorted stray dogs Pamela had collected through the years ran to greet the car as it came to a quick stop in front of the cottage. She walked toward the front of her home and watched tentatively as the dogs surrounded the Jeep.

A tall man with thick, dark brown hair and sunglasses stood up in the cab of the Jeep and peered down at her.

"Hey there," he said then glanced at a slip of paper in his hand. "Is this Second Chance Wildlife Rehabilitation Center?" he asked in a deep voice.

"Yes. Is there something I can do for you?" Pamela gave the man a curt nod of her head as the dogs around the car growled almost in unison.

"You want to call off the posse?" he said as he waved to the five dogs surrounding his Jeep.

Pamela folded her arms over her chest. "First, tell me who you are, and what you're doing out here?" she demanded as she tried to walk to the car, pulling Rodney along with her as he continued to cling to her leg.

The stranger removed his sunglasses. "Your facility requested a service worker to come out and help clean cages, right?" He shrugged his wide shoulders at her. "I'm your service worker," he declared.

"The probation office sent you?" Pamela frowned. "But they called and told me you were supposed to come next Wednesday. Today's Saturday."

"It's my day off and my probation officer said it would be all right." He made a move to step down from the Jeep, but the snarl of a tall, black Catahoula mix stopped him.

"Quincy," Pamela called out to the dog. "Go back to the porch." She pointed to the porch at the front of the house. Quincy, along with the rest of his canine pack, obediently obliged and made their way slowly to the porch steps.

Pamela waited for the dogs to settle down on the shady front porch before she looked back at her new service worker. "I'm Pamela Wells, the owner. Your probation officer told you what is expected around here? I don't tolerate drinking, cursing or—"

"Lewd or rude behavior," the man said, interrupting her as he stepped down from the Jeep. "Yeah, I got the memo. Don't worry, Ms. Wells, I will be like a choir boy in church while I am here."

"What's your name?"

"Daniel, Daniel Phillips." He hung his sunglasses on the neck of his white T-shirt as he looked her up and down. "You don't have a stable hand or someone to clean up around here?"

Pamela noticed that his round, dark brown eyes appeared almost black and had a seductive quality to them. She nervously cast her eyes to the ground. "I'd have to pay for help. This facility runs on a shoestring budget already. To hire someone would break me. Besides, there's not much to it." She noticed his expensive-looking leather boots. "You ever worked with wild animals before?"

Daniel laughed as he took a step closer to her. "Only the human kind. I deal with a lot of wild people at work."

Pamela glanced up at the man before her. He was dressed in old faded blue jeans and stood a good bit taller than she. He had a slender build, muscular arms, a broad chest, and long legs. His face was rectangular with a wide forehead and chiseled jaw. He did not look any older than his early thirties. A scar under his left eye made him appear more sinister than innocent, making Pamela suspect that this was not the first time Daniel Phillips had found himself under the direction of the courts and a probation officer.

She quickly checked her disconcerting thoughts. "Where do you work?" she asked, trying to sound more confident than she felt.

"Pat O'Brien's in the Quarter. I'm a bartender there."

"You're a bartender in the French Quarter?" Pamela asked, raising her brows at him.

"Yeah, I've worked at a couple of places in the Quarter. The Voodoo Lounge on Decatur, Muriel's on Jackson Square, and even did a few months at The Dungeon." Daniel carefully examined the slender woman before him.

Pamela found his dark eyes disturbing. She knew from experience that her slim figure and shoulder length dirty blond hair made her an easy target for a man's overactive imagination. But it was the way Daniel looked at her that rattled her so. It was almost as if he were sizing up her potential as a meal rather than a quick roll in the sheets.

He turned his eyes away from her and browsed the facility surrounding them. About a hundred yards from the rear of the house was an old battered blue barn with a few other smaller out buildings to the right of it. Located close to the barn, at the edge of the cleared property, were several tall wood-trimmed cages. Each cage was covered with wire, had a tin roof, and a water faucet attached right outside of the entrance. Majestic oaks were scattered about the property as well as next to the blue and white house. An open shed to the left of the property had a tractor, a white Ford pick-up truck, and two ATVs inside of it.

"You told my probation officer you needed someone to help out around here," he said as his eyes continued to scan the property.

"Yes, with spring finally here we will be swamped with babies soon. I've already gotten quite a few baby squirrels. The cages you will be cleaning are where I wintered several different animals. They have all just recently been released."

"What kind of animals do you usually get here?" Daniel kept his eyes on the trees along the edge of the clearing beside the house.

"Fox, rabbit, skunk, gray squirrel, fox squirrel, raccoon, opossum, bats, nutria, and an occasional river otter. But I have rehabbed chipmunks, beaver, a few owls, and once, a baby coyote."

"What about deer?"

"As a permitted wildlife rehabber, the Louisiana Wildlife and Fisheries does not want us working with deer. There has been an increase in a certain kind of wasting disease in the Louisiana deer population and most injured deer are put down, along with any fawns. Deer are also very hard to return to the wild once they have bonded with humans."

Daniel turned back at her. "So is this all there is to the place?"

"Why? What did you expect?"

He shrugged. "I don't know, something like the Audubon Zoo maybe."

Pamela focused her gray eyes on his. "This is not a zoo," she responded, indignantly. "It's a wildlife rehabilitation facility. We care for orphaned and injured wildlife and do not keep animals for display to an indifferent public. If more people knew about what we do here, they would, hopefully, be less willing to support zoos and more apt to make donations to a cause that puts animals back into their natural habitat." She gave the man another going over with her eyes as he stepped closer to her side. "What were you convicted of? I often have volunteers on the site and I want to make sure—"

"I'm not a serial rapist, Ms. Wells," Daniel proclaimed in a perturbed tone of voice. "I hit a guy in the bar where I work for roughing up his date. He filed charges and I was busted for assault and battery. My sentence was one hundred hours of community service. Satisfied?"

"Did they throw in any anger management classes with that community service?" she quipped.

Daniel smiled, cockily, revealing a row of perfectly white teeth. "No, the judge didn't seem to think I needed any." He stared into her face for a moment as if trying to figure her out. "So am I to call you Ms. Wells the entire time I'm here, or will Pamela be all right with you?" he questioned.

"Pamela is fine. We don't stand on formality around here." A loud sniff came from around Pamela's feet. She looked down at the ground to see Rodney standing behind her legs, staring at the stranger.

"One of the rehabilitated returned to the wild?" Daniel asked as he nodded to Rodney.

Pamela leaned over and picked up the overweight ring-tailed creature from the ground. The animal cuddled against her chest and warily watched the man standing next to her.

Pamela shifted the heavy animal in her arms. "This is Rodney. He was rescued from a hawk when he was about two weeks old. He's over a year now and I can't get him to leave. He thinks he is one of the dogs."

Daniel reached out to pet the raccoon, but the animal growled at him.

"He doesn't like strangers," Pamela quickly added. "All of the animals in this facility are wild. Do not pet them or try to treat them like a cute and cuddly lap dog."

"And are there any more like him?" he asked as he motioned to the raccoon nuzzling up against Pamela's neck.

"A few. You'll meet them later. For now, I'll show you to the cages that need cleaning." She turned away and started toward the row of cages and sheds located a short distance from the back of the house.

Daniel directed his attention to the blue and white wooden cottage on his right. The home appeared clean and well taken care of. But on closer inspection some shingles on the roof had cracked and were falling away, and the paint covering the wooden boards along the side of the house had begun to bubble up and peel off.

The house looked older, like many scattered around the countryside of Louisiana. It was an Acadian cottage that had been built when horse farms and cattle ranches had filled most of St. Tammany Parish. But such communities had long since given way to manicured subdivisions and posh country clubs as hurricane weary New Orleanians had left the city and taken over the lands north of Lake Pontchartrain.

"How many acres have you got here?" he asked, following her.

"Fifteen. There are another fifty acres behind this property that belongs to one of my patrons. So the animals have a large refuge to roam far away from any humans."

Daniel watched as the raccoon rested his head against the woman's shoulder as she carried him. "Is there any money in this sort of thing?"

Pamela stopped walking and turned to him. "There is no money here if that is what you're asking. Everything is for the animals," she said, scowling at him. "So if you are thinking you can steal from me, borrow equipment, or make a tidy profit from your time here, think again," she curtly added.

Daniel raised his hands up in submission. "Hey, don't get all bent out of shape, Pamela. I was just wondering why anyone would go to this much trouble for a bunch of stray squirrels."

Pamela shook her head in disgust, leaned over, and rubbed her cheek against the raccoon's fluffy face. "The cages are this way."

She quickly turned and started for the cages at the end of the clearing, leaving a wide-eyed Daniel to follow behind her.

* * * *

An hour later, Pamela was sitting on the back porch of her cottage feeding a three-week old baby gray squirrel with a small syringe.

"So what's this one's story?" a woman's voice asked behind her.

"Fell out of a tree and was dropped off last night by a lady from Ponchatoula," Pamela said, not looking up from the small gray shadow of fur as it sucked voraciously on a syringe filled with formula. The helpless creature's eyes were still closed and resembled a baby rat rather than a squirrel. Pamela delicately rubbed the animal's cheek to encourage it to continue to suckle.

"And how many is that now?" the voice persisted.

Pamela turned around and was immediately hit head on by a pair of pale blue eyes. The young woman standing behind her was short, round, had sharp features, and long, light brown hair pulled back in a ponytail.

"Fifteen gray squirrels. Why are you keeping count, Carol?" Pamela replied.

Carol Corbin was Pamela's accountant, manager, board member, and all around arranger of everything impossible. When the facility needed a new refrigerator, Carol found it. When the roof on the barn needed to be replaced, Carol got someone to donate the materials and found workers willing to help out. She was the glue that kept Pamela's little sanctuary held together.

"I thought you were going to tell everyone we have reached our limit as far as baby squirrels go," Carol said, placing her hands on her hips and frowning at Pamela.

"One more won't make any difference." Pamela shrugged as she glanced down at the tiny creature in her hands. "Besides, I don't have any raccoons or skunks in yet this year, so I can take in more baby squirrels."

Carol sighed. "Last year you kept saying you were going to cut back and we ended up with twenty-two baby gray squirrels, eighteen fox squirrels, fifteen baby raccoons, ten injured bats, nine rabbits, eight baby possums, six skunks, four fox kits, and one deranged owl."

"Lester is not deranged," Pamela clarified. "He just has issues."

"He lives on ham and eggs and thinks hunting is something you watch other birds do on the National Geographic Channel. Has he ever left the tree outside of your bedroom window?"

"He's working on it," Pamela defended, turning away from Carol. "Just last week he got down on the ground and walked over to my back porch," she proudly reported.

Carol folded her arms over her chest. "Let me guess, chocolate?"

Pamela shrugged. "Rice Krispie treats, but it's a step. It's the first time he has left the tree since he got here." She gently pulled the syringe out of the mouth of the baby squirrel in her hands.

"I know you created this place as a haven for the wildlife, but you have to be realistic. The donations are not flowing in like they used to and the budget is getting tight, real tight. You're going to have to accept the fact that we need to cut back on the amount of animals we take in. Between the formula, food, and vet bills, we are barely making it," Carol informed her.

Pamela kept her eyes on the bowl of formula as she refilled her syringe. "I could apply for another of those federal grants for wildlife rehabilitation. They have helped us out in the past."

Carol shook her head. "You know how much red tape and paperwork are involved with those grants. And after all the recent state and federal budget cuts, the competition for grant money to fund wildlife programs has become fierce. Besides, any grant could take several months to come through and we need an influx of cash now."

Pamela placed the syringe back in the baby squirrel's mouth. "I could go to Bob. He always said he would cover us if things got tight."

Carol took a seat on the porch next to Pamela. "You went to him last year when the air-conditioning had to be replaced in your house."

"But he would come through if I asked him," Pamela insisted.

Carol placed a concerned arm about Pamela's shoulder. "And how would Imelda feel about that? You two almost came to blows last year over the air conditioner."

Imelda was Carol's name for Bob's second wife, Clarissa. A social climbing court reporter, Clarissa Turner had married him three months after Bob and Pamela's divorce was final. She was a green-eyed beauty who had an affinity for designer clothes, lavish parties, and was known around town for her obsession with shoes. It was a running joke that Bob had bought their expensive mansion in the Garden District of New Orleans just to make room for all of Clarissa's shoes.

"Clarissa is not as bad as you make her out to be, Carol. She cares about this place," Pamela asserted. She gently started rubbing the squirrel's pink stomach as it sucked on the syringe.

Carol laughed and quickly removed her arm from Pamela's shoulder. "Are you kidding me? The only time the woman shows any interest in this place is when she is trying to get her name in the society pages of the *Times-Picayune*. And even when she does manage to get us any publicity, she insists that all of the donations be sent to her and not directly to you. Probably so she can buy that Chinese baby she keeps talking about adopting."

Pamela pulled the syringe away from the baby squirrel and placed it back in the bowl of formula. "You know Bob doesn't want to adopt a kid. He never wanted kids."

"Then why did he divorce you?!" Carol said, raising her voice. "I thought you told me Bob wanted the divorce because you couldn't have children."

Pamela wrapped the baby squirrel in the towel she had sitting on her lap. "Bob didn't leave me because I couldn't have children. He left because I have lupus. He could not stand the thought of having a chronically ill wife."

"So much for in sickness and in health," Carol commented as she patted Pamela's shoulder. "Bob always was a bit of a backstabbing son of a bitch, if you ask me. I guess that's why he became such a successful attorney." She stood up and looked down at Pamela. "But you can't always depend on him to solve your financial problems, Pamie."

"Don't call me that, Carol." She frowned. "You know I hate that name." She paused for a moment as she rubbed the small squirrel's round, pink stomach. "Anyway, there is always the settlement fund, if I need money," she added.

Carol stomped her foot defiantly on the ground. "No, the money from your accident is your nest egg. You depleted half of it when you got this place up and running. As your accountant and your friend, I cannot stand by and let you squander anymore of it.

That money is for when you really need it. In case you get sick and…" Carol left the sentence unfinished.

The "what ifs" had been hanging over Pamela's head like a noose ever since she was first diagnosed with her chronic disease. It was not a possible death sentence that she feared. No individual afflicted with such a disorder feared death; they feared loosing control of their life. Lupus had robbed her of her marriage, her chance at motherhood, her health and, at times, her sanity. But she had secretly vowed that she would never let it take away her one form of happiness: her sanctuary.

"You worry too much, Carol." Pamela stood from the porch still holding the towel in her hands. "You know I would rather have that money go to helping these animals than paying doctor bills."

"You can't go on forever, Pamie. One day you will have to slow down and hand this place over to someone who has the money and the connections to keep it going."

"Don't bring that up again, Carol. You and I both know what Bob will do to this place if he ever gets his hands on it. Or even worse, if Clarissa gets her hands on it," Pamela said, raising her voice slightly. "She would kick all of the animals out and turn it into an exclusive retreat for overweight French poodles."

"Well, if you can't keep up with the taxes and the overhead, that, or something equally disturbing, will happen," Carol affirmed.

"As long as Bob's name is on the mortgage, I'm stuck with him as a silent partner. Until I'm financially viable, I'll never be rid of him, you know that."

"Then let's find another patron, a richer one."

Pamela frowned at her. "What do you suggest I do, Carol? Tack on a pair of pasties, head down to Bourbon Street, and sleep with the first man that flashes a blank check in my face?"

Carol laughed. "That would be a start." She shook her head and focused her pale blue eyes on Pamela. "Honestly, if I had your package I would be out there hunting for the first man I came across with a pulse and a high credit score. You spend every day and night up to your elbows in animals. When was the last time you even had a date?"

"I don't have time to date!" Pamela shouted.

"No, you don't want to date." Carol crossed her arms over her chest. "Last year, that fine looking vet kept making excuses to stop by. He asked you out a dozen times. What was his name?"

"Gary Levy."

"So why didn't you go out with him?"

Pamela could feel the tiny squirrel squirming around inside of the towel in her hands. She took a breath and let it out slowly. "Men don't want me, Carol. I'm too old and once they find out I have–"

"Forty-one is not old!" Carol chimed in. "And have you seen the way half of the deliverymen look at you when they come in here? Trust me, men want you and they won't give a damn about your disease. Bob is not representative of the entire male population, Pamie. Just because he reacted the way he did to your lupus does not mean that another man will be such a heartless asshole." She threw her hands up in the air and laughed. "Christ, everyone has got something wrong with them. No one is perfect."

Pamela nodded and tried to force back the slow grinding tension rising from the pit of her stomach. "But everyone does judge you when you have lupus. Many people don't know anything about my disease, and I don't want a man to only consider my limitations before he ever gets to know my possibilities."

Carol stood in silence before her, as Pamela watched the woman's pale blue eyes sink in resignation.

"All right," Carol said, waving her hand in the air. "Lecture over. But I want you to at least consider dating someone." She winked. "Preferably someone rich, but I'm not picky. I would go for someone moderately comfortable if it will get you laid."

"Carol!" Pamela tried to look shocked, but instead found she was fighting to stifle a girlish giggle. "My sex life, or lack thereof, is none of your business."

Carol rolled her eyes. "Honey, your sex life is my only business. Because any man that can get into your jeans will not only have to love animals, but will have to find a way to make you think he loves animals. And the only way any man will successfully be able do that is with a fat checkbook."

"Really, Carol you make me sound like some—"

"Who's that?" Carol quickly asked as she looked out toward the cages along the edge of the cleared property.

Pamela followed her line of sight until she saw Daniel. He was naked from the waist up, hosing out cages at the other end of the clearing. She stood there frozen for a moment as she watched his water-covered chest glistening in the mid-morning sunlight.

Pamela gasped. "Shit!"

Carol turned to her. "What is it?"

Pamela nodded in Daniel's direction. "That's the guy the parole office sent over to clean cages."

Carol raised her eyebrows as she stared at Daniel. "Him? Man, we need to call them more often."

"Not funny." Pamela handed the towel with the baby squirrel inside to Carol. "The guy needs to put his shirt back on. This is not a Chippendales nightclub. This is a family friendly facility, for God's sake!"

"Oh, please!" Carol laughed. "That is the first fine piece of man meat I have seen since I went into the city and got shit-faced at Pat O'Brien's last year."

"Yeah, well, maybe you saw him." Pamela headed toward the back steps. "He works as a bartender at Pat O'Brien's."

"Oh, this morning is just getting better and better," Carol remarked.

Pamela glanced back to her just as she reached the bottom step. "It won't be so good when twenty prepubescent Girl Scouts and their mother's pull up and see a half-naked man on my property."

Carol smiled at her. "Pamela, right now it's not the Girl Scouts getting bent out of shape by the half-naked man. It's you."

BROKEN WINGS

Pamela stormed down the steps and across the green grass toward the back row of cages. She could feel her anger coming to a steady boil as she watched the man flexing his muscles as he scrubbed the outside of the cage. All she could see was his nude upper body glaring at her from across the yard. In her head, she could hear the screams of frightened Girl Scouts as their mother's insisted they quickly depart the depraved wildlife center.

"What do you think you are doing?" Pamela snapped as she came up to Daniel's side.

Daniel glanced over at her and then down at the scrub brush in his hand. "What does it look like I'm doing?" His dark eyes flashed with irritation. "And what the hell did you keep in this cage? It stinks!"

"Four fox kits. Their urine is almost as bad as a skunk's spray."

Pamela felt her stomach do an uneasy flip as she watched the man's eyes slice into hers. She walked over to the side of the cage where he had hung his white T-shirt to keep it from getting wet. She angrily pulled the shirt off the wire cage and turned to Daniel.

"Put your shirt back on." She handed the T-shirt to him. "This is not some bar in the French Quarter where women throw money at you to see your bare chest. I've got a busload of Girl Scouts coming today and the last thing I need them to see is your half-naked ass in my facility."

He grinned. "It's not my ass that's naked, Pamela." He threw the scrub brush on the ground and wiped his hands on his jeans. "I'm sorry. Since so many women throw money at me to see my half-naked body, I figured you wouldn't mind."

"I don't give a damn if you parade around here buck naked, but when I have guests coming, guests who could be potential benefactors, then I do care."

Daniel reached out and took the shirt from her hands. Then Pamela saw the three circular scars on the man's chest and right shoulder. The scars were unmistakable to Pamela: gunshot wounds. Having worked as an EMT on the dangerous streets of New Orleans, she was well acquainted with scars of that type. It was the first thing she had searched for on any victim of violent crime. Most recipients of gunshot, or knife-related injuries, bragged about their past encounters and were proud to discuss each and every scar on their body. She had seen boys no more than fourteen show off their old wounds like medals of honor garnered for service in a war no one was ever meant to win.

She redirected her eyes from his chest to the ground. She hated being right about people, especially when her thoughts tended to emphasize the negative rather than the positive. But she felt assured that her initial instincts about Daniel Phillips had been correct.

Daniel put his T-shirt back on and picked up his scrub brush from the ground. "I'll try not to further offend your delicate sense of decency."

Pamela gave him a smug grin and folded her arms across her chest. "Listen, I really don't give a shit what you think of me—"

He held up his long, slender hand stopping her tirade. "Shit does not suit you. Why don't you try darn, or even damn, but not shit. You don't look like the kind of woman who should use such profanities."

"What in the hell is that supposed to mean? What kind of woman do you think I am?" she shouted.

He grinned as he pointed the scrub brush at her. "Your looks and manners scream of an upper class kind of background. Your pale skin and delicate features mean you have probably never done a hard day's work in your life. And this place?" He waved his hand around the facility surrounding them. "Only a bored housewife looking to show off her altruistic side to her posh friends would waste her days chasing flea-infested fuzz balls around a makeshift petting zoo."

"Well, at least I don't have three gun shot wounds in my chest. And how did you come by those, Mr. Phillips? Protecting the patrons of your bar from mass slaughter?"

"Why you little..." he let the words die on his lips. "You don't know anything about me, Ms. Wells. And do not even begin to think that because I have a few scars on my body that I have led a depraved—"

".9 mm I would think by the look of the entrance wounds," Pamela stated, cutting him off.

Daniel stopped and stared at her for a moment. He cocked his head to the side. "How in the hell did you know it was a .9 mm?"

Pamela raised her chin and gave him a condescending gaze with her cool gray eyes. "Every bored housewife knows the difference between—"

"Hey!" A voice shouted behind them.

Pamela and Daniel turned to see Carol standing there waving her hands frantically in the air.

Carol walked over to Pamela's side. "Do you two want to keep it down to a dull roar over here? I got a busload of girls dressed in funky green outfits that are asking where all the screaming is coming from."

"They're here? Already?" Pamela bit her lower lip and looked back toward the house.

Carol nodded. "Yes ma'am; to the Girl Scouts, being on time ranks right up there with cajoling people into buying truckloads of tasteless cookies."

"Carol!" Pamela glared back at her friend. "Keep your voice down." She turned to Daniel. "I think you and I are finished here, Mr. Phillips. You can pack up and get the hell off of my property."

"Ignore her," Carol said, sticking out her hand to Daniel. "She just has PMS; fires everybody when she's in a crappy mood. I'm Carol Corbin, Pamela's accountant and second in command around here."

Daniel took the round woman's hand. "Daniel Phillips."

"Carol, stop undermining me!" Pamela exclaimed.

Carol took a step back from Daniel. "Give the guy a break, Pamie. He took off his shirt, so what?" Carol grinned at Daniel. "Loved your beefcake display, by the way. It added a real zing to my morning." She patted Pamela on the arm. "Pamie's too."

Daniel ran his hand through his thick, brown hair. "Really? I got the distinct impression Ms. Wells was not at all pleased with my beefcake display."

"Trust me, unless you have fur covering some unseen portion of that body of yours, she won't be interested," Carol said with a dismissive wave of her hand.

Daniel raised his dark brows. "Lesbian?"

"Worse. Frustrated, if you know what I mean," Carol confided as she winked at Daniel.

"All right!" Pamela called out as she stepped in between them. "Enough." She waved her hand at Daniel and sighed. "You can finish out the day, Daniel." A sudden jolt of pain gripped Pamela's elbow. She winced as she pulled her arm against her chest.

"You okay?" Carol asked.

Pamela grimaced again and then nodded. "Just a bad day." She gave Daniel one last reproach with her eyes and turned away. She started back to the house, still cradling her arm against her body.

Daniel watched as the pale, slender woman slowly made her way to the blue and white cottage. "She all right?" he asked as he nodded after Pamela.

"She has bad days. They seem to be coming more often lately," Carol disclosed as her eyes followed Pamela. "Trying to keep this place going is taking its toll on her."

"Why doesn't she give it up?" Daniel asked.

"This place is all she's got. It's the only thing that keeps her from completely falling apart. She tries to act brave, but the stress is wearing her down. And God knows her body doesn't need anymore stress."

"Is something wrong with her?"

Carol sighed and turned to Daniel. "The medical term for what she has is systemic lupus erythematosus. It's more commonly known as lupus."

"Lupus? I'm not sure of what that is," he said, furrowing his brow.

"Pamela's immune system has trouble telling the difference between her body and a foreign body, like a virus. It attacks her joints and can destroy major organs, like her kidneys, liver, lungs, and heart."

Daniel felt his gut recoil with reproach as he reflected on his previous exchange with Pamela Wells. He wiped his hand across his face. "Christ, I didn't know. I shouldn't have been egging her on the way I did. Will she be all right?"

"She's not broken, only bruised, Daniel. Her lupus causes pain and swelling in her joints. It comes on suddenly and can last for an hour or a day. She manages with it but some days are worse than others. Anyway, she doesn't like to be handled with kid gloves. The woman is a lot tougher than she looks. My father always said she was one of the toughest women he ever met."

"Your father knows Pamela?"

"Knew her; he died a long time ago," Carol corrected. "He was her partner when she worked as an EMT in New Orleans."

Daniel's face dropped. "She was an EMT?"

"Yep, a pretty good one, so I was told. Gave it up after the accident."

"What accident?"

"She and my dad were transporting a patient to the emergency room when they were hit head on by a drunk driver. Apparently, Pamela broke her ribs in the collision, but that didn't stop her from trying to save my father's life. After my father was pronounced dead at the scene, Pamela finally agreed to let the rescue workers take her to the closest hospital. Once in the emergency room, Pamela's condition quickly deteriorated. The next day she woke up in the ICU with a chest tube and a large incision down her abdomen. Her broken ribs had punctured her right lung and she had ruptured her spleen." Carol smiled. "Like I said, she is a lot tougher than she looks. After that, she kept tabs on me and was a good friend to my mother. When I finished college, I offered to come out here and help her run this place." Carol gazed about the facility. "Yeah, this has always been her dream. Save the world by saving one flea-infested fuzz ball at a time."

Daniel shook his head. "You heard that?"

Carol laughed. "Me, and all of the jolly green midgets scampering off of the yellow school bus heard it." She studied Daniel for a moment. "You got quite a way with words, Mr. Phillips. Where did you hone those oratory skills of yours, or do all bartenders possess such a colorful vocabulary?"

"Only the ones with Harvard educations."

Carol grinned. "Harvard, eh? Well, there seems to be more to you than meets the eye, Mr. Phillips."

"Carol!" Pamela's voice boomed across the compound toward them.

Carol turned back to the house. "Ah, my master's voice." She glanced back at Daniel. "I know you may think Pamela an uptight prude, but she is one of the best people I know, and I would really be disturbed to see you upsetting her any further."

Daniel grinned, playfully. "How disturbed?"

Carol smiled. "Lets just say I got an A+ in my torture and intimidation classes at college."

"Where did you study? Fort Bragg?" Daniel asked, looking amused.

"No, University of New Orleans. Any good accounting program makes such courses compulsory for their students. Where do you think IRS agents come from?"

Carol quickly turned on her heels and headed toward the waiting Girl Scouts, leaving a bewildered Daniel Phillips to his dirty cages.

CHAPTER 2

Daniel busied himself around the facility, cleaning cages and restocking them with hay and assorted scrap cloth. As he tried to concentrate on the job at hand, he could not help but let his eyes wander across the clearing to the slender blond leading a group of eager-faced girls dressed in green uniforms. Pamela Wells was enlivened as she pointed out the different animals still housed in their cages to the Girl Scouts. Her heart-shaped face almost glowed as she talked about each and every animal. She appeared relaxed as she laughed and interacted with the children; not at all like the rigid and uptight woman he had first met. She looked different, more approachable, more attractive even. He reflected on all that he had learned of her through Carol and frowned. He should have tried harder to make a good first impression with Pamela Wells and kept his eyes focused above her bust line. But he always physically evaluated every woman he met; it was just the nature of sex, he reasoned. He could not help it if he found the distant Ms. Wells attractive.

Daniel quickly silenced his runaway libido. He knew this was the type of woman he should keep out of his thoughts. She had the face and figure that could haunt a man for a very long time, but the high walls in which she had encased herself made Daniel wary of getting to know her better than he already had. For a woman who should have everything going for her, he wondered why she seemed to be running away from all that she could offer any man. It was as if she had purposely closed off the most attractive portions of herself to ensure no man would ever want to get too close.

Daniel laughed to himself as he finished putting the last bit of the scrap cloth into one of the cages.

"You're no prize either, Daniel Phillips," he quietly scolded.

But as he observed Pamela engaging the young girls in front of a cage of bouncing rabbits, he wondered if he hadn't been a bit rough on her. And when Pamela turned her gray eyes to him from across the clearing, Daniel felt his frustration with the woman give way to a more intriguing feeling.

"Maybe I should start over with the elusive Pamela Wells," he mumbled as he let a slow smile spread across his lips.

Everyone deserves a second chance, his mother had always told him. No matter if they are friend or foe, second chances are fate's way of showing you just how wrong first impressions can be.

* * * *

After the busload of Girl Scouts had left her facility laughing and filled with happy memories, Pamela settled her aching body on the green couch in her living room/office. Scattered about the old rolltop desk in the corner and piled up on the hardwood floor were stacks of bills and wildlife magazines. Located behind the living room was a yellow kitchen with two refrigerators; one marked for human food, the other for animal food. In the breakfast area, on top of a round breakfast table, was an assortment of square plastic containers with small, circular air holes drilled into the sides and lids. Inside the containers, mounds of felt strips could be seen moving with an occasional baby squirrel head peeping out from beneath its protective coverings. On the opposite wall from the kitchen was an old television and satellite dish receiver sitting on an oak entertainment center. Next to the entertainment center was a long wooden table with a laptop computer, printer, and large wire cage on top of it. Inside the open cage a very round gray squirrel sat contentedly eating a pecan.

"Louis," Pamela said as she looked at the squirrel. "I'm exhausted."

The squirrel took no notice of Pamela and continued to enjoy his nut.

A knock at the front door made Pamela sigh and reluctantly get up from her couch. She walked across the living room to the door and opened it.

Daniel was there, holding up a piece of white paper. "I need you to sign off on my time sheet before I go," he said, nodding to the paper in his hand.

She moved back from the door and waved him into her home. "Come in. I'll just get a pen."

Daniel stepped inside and took in the cluttered living room. "I think your animals live better than you do."

Pamela ignored his comment and went over to her rolltop desk. After shuffling around some papers to find a pen, she turned back to Daniel.

"Is that another of the successfully rehabbed?" he asked, pointing at Louis in his cage.

Pamela smiled affectionately as she nodded to the squirrel. "No, this is my baby boy, Louis." She walked over to the cage and reached in to gently rub the squirrel's head.

Louis, more interested in his nut than the affection, never stopped munching.

"He was a Katrina baby. He injured his back in a fall from a tree during the storm and could never be released. He can't climb very well, or jump, like a normal squirrel. He was just one of the many victims of that storm. The kind the media didn't bother to tell you about. We got a ton of injured and orphaned wildlife in after Katrina. But there was no extra funding for us, no government grants, no FEMA money, and no help to take care of all of the wildlife we were given." She rubbed the squirrel's head once more. Louis tilted his head slightly to the side as he ate his nut so Pamela's fingers could scratch just the right spot. "As wildlife rehabbers we are supposed to put all animals that can't be rehabilitated to sleep, but I just couldn't do that to him. So he lives in here with me."

Daniel watched the way the woman's gray eyes shined when she handled the squirrel. She seemed so different when she spoke of her animals. Every ounce of coldness he had seen in her earlier that day instantly vanished.

"You really love animals, don't you?" he quietly said.

Pamela snickered. "I wouldn't go to all of this trouble if I didn't. Animals are the victims of our society. We raise them in cages to feed on them, chase them out of their habitats, abuse them for their coats, and treat them as furniture in our homes. If you ask me they are the meek, and one day—"

"The meek shall inherit the earth," Daniel said, finishing her words for her.

Pamela nodded. "Yes. They are living beings with emotions and souls, just like us. If the human race can't be kind to animals, then how in the hell are we going to be kind to each other?"

Daniel felt his usually impenetrable resolve weakening as he looked at the quirky woman standing in her cluttered living room. He took a step closer to her. "I should apologize to you for the things I said earlier. I was out of line."

Pamela waved a weary hand in his direction. "Forget about it." She moved across the room toward him. "Let's just say we had a misunderstanding and leave it at that."

"I would like to make it up to you."

Pamela eyed him suspiciously.

Daniel just smiled. "This house could use some work. Why don't you let me do some repairs for you? I could patch up the broken shingles on the roof and repaint the exterior for starters."

Pamela stood for a moment trying to gauge the depth of his sincerity.

"That is work I cannot apply to your community service," she finally said.

"I don't care about that." Daniel shrugged off her concern. "I just want to help out a little. You look like you could use it. Anyone dedicated to a good cause deserves a little help, don't you think?"

Pamela shook her head and took the white piece of paper out of his hand. "Thanks, but no thanks, Daniel. We can get along just fine without your charity."

Pamela took the paper over to a nearby end table and hastily scribbled her name on it.

"Look, I know you think I'm some kind of thug," Daniel began behind her. "But I would like to help out here. I saw you with those Girl Scouts today; the way you lit up when you showed them the animals you are helping here. And I have to admit I was wrong about you. You come across as a real snob but—"

"I do not come across as a snob!" she refuted as she spun around to face him.

"Yes, Pamela, you do. You try and hide the real you from everyone because you think—"

"Don't do that," she angrily cut in.

"Do what?" he questioned, taken aback by her hostility.

"Pretend that you know me. We just met this morning. You know nothing about me."

He ran his hand through his dark hair, trying to control his growing sense of frustration with the woman. "I know a lot more than you think," he mumbled.

Pamela stubbornly folded her arms over her chest. "Okay. Let's hear it. What do you think you know about me?"

Daniel folded his arms over his chest and stared her down. "You're stubborn for starters. You're tougher than you look, or at least you try to be. You prefer to do everything yourself. You think no one takes you seriously because of your beauty, so you work even harder to be seen as woman of intelligence. You're suspicious of strangers, probably a vegetarian." He playfully raised his eyebrows. "And you don't like asking for help, even when you need it."

"Congratulations, you have probably just described half of the female population in the United States."

"Not the half I've known. And none of them have been like you," he said as he inspected her again with his dark eyes.

"Your bedpost must be quite the conversation piece," she remarked.

He smirked at her. "I've been around enough women to know when they are looking for a savior, a father figure, a sinner, or a saint. Most women want help, especially from a man. You seem to resent help from men."

She turned around, picked up the white slip of paper from the end table, and walked over to him.

"Is that your expert opinion? How comforting it must be for you to know that all of your horizontal study has afforded you the opportunity to pass judgment on me." She watched him take the signed form from her hand.

"I wasn't passing judgment, just making an observation," he calmly stated as he folded the form and put it in his pocket. "And I'm not an expert on women. No man will ever accomplish that feat," he added with a grin.

She raised her chin defiantly to him. "So how do a few random one-night stands give you insight into what a woman wants or needs from a man?"

He peered into her eyes. "I can usually figure out what a woman wants from me within the first few seconds. They all have a pretty damn predictable set of criteria, or at least I thought so until today. But you aren't looking for anything from anybody. You only show your emotions to your animals, don't you?"

Pamela kept her eyes on his. "In my experience, animals are safer to care about than people. My mother was one of those women who always required help from other people, especially men. She spent her entire life looking through the bottom of a vodka bottle for someone to make everything wonderful for her. The only problem was, by the time she sobered up and figured out that only she could make her life wonderful, she died."

Daniel sighed as a ripple of regret passed through him. "How old were you when she died?"

"Thirteen."

"What about your father?"

"My father was the one who raised me. My mother wasn't exactly the maternal kind."

He gazed about the living room. "Is that why I don't see any family pictures on the walls?"

"What are you, a shrink?" She went around him and made her way to the front door. "I want to thank you for coming out and helping us. If I ever need your services again, I'll let your probation officer know."

He followed behind her. "You're not getting rid of me that easily. I told you I would be back to fix up your place."

She turned back and glared at him. "I don't want you coming back."

"Afraid I'll steal the family silver?"

"Something like that, yes," she replied as she opened the front door.

He came up to her. "For a woman who doesn't like being judged, you are sure quick to judge others."

"One of my many, many flaws," she asserted with a sarcastic smile.

"Fine," he said as he walked out the door. "Perhaps you should start taking chances on people, Ms. Wells, instead of always taking chances on animals."

"Duly noted. Thanks for coming, Mr. Phillips," she stated, and then slammed the door behind him.

Pamela went back to the couch and plopped her aching body down on the soft fabric. Looking over at Louis in his cage, still munching away on his pecan, she wished at that moment that she could be like her squirrel. She wanted to be left alone, unperturbed by the world around her, and able to find pleasure in the taste of a simple nut.

CHAPTER 3

Three days later Daniel returned. The back of his Jeep was crammed full with roofing materials and paint. Across the roll bars on top of the Jeep, he had secured his ladder. When he pulled up in front of the blue and white Acadian cottage, there was no one around. But before he had even turned the engine off, the pack of stray dogs that hung out on the front porch made for his car.

Daniel sat in his Jeep, not wanting to face the snarling teeth of Pamela's overzealous four-legged burglar alarm. The pack ranged in size from a small chiweenie to the monster Catahoula mix named Quincy. A few minutes later, Pamela emerged from the house, gingerly carrying a towel in her hands. She stopped on the porch and caught sight of his Jeep.

"Guys, calm down," she called to the barking dogs.

Instantly, the pack backed away from Daniel's Jeep and headed to the porch.

"I'm glad to see that the posse is always on patrol," Daniel said as he climbed out of the Jeep.

Pamela came down the steps to the gravel drive. "What are you doing here?"

Daniel waved to the back of his Jeep. "I told you I was going to fix up your house."

Pamela walked up to the car. "And I told you I didn't want your help."

"Lucky for you I'm one of those men who doesn't pay a whole lot of attention to what women tell me," he smartly remarked as he went around to the back of his Jeep.

"So what? Are you are just going to ignore my wishes and fix up my house anyway?"

"Something like that, yeah." He smiled at her as he pulled a roll of roofing felt out of the back of the car.

Carol came out on the front porch, carrying a cup of coffee in her hands. She waved at Daniel. "Couldn't stay away, huh?"

"Nope," he answered as he carried the roll of felt over to the side of the house.

"Carol!" Pamela cried out. "Tell this man to leave. I don't want his charity."

"Well, I do," Carol admitted as she made her way to the edge of the porch. "Your house could use some work. It's beginning to look like something one of those weird animal hoarders would live in."

"Don't consider it charity," Daniel told Pamela as he walked to the Jeep. "Consider it a donation."

"Yeah, Pamie," Carol added from the porch. "Consider it a donation."

"You two are impossible." Pamela ran back up the porch steps still carrying the towel in her hands. "Fine, do what you like. I have babies to feed," she grumbled over her shoulder, and stormed back into the house.

Carol raised her mug of coffee to Daniel. "I think you're growing on her," she said with a playful grin.

Daniel just shook his head and lifted a can of paint from the back of his Jeep.

Once back inside the house, Carol found Pamela sitting on the floor of her kitchen, holding a tiny baby gray squirrel in her lap. She watched, fascinated, as Pamela fed the animal formula drop by drop with a small syringe. It amazed her at times how much patience her friend always seemed to have with these animals. But when confronted by someone like Daniel Phillips, Pamela became like a snapping turtle, eager to bite off the man's fingers with her powerful jaws.

"You could give the guy a break," Carol proposed as she leaned against the entrance to the hallway.

"He's a bartender from New Orleans who beats up his customers. Now why should I give him a break?"

"He also studied at Harvard."

Pamela frowned. "How do you know that?"

"He told me."

Pamela glanced up at Carol and then she snickered. "And you believed him?"

"Of course," Carol shrugged as she took another sip from her coffee mug. "They're not all out to get you, you know."

Pamela turned her attention back to the baby squirrel in her hands. "What are you talking about?"

"Men. You think every one of them has some ulterior motive for talking to you or doing anything for you."

"Men always have ulterior motives, Carol. That's what makes them men."

"The guy drove up here from the city, bought supplies to fix your house, and hasn't so much as asked you for a cup of coffee, let alone a date. So what's your problem with him?"

Pamela shook her head. "I have a hard enough time letting people I know into my life. How do you expect me to accept a stranger just like that?"

Carol lazily pushed her body away from the wall. "I've got to head over to my office and get some work done." She placed her mug down on the old brown and white tiled counter in the kitchen. "Sometimes people come into your life for a reason, Pamie. Just like the animals. You always said every animal that you have rehabbed has changed you in some way. People can do the same thing, but you have to let them in first so you can find out how they will change you." Carol walked over to the couch and picked up her five-gallon purse. "You once told me your biggest fear was being a burden to someone. And I have often wondered if that's the reason you have fought so hard to be alone. But the one thing you've never stopped to consider is that you will never be a burden to anyone who loves you."

Carol placed her purse over her shoulder and then walked to the front door. She opened the door and without looking back quietly exited the house.

Pamela felt her heart sink as she mulled over Carol's words. Inside she wished it could be that easy for her; to just accept people into her life and not give a second thought as to the consequences. But like a prophet privileged to see the future, Pamela knew exactly how any relationship with the impossible Daniel Phillips would end. And the thought of giving in to those long dormant desires scared her more than a lifetime filled with frozen dinners for one.

* * * *

After feeding all of the baby squirrels inside of her house, Pamela ventured out to the front porch to look for her uncannily quiet handyman. She found him on the side of her house, frozen atop his ladder and starring into the oak tree next to her bedroom window.

She came up alongside of his ladder and gazed up at him. "Is something wrong?" she asked.

He did not move, but appeared to talk very slowly out of the corner of his mouth. "There is a big ass owl up here staring at me like it's going to rip my eyes out."

Pamela laughed and started to climb up the ladder behind him. "Oh, I forgot to tell you about him. That's Lester. He won't hurt you."

As Daniel looked down at her, Lester let out an ear-splitting screech.

"Oh, Lester, hush up," Pamela scolded as she waved her hand at the large brown owl.

"Jesus!" Daniel grabbed for his chest. "That thing wants to kill me."

Pamela came up right below him on the ladder. She reached out to the tree and began to stroke the owl's wing. "He's really a pussycat when you get to know him. He already ate this morning so I can guarantee he has no interest in you. That is unless you are carrying any chocolate on you."

Daniel caught his breath. "Chocolate?"

"He loves chocolate. Only comes out of the tree for it. Otherwise he stays up there all day and all night."

Daniel rubbed his hand across his sweaty forehead. "I've been sitting up here for thirty minutes afraid to move or make a sound in case that thing went after me." He shook his head. "And then you come out here and tell me the damned owl only eats chocolate." He stared down at Pamela. "What kind of place are you running here?"

"Oh, Lester eats ham and eggs, too. I only give him chocolate on special occasions," she confided with a smug grin on her face.

Pamela started back down the ladder and Daniel quickly followed behind her. When they reached the ground, Pamela noticed the man's dark blue T-shirt was soaked through. She did not think it was warm enough for him to be overheated.

"Are you all right?" she asked as she watched his eyes dart back and forth across the compound.

He wiped his hand across his sweaty brow. "I just don't like being cornered like that." He leaned over and grabbed his knees.

Pamela saw how his hands gripped on to the fabric of his jeans until his knuckles turned white.

She put her hand on his shoulder. "Let's go sit down over by the porch," she softly suggested.

Daniel stood up and took a few deep breaths.

To Pamela, the man appeared to be trying with all of his might to regain his composure. She noted his respirations and reached over to check his pulse.

"I'm fine," he insisted, pulling his wrist away from her.

"You're not fine." Pamela put an arm about his waist. "Come on," she urged as she ushered him to the front of the house.

Daniel let her guide him to the porch. She shooed the dogs gathered there away to make room for them to sit. Five dogs instantly scattered and ran to the back of the house. She eased Daniel down on to the step.

"I'm going inside to get you some water. Stay right here," she ordered in a firm tone.

Daniel rubbed his face with his hands and nodded.

Pamela ran into the house and grabbed a glass from the kitchen cabinet and filled it with water from the tap. When she returned, she found Daniel standing by the porch railing. Studying him from the steps was Rodney the raccoon. She walked over to Daniel and handed him the water. His hands were shaking as he took the glass from her.

She nodded to the raccoon. "He came to check up on you."

Daniel took a few deep gulps of the water and then motioned to the raccoon. "I thought he was debating on whether or not to attack me."

Pamela noted the way Rodney stood on his hind haunches and sniffed at Daniel. "No, he's concerned. He senses your distress. Animals can do that." She turned back to him. "They know when someone needs help," she added.

"Maybe it is because they're wild animals. They're just more in tune with nature, or whatever you rehabbers call it," Daniel reasoned.

"Wild is only a term used to measure degrees of distance between us and them. We call something wild because we do not know it. But once you form a bond with a creature, and become part of its family, you discover it was never wild, simply afraid." She watched his hands as they tightly gripped the glass. The beads of sweat were still forming above his upper lip and forehead, despite the cool spring morning. "Can I get you anything?" she asked, suddenly feeling helpless without her array of EMT equipment to aid her.

Daniel shook his head and tried to wave off her concern. "I'll be all right. You got anything stronger than water in your house?" He then took another long sip from the glass.

"I've got one bottle of vodka and half a bottle of cognac."

Daniel raised one eyebrow at her.

Pamela just shrugged. "I like to take a sip of cognac when I can't sleep. It helps to calm me."

"I suspect it's a good pain reliever too," he stated, handing the empty glass to her. "I saw you grabbing your arm the other day. Carol told me about your lupus."

Pamela sighed as she took the glass from him. "Carol has a big mouth."

He leveled his dark eyes on her. "And she cares for you a great deal. She even threatened me with torture if I ever hurt you."

That made Pamela laugh.

Daniel watched the pale woman's face fill with color. She had a light harmonious laugh that reminded him of wind chimes stirring in a gentle breeze.

"That's something you need to do more often," Daniel said, smiling into her face.

"What?"

"Laugh. You look good when you laugh. And your eyes are not all cold and distant, like they usually are."

Her smile fell away. "My eyes are not cold and distant."

Daniel tilted his head slightly to the side and frowned. "They are when they look at me."

Pamela gazed down at the porch deck beneath her feet. She knew she had been staring at the man as if he were some plague-carrying vagrant. But that was the way she always looked at people. It was her safety mechanism, in a way. And even though keeping everyone at a distance had guaranteed she would live a lonely life, at least it was a life she knew she could live with.

She rubbed her tennis shoe against a crack in the wood on the porch deck. "Yeah, well, you're a thug, remember?"

Daniel leaned to the side and playfully nudged her shoulder. "Still think I'm a thug?" he asked with a grin.

Pamela turned and examined his face for a moment. He was a handsome man, she decided, and wondered why she had never thought of him as attractive before. His looks were more suited for a man of adventure rather than a model or actor. He appeared to be someone who should be flying planes or, at least, jumping out of them. His eyes were the only part of his features that she found unsettling. The darkness of them seemed to hint at some hidden pain behind his welcoming smile. Like he had been to hell, and the visions he had seen there were still burning through his soul. She found it odd how you can look into a person's face a thousand times, and then suddenly, one day, you glance over and feel as though you are seeing them for the very first time.

"Perhaps you should call it a day," she suggested.

Daniel shook his head. "No, I came here to help you out, and I'm fine now. I just got a little shaken up by that crazy bird of yours."

"You were more than a little shaken up, Daniel."

He moved toward the steps. "Sorry, I just overreacted. I'll get back to your roof," he said over his shoulder. He quickly walked down the steps and around the side of the house.

Pamela felt a sense of relief when Daniel disappeared from view. It wasn't that she didn't like his company; it was more that his presence seemed to unhinge her. Being around Daniel turned her mind into that of a self-conscious adolescent again. Perhaps what she felt were the dying embers of her youth making a last ditch effort to ignite her interest in the opposite sex. But she knew she had come too far in her life to ever entertain the idea of allowing a man like Daniel in. She had enough adrift souls dependent on her for their survival, and she had no room in her heart to try and right another.

* * * *

Later that morning, Pamela returned from feeding the animals in their outdoor cages to find Daniel hammering away on her roof. He diligently labored to pry the cracked shingles from the roof, throw them to the side, and hammer the new ones into place. Pamela wondered if he had ever worked in construction, or if replacing roof shingles was something he had learned from his father. She stopped, shook her head, and silently chastised her overzealous curiosity. Suddenly angry that she had allowed her mind to fill with such frivolous thoughts, Pamela marched to the front door.

Once she stepped inside the door to her home, the constant thud of the hammer seemed to reverberate throughout her house.

No room was free of the overhead banging. She noticed even Louis, the squirrel, had hidden himself inside of the sleeping sack in his open cage to try and get away from the noise. Unable to take the intermittent hammering, Pamela walked to her hall closet and took out the Winchester rifle she kept there. She added a few extra shells to the front pocket of her jeans and checked to make sure the rifle was loaded. She eyed Louis once more and observed the array of sleeping baby squirrels in their containers on her kitchen table.

"I don't have to feed you guys for another hour, so I'm going out to check feeders," she said to the animals.

Rifle in hand, Pamela headed out the door. As she walked down the steps of her back porch, she toyed with the idea of telling Daniel where she was going, but quickly decided against it. She figured it would be best to avoid further interaction with him and then maybe her disturbing feelings about him might just go away.

Pamela made her way to the open shed that housed her truck, tractor, and ATVs. She went to the larger of the two ATVs and searched under the seat for the keys. After she had secured her rifle, she started the vehicle and headed for the woods.

A few feet into the thick brush around her property, she found the old trail she used to travel to the feeders that sustained the released animals throughout the cold winters. Normally the feeders would be empty this time of year, but because of the unusually cold winter Louisiana had just endured, Pamela had opted to stock the feeders for another month until spring was firmly entrenched. As she maneuvered the ATV through the high shrubs and around the low tree limbs covering the trail, she continually checked for her rifle. No one should ever be caught out in the thick brush without a weapon. Most animals would run from the approaching sounds and smells of a human, but wild boar, indigenous to the area, were especially aggressive in the spring. Mothers had baby piglets to protect from predators, and they could badly maim, or even kill, when encountered.

After ten minutes of negotiating through the dense vegetation, Pamela came upon a small clearing and the first of four feeders located on her property. The feeder was nothing more than an empty metal barrel with large holes drilled into the sides along the bottom. A mixture of corn, seeds, and nuts would be poured into the top of the barrel and as the animals removed the food from around the bottom of the barrel, more food would filter out through the holes.

Pamela pulled her vehicle up next to the feeder and left the motor running as she climbed off the ATV and went over to the barrel. Lifting the heavy top of the barrel and looking inside, she could see that the barrel was still full of food. Pamela let the lid drop with a bang and then stepped back to her vehicle.

A loud rustling from the bushes off to her left distracted her. Instinctively, Pamela reached for her gun on the back of the ATV and stood watching the brush where the noise had emanated from. Then a long angry grunt came from inside the dense foliage in front of her. As her body tensed, she lifted the rifle and aimed in the direction of the noise. Seconds later, a huge black ball of fur came barreling out of the brush directly toward her. She fired one shot above the creature's head and saw the animal immediately halt. It was a large black bear, probably female, Pamela surmised. Black bears were common in Louisiana, but they usually never ventured this far south. The animal stared at her, rocking back and forth on its front feet, as if debating the prudence of pursuing an attack. Then from the brush behind the bear, a small black face emerged, and then a second face popped out next to the first. Pamela stood motionless while keeping her eyes peeled on the mother black bear. The stand off seemed to go on for several agonizing minutes, until the bear emitted a low, deep growl. Pamela raised the barrel of her rifle and fired.

* * * *

"Pamela!" Daniel's frantic scream pieced through the woods.

He ran toward the sound of the gunshots and called out again and again for the woman.

"Pamela, can you hear me?" he shouted and would stop running only long enough to listen for a reply. But there was none.

He ran on, figuring he must be coming closer to the origin of the two shots he had heard. But as he fought his way through the brush, he could feel that familiar pang of dread start to tangle his gut. His heart was racing and his breath seemed to burn like fire in his chest. *The panic, God the panic*! he thought to himself. It was eating him up. He tried to think of the techniques he had been taught to control the powerful flood of adrenalin in his veins, but no peaceful thoughts of sandy beaches or cool ocean breezes were going to allay the absolute terror that was raging through his body. What if he couldn't find her? What if she was wounded, or worse? Frightful scenarios, with the force of a tsunami, began to slam, one after the other, into his mind. Then, he heard the sound of an engine idling close by. He jumped through some of the brush to his left and soon found himself in a small clearing. There, standing next to a tall oil barrel, was Pamela.

She spun around to face him. The rifle, still at the ready in her hands, was pointed at his chest.

"Are you insane?" she yelled at him as she lowered her rifle. "I could have shot you!"

Daniel stopped, bent over, and tried to catch his breath. "I heard the gunshots…and thought you might be hurt…I took off from the house to come…and help you."

"And surprising a woman with a loaded gun was going to help me? Do what? Spend the next eighteen to twenty in prison?" she shouted.

Pamela spotted several small trickles of blood flowing down his arms. She ran to his side and inspected his arms. "Jesus, Daniel. You're all sliced up."

Daniel stood up and, still gasping for breath, yelled, "What in the hell are you doing out here? And why did I hear gunshots?"

Pamela never looked up from the man's bleeding arms. "We have got to get you back to the house."

At that moment, he felt the shaking begin. It always started in his knees and worked its way up. Soon, it would reach his hands and face and he would not be able to hide it from her this time. He eagerly scanned the brush surrounding him. There was nowhere to run and hide.

"Daniel!" Pamela's voice registered in his brain. "Daniel, are you all right?"

He felt his body caving in. The panic was ripping through his muscles and tissue, taking over his will to fight and his desire to maintain control.

Pamela watched as Daniel sank to his knees. He reached up and placed his face in his trembling hands, and then he started to hyperventilate. His gasping breath rattled in his throat as his body seemed to be taken over by convulsions. Pamela knelt down in front of him and pushed his hands away from his face. She looked into his eyes and immediately saw that unmistakable expression.

"Goddamn it," Daniel growled beneath his breath. "Not here. Not now." His eyes burned into hers. "Not with you." He wrapped his bleeding arms about his body and started to rock gently back and forth. "Go away, Pamela. Leave me alone," he ordered in a shaky voice.

Pamela calmly placed her hands about his face. "Daniel, I'm not leaving you. I am right here." She knew she had to get him out of there. "I have to get you back to the house," she declared.

He covered his ears. "The gunfire! I can still hear the gunfire!" he mumbled.

Pamela ran back to the ATV and put the vehicle into gear. She pulled it right alongside of Daniel. She got off the four-wheeled vehicle and went back to him.

"I need you to focus, Daniel," she directed as she placed her hand under his chin and tried to draw his eyes to hers. "I want you to listen to me and do as I say. I need you to get up and get on this four-wheeler."

She watched as Daniel nodded his head and fought to gain control of his rapid breathing. She helped him to his feet and lifted his leg over the back of the vehicle. She then climbed on to the seat in front of him and rested her rifle across her lap.

She turned back to Daniel. "Put your arms around my waist and hold on as tight as you can."

He did as she instructed. Pamela could feel his respirations beginning to calm, but his shaking body was now soaked through with perspiration. His sweat mixed with blood seeped through her own shirt and created a chill against her skin. She took a breath and slowly started to make her way out of the clearing, her body straining with tension as she maneuvered the ATV through the dense woods. Pamela did not feel her body relax until she saw the familiar blue and white cottage looming before her.

* * * *

"A bear?" Daniel said as his dark eyes stared transfixed at Pamela.

He was sitting on her green couch, naked from the waist up and wrapped in a blanket. He had bandages down both his forearms, along with a few minor scratches on his face, and was holding a half glass of cognac in his now steady hands.

Pamela was sitting next to him nursing her glass of orange juice. She had removed her bloodstained clothes and put on her favorite robe. "A mother bear. She came out of the brush and found me standing next to the feeder. She was probably bringing her babies to eat."

Daniel shook his head in disbelief. "A bear in Louisiana?"

Pamela nodded. "Not something we see a lot of around here, but black bears have been spotted in this area before. Not many places for them to hibernate, but she seems to have managed."

"She could have mauled you, or worse," he calmly remarked, and then he took another sip of the amber liquid from his glass.

"I shot over her head and scared her off. I'm good enough with a rifle should she have decided to charge me." She shrugged. "But I would have been raising those babies instead of her. And a couple of baby bears would simply wreak havoc on my rehab facility. They are very mischievous and also very destructive."

He tilted his head slightly to the side as he studied her for a few moments. "You're a lot tougher than you look, right?"

Pamela smiled. "Yes, I am."

A few uncomfortable minutes of silence passed between them.

"Are you going to tell me what happened out there?" she finally asked in a soft voice.

Daniel sighed and placed his glass on the coffee table in front of him. "I had a panic attack, that's all. It happens every now and then when I get stressed."

She leaned in closer to him. "And is that what happened this morning with Lester, the owl?"

Daniel nodded. "If I get stressed out, or angry, they tend to come in clusters." He gave her a reassuring smile. He hoped his casual demeanor would make her think that his episodes were no big deal.

Pamela tried to read his feelings at that moment. His features said one thing, but his eyes said another. If she had been less experienced with medical conditions, she might have actually believed his nonchalant reaction.

"Panic attacks, huh?" She reached over and patted his knee. "Nice try, Daniel. But I'm not some airhead blond trying to flirt with an attractive bartender."

Daniel grinned at her. "Attractive?"

Pamela ignored him. "Panic attacks are usually a symptom of some underlying disorder. And back in the woods you mumbled something about gunfire. You said you could still hear the gunfire." She sat back on the couch but never removed her eyes from his. "What gunfire?"

Daniel took in a deep breath and lowered his gaze to the glass on the table in front of him. His voice became very faint as he spoke. "I did two tours of duty in Iraq."

Pamela raised her eyebrows at him. "Really? When did you join the military?"

"After September 11th. I remember watching the towers go down on the television and thinking, I have to do something. So I dropped out of graduate school and enlisted."

"Graduate school?" she questioned.

"I was at Harvard, completing my MBA. When my old man found out I quit grad school and enlisted, he blew a fuse." He laughed, slightly.

"I'm sure your father was probably terrified for you. You were going off to a strange country to fight a war."

"Not quite. He was grooming me to take over his business. He wanted me to finish my MBA and go to work with him."

"The scars on your chest. You got those in Iraq, didn't you?" she asked, trying to keep her voice calm and steady.

Daniel sat back and ran his hands over his face. He shook his head. "We were on foot in what we thought was a pretty secure section of Baghdad. We came around a corner and walked right into an ambush. I took the first one in the leg and then the next three…" He paused. "Well, you saw the scars."

She sat back on the couch next to him, admiring his strong profile. "When did you get out?"

"Six years ago after I was shot." He shrugged. "I traveled around the country a bit and then I went to bartending school for the fun of it. I don't sleep well and I figured if I was going to be up all night I might as well get paid for it."

Pamela shook her head. "What you are describing, Daniel, is more than just—"

"It's called PTSD, post traumatic stress disorder," he interrupted. "That's what the army shrinks said it was."

"So you have seen someone?"

Daniel snickered. "I've seen several someones. They all say the same thing. They try to give me pills, try to hypnotize me, desensitize me, detoxify me, and demoralize me." He got up from the couch and walked over to the window next to Louis's cage.

The squirrel watched as Daniel came up to him. The creature's little eyes curiously took in the stranger without showing the least bit of fear. Louis then climbed out of his cage and slowly made his way over to the tall man.

Daniel warily watched as the squirrel came closer to him.

Pamela rose from the couch and went over to the cage. "It's all right," she assured him. "He doesn't bite. In fact he is quite a sweet little boy."

She took his hand and guided it toward Louis. At first, Louis seemed a little nervous about the big hand approaching, but then he let Daniel touch his head. After a few seconds, Daniel was able to gently stroke the top of the squirrel's head.

"Now reach around and stroke under his chin," Pamela instructed.

Daniel did as he was told and was happily surprised when the little creature lifted his front paw for Daniel to rub his fuzzy white underbelly.

"Look at that. He likes it." Daniel laughed.

"Actually, it is something all squirrels do when you rub under their chins. I call it the squirrel reflex."

Then Louis decided that he had had enough attention for the time being and moved away from Daniel's hand and back into his cage.

"I've never petted a squirrel before," Daniel said, his face bright with enthusiasm.

"Not many people have," Pamela admitted. "Do you want to feel something truly amazing?"

Daniel explored her cool gray eyes. He felt a pang of desire blaze through him as he took in every detail of her face. His excitement dwindled to disappointment when Pamela turned away from him and walked over to the other side of the living room.

She went to the containers housing her myriad of wildlife babies and opened one. She came back to Daniel holding a small gray and brown lump of fur in her hands.

"Hold out your hands," she told him.

Daniel watched anxiously as Pamela placed a six-week-old squirrel in his hands.

The creature's eyes and ears were open and the body was covered with a silky brown and gray fur. He could feel the little life squirming in his hands, as tiny teeth nipped at the calluses on his palms.

Daniel looked up at Pamela. "It's so small, I feel like I might crush it."

"Would you like to feed her?"

Daniel raised his dark eyebrows at Pamela. "Are you sure?"

She gave him an encouraging smile. "I think it might be just what you need right now."

* * * *

BROKEN WINGS

Half an hour later, Pamela looked on as Daniel sat on the floor, carefully feeding formula to his fifth baby squirrel. The man seemed to revel in the way the eager little mouths sucked at the small syringe. He carefully rubbed each and every pink tummy after feeding to aid with digestion, just as Pamela had instructed. He was enthralled with the tiny creatures, studying their faces, and caressing their little feet. The joy he seemed to find made Pamela feel as if the disturbing events of the day had almost never happened. Almost.

"No wonder you like doing this." Daniel glanced up from the squirrel in his hands. "They are so helpless and have such trust in you. They let you feed them and rub them without the slightest bit of reservation."

Pamela walked over to his place on the floor. "Wait until they get older and can squirm and bite. Then feeding them with a syringe becomes a real challenge."

"Why do you use a syringe? I've always seen those bottles sold in stores with the kitten and puppy formulas. I thought you would be using them to feed your babies."

"Nursing bottles can cause aspiration—formula in the lungs—in a lot of infant wildlife. Rehabbers always use syringes to make sure the animal doesn't aspirate."

"When do they get off the formula?"

"At eight to ten weeks I start weaning them. I'll get them into some small cages, out of these plastic containers, and start to offer solid food. Usually I give them a selection of apples, berries, beans, and corn, along with a little sweet potato, as well as wheat bread or crackers. Once they are completely off formula, I will transfer them to the bigger cages outside that you were cleaning the other day. And when they are able to crack a nut with their teeth, they are ready to be released."

He gazed down at the little ball of fur in his hands. "That must be hard. You must get so attached."

"To some, yes, I become very attached. Almost from the first moment you begin feeding them, you recognize traits of each baby's individual personality, no matter how alike they may appear. Some are stubborn, shy, feisty, or some are like little bulldozers; they will plow through anything that gets in their way. Most people think they are just animals and wonder how they can have different personalities. But getting to know them is just like getting to know another person. At first you see only the outside, but with time you learn to memorize every idiosyncrasy, every inflection, every movement until one day…" She shrugged. "They become a part of you. And for the rest of your life, their memory will live on in your thoughts and in your dreams."

"Do they ever not want to leave?" Daniel asked. "I mean they have it pretty good here and it is a big old scary world out there."

"Some hang around for a long time, like Rodney. Usually the males stay longer than the females." She gave him a teasing grin. "But many do come back to visit me. The mothers bring their babies to me and show me their families. That makes what I do worthwhile. I guess it is their way of saying thank you. They make me a part of the tribe, so to speak. They remember me, and you cannot ask for more than that from anyone."

Daniel carefully placed the small baby back in its plastic container. He watched as the tiny creature crawled over to join the rest of the litter, which was hidden underneath a mound of cloth strips. He put the lid back on the square plastic box and placed the container with the others against the wall on his left. He looked past Pamela to the window located across the room, and felt a pang of disappointment run through him as he saw the fading light peeking through the light brown curtains.

"It's getting late," he stated as he stood up from the floor. "I should get back to your roof while there is still some daylight left."

Pamela shook her head. "No, you're not going back up there today."

"I'm fine now." He leaned his head slightly closer to her and gave her a cocky grin. "I'm a lot tougher than I look," he added.

"I'm sure you think you are, but I'm not letting you get back up there with all that cognac in your system."

Daniel's deep laugh filled the cramped living room with a sudden rush of warmth Pamela had never felt before.

"My dear woman," he began. "I have been known to put a hell of a lot more than that away on any given night behind the bar. Trust me, I'm stone cold sober."

She frowned. "You drink at work?"

He took another step closer, letting his body ease right up next to hers. He stared down into her gray eyes. "I'm a bartender, drinking on the job is required."

"You don't seem like a bartender to me. You're well educated, resourceful, and have a curious mind. I'd say there is more to you than just tending bar and getting in fights with customers."

He stared up at the ceiling, appearing to mull over her observations. Then he gave her an amusing smile. "Sorry, that about covers it for me. Drinking and fighting are what I'm best at."

"But you can replace shingles on a roof? There must be other things you're good at?"

"There are other things I can do, but I'm not necessarily good at them. And most men know how to replace shingles on a roof. A compulsion for making minor household repairs is just one of the side effects of testosterone."

Pamela immediately broke out into a fit of laughter.

A perplexed look came over Daniel's face. "It wasn't that funny," he commented.

Pamela wiped a happy tear from the corner of her eye. "It's just that my ex-husband always said manual labor was the result of not having enough intelligence to know how to avoid it."

Daniel furrowed his brow at her. "Sounds like a great guy. How long were you married?"

"Eight years."

"May I ask what happened?"

Pamela waved her hand casually in the air. "When I was diagnosed with lupus things started to fall apart. Bob tried to be the dutiful husband and help me through the bad patches, but after a few years he couldn't handle it any more. So he asked for a divorce."

"What an asshole," Daniel said as he frowned at Pamela. "Why on earth did you marry him?"

"We met right after I was in a pretty bad car accident. He became my attorney and handled my lawsuit against the drunk driver who hit me. We wound up spending a lot of time together. Lunch meetings became dinner meetings and then our meetings turned into dates. I thought he was charming, kind, and would always be there for me. I was wrong." She wrapped her arms about her body. "You ever been married?" she asked.

He shook his head. "No. I'm not cut out for long-term relationships. Most women get sick of my shit and quickly move on. It's better that way. What happened today is something I never let anyone see. At times it becomes really hard hiding my PTSD from the world, but so far I have been able to keep most of my symptoms under control."

"And when you can't keep it under control anymore?"

"Then it will be time for me to move on. I'll find a new town, and new people, who don't know anything about me."

"Is that what you have been doing? Moving from one town to the next to try and hide your condition?"

He turned away from her and went back to the couch. He removed the blanket from around his shoulders and picked up his bloody T-shirt. "It's worked pretty well for me so far."

"But you can't go on like that forever, Daniel."

He pulled the T-shirt over his head. "You don't get it, Pamela," he said with a hint of frustration in his voice. "For someone like me there isn't a forever. Right now is about all I can handle."

She stood in silence as she watched him neatly fold up the blanket and place it on her couch. He then picked up the half full glass of cognac and downed the contents in one long swallow.

"If you aren't going to let me back on your roof, then I better head back to the city," he grumbled as he banged the glass down on the coffee table.

"Maybe you shouldn't be driving right now. Why not wait a while longer before you get behind the wheel?"

"I'm fine," he said, avoiding her eyes. He moved to the front door. "I'll come back tomorrow after lunch and finish the roof."

He reached for the doorknob. "Thanks for today, Pamela. I know what you must think of me, but I promise I will be out of your life soon." And with that he opened the door and stepped out into the fading afternoon light.

Pamela felt her body jump as he slammed the door shut behind him. She closed her eyes and cursed her own insecurities for not allowing her to tell him what she was thinking. Her hands curled into fists as she tried to suppress the flood of emotion that was suddenly inundating her. She did not want to feel her heartstrings tug for another, not another human anyway. She could not risk letting someone else in and she had spent enough time with the opposite sex to know that relationships only ended up being mistakes that she wished had never happened. No, it was best not to entertain any emotional feelings for Daniel Phillips. Her animals fulfilled her and she knew the silly banter between two lonely people would never amount to anything. Besides, a man like Daniel Phillips would only use her and move on, and she had endured enough heartbreak for one lifetime.

ALEXANDREA WEIS

CHAPTER 4

The following afternoon Pamela was trying to stuff a few heads of cabbage into an old refrigerator when Daniel walked into the barn.

"What's with all the boxes of food?" He asked as he examined the boxes of old cantaloupes, radishes, apples, turnip greens, and other assorted fruits and vegetables scattered around the barn floor.

"Hey. I didn't think I would see you back here again," she casually stated as she tried to rearrange some old cantaloupe in the refrigerator.

"I told you I would be back."

She did not look up at him, but kept her eyes focused on the contents of the refrigerator. "Yeah, well, people may say one thing, but do another."

"You'll find I'm a man of my word, Pamela." He came up to her side and waved his hand to the boxes. "So what is all this?"

"I just made my run," Pamela replied, grabbing some cherry tomatoes and putting them in a second refrigerator.

"Your run?"

"I have a 501C non profit organization so businesses can donate goods to my facility and write it off as a charitable donation. The grocery in Folsom saves all of their old produce for me, and I go to collect it three times a week."

Daniel picked up a soft cantaloupe. "Is this stuff edible?"

"It is to a fox, rabbit, squirrel, raccoon." She waved her hand at him. "You get the idea."

He nodded as she continued to fill the refrigerators.

"The feed store in nearby Covington donates broken or torn bags of seed and deer corn, a local grade school collects old clothes for bedding, and I have a building contractor who gives me scraps of wood I use to build nest boxes," she explained as she shoved some wilted kale into the refrigerator.

"Nest boxes? Like the ones birds use?" Daniel asked.

Pamela nodded. "Squirrels too. I also build dens for the foxes, climbing trees for the raccoons, houses for skunks, basically anything an animal will need to help them adapt to being released back into the wild."

"You've got quite an operation going here," he commented.

She walked over to a box of zucchini mixed with broccoli. "Took me a while to get everything set up, but it's finally come together in the past year or two."

"So how did you get into this?" he asked as he started helping her unpack some of the boxes.

She picked up the box and stepped back to the refrigerator. "I lived in the city with my husband and a neighbor brought a baby squirrel to me." She put the box down on the floor. "I had always been an animal nut as a kid. I raised orphaned kittens and took in stray dogs all the time. Drove my father crazy. But I had never taken care of a squirrel, so I got on the Internet and learned all I could." She smiled and her face warmed over with memories. "Her name was Widget and she taught me how to love squirrels. Soon I began to connect with permitted wildlife rehabbers in the area and learned more about raising baby squirrels and other small mammals. Right after I got my wildlife rehabilitation permit from the Louisiana Wildlife and Fisheries, my husband asked for a divorce. Bob never liked animals much. So I moved out here and decided to pursue rehabbing full time."

Daniel stared at the woman as she stuffed some zucchini in the refrigerator. It was then he noticed the scratches on her forearm peaking out from under her long-sleeved shirt.

"What happened?" he asked as he pointed to her arm.

Pamela looked at her arm and seemed amazed by what she found there. "Oh, one of the baby squirrels was running all over me this morning. Their nails are really sharp when they are young. I'm always getting scratched up."

"Isn't that a little dangerous for you considering your lupus? It's an immune system disorder, right? So shouldn't you try and protect yourself from diseases?"

Pamela gave a frustrated sigh as she reached for some broccoli. "I know I should be more careful. Sometimes the scratches get infected, mostly from the raccoons. Their scratches are the worst for me. If I have problems, I notify my doctor and he calls something in to the pharmacy for me." She rolled her eyes. "But only after he has given me a long lecture about why I should quit rehabbing."

"That would be enough to stop a lot of other people with lupus," he argued.

She shoved the broccoli into the refrigerator. "When I was first diagnosed, I spent a lot of time on the computer doing research, even joined a couple of support groups, but all that did was constantly remind me of my lupus. I didn't want to be one of those people who spent every waking moment obsessing about their condition. I decided I needed something else to occupy my mind."

Daniel glanced around the barn. "And this is what you found?"

She walked over to a box of romaine lettuce. "I love what I do, and it keeps me going," she affirmed. "I don't jump motorcycles over cars, get blown out of a cannon twice a day, or break horses. I think what I do is pretty tame compared to others." She picked up the box and moved back to the refrigerator.

Daniel patted the refrigerator door. "You need another one of these."

She placed the box of romaine lettuce on the floor next to his feet. "I need two more. It's on my to-do list."

Daniel took in the six-stall horse barn. There was a large tack room next to him, where Pamela had stored several garbage tins filled with seeds and corn. The refrigerators were located outside of the tack room door. She had hay piled up in one stall and old wood planks in another. In a third stall, she had a selection of power tools spread out on a makeshift table. In another were several wire cages piled one on top of the other.

"What do you use this place for?" he asked.

Pamela followed his eyes around the barn. "Storage for the time being. I would like one day to take out all of the stalls and turn this place into the nursery, medical ward, and food prep site. To do that I would have to knock out all the stalls, divide it into separate areas with walls and sheetrock, add air and heat, as well as gut the disgusting bathroom next to the tack room to make it usable." She shrugged as she turned back to Daniel. "It's on my to-do list."

Daniel shook his head. "That's a long list."

"You should have seen the place when I first took it over. I try to remove one thing a year from my list, but that is completely dependent on the amount of money it takes to fix whatever meltdowns may occur around here. One broken appliance that needs to be fixed, or worse, replaced, can really set me back."

She finished putting the last of the romaine lettuce away and could feel Daniel's eyes on her. Either she was becoming paranoid, or she could truly sense every time the man looked at her. The only problem was she was not sure what he was thinking when he did observe her. Normally, she could have cared less what someone like Daniel Phillips thought of her. But as she spent more time with him, she found herself becoming more obsessed with what he was thinking and why.

She wiped her hands on the back of her jeans and started picking up the empty boxes from the floor. Daniel stepped in and started helping her.

"What do you want to do with these?" he asked, holding an armload of boxes.

"Let's take them out to the burn pile," she instructed, heading to the barn entrance.

Daniel followed her out of the barn and toward a large pile of boxes, dead tree limbs, discarded nesting hay, and old newspapers set up close to the edge of the cleared property.

BROKEN WINGS

As Pamela stepped in front of the burn pile, Daniel noticed two squirrels running from the nearby brush to her side. He stopped and watched as Pamela bent over to speak to the squirrels. The animals darted about her feet, and around some of the boxes gathered on the ground, before heading back to the brush.

Daniel came up to her side and tossed the boxes in his arms on top of the mound of rubbish. "Does that usually happen?" he asked.

Pamela nodded. "Two of my male squirrels from last season, Moe and Larry. They hang out in the trees on this side of the clearing and sometimes come to see me. When I am walking about the property I usually have a few of the animals I have rehabbed running up to me looking for treats or just to visit."

"I thought they were supposed to be wild. Won't interacting with you teach them not to be afraid of people?" he asked as he picked up the boxes scattered about his feet.

"No, they're wild. They won't go to strangers. I'm family," Pamela replied as she tossed the last of the boxes on to the burn pile. "Thanks for helping me," she stated, turning to him.

"I'll bet that hurt," he said, wiping his hands together.

She knitted her brows. "What are you talking about?"

"You hate having people help you. Must be hard enough for you to admit that you need help, let alone thank someone for helping you."

"I was being polite," she admitted, raising her voice just a bit.

He laughed. "Now you're getting defensive."

She opened her mouth to respond to his accusation but decided against it. "I have baby squirrels to feed," she informed him and turned away, heading back toward the house.

"Can I help?" Daniel asked as he followed her.

Pamela stopped walking and faced him. "I thought you were going to work on the roof." She paused and watched as his expression became somber. "I didn't realize. I mean you want to feed the babies?"

His dark mood instantly lifted and he gave her a warm smile that seemed to soften the coldness in his eyes. "Yes, I know you want me to get started on the roof but…"

"No, it's not about the roof. I'm just surprised that you want to feed the babies again. Most people, especially men, aren't very interested in helping feed babies. They think it's…" she tried to find the right word.

"A woman's job," Daniel said, filling in the blank.

She nodded.

He looked sheepishly at the ground. "Well, I don't think that. I really enjoyed handling the little flea-infested fuzz balls."

Pamela could not help but laugh at him. "Well, come on then. I'll even show you how to mix their formula."

Back at the house, Pamela taught Daniel how to mix powdered formula with water and yogurt in a blender.

"The yogurt aids their digestion and adds a little thickness to the formula," she said, removing the formula from the blender and pouring some of it into two small bowls. She then took the bowls to the microwave.

"Where do you get your formula?" he asked, watching her place small nipples on the end of some syringes.

"Every rehabber has a different theory about formula. A lot of rehabbers go with the company I use because they don't have as many chemicals in their formula. Some buy another brand and some make their own out of milk. If you want to start a fist fight among rehabbers, bring up which is the best formula to use for babies." She took the warmed formula out of the microwave and carried the bowls over to the kitchen table.

She sat in a chair next to the table as Daniel took a seat across from her. She handed him a syringe and a bowl of formula.

"Grab a container and get to it," she ordered as she waved her hand at the pile of containers between them.

Daniel eagerly lifted the first baby out of the small clear plastic container. His eyes softened as he handled the tiny creature. And when he put the nipple into the animal's mouth and watched it eagerly begin sucking down the formula from the syringe, he smiled.

"You really enjoy this, don't you?" she asked, observing him.

"Yes, I really do," he said, briefly glancing up at her. "Makes me feel like I'm doing something worthwhile. I'm not standing behind a bar mixing drinks with names like 'Demolition Brew' to serve some moron who defines having fun as getting stupid drunk in a bar every night. It's very simple with these guys. Life is about staying full, finding someone to rub your belly, and having a warm place to sleep. Having the right kind of car or wearing an expensive designer label is not important to them. They already know what matters. And that makes you remember what is important in life."

"And you got all that from feeding baby squirrels?"

"And being here, in your place."

Pamela reached into the closest container and picked up the baby squirrel inside. "I'm happy your time here has helped you gain a better perspective. Shame it doesn't do that for everyone."

He nodded in agreement. "Most people are too afraid to look at who they are on the inside because they won't like what they find. Instead they concentrate on their reflection in the mirror, and believe that by making themselves prettier, thinner, or younger, they will be more admired by others, and become a better person in the process. The world would be a better place without mirrors, in my opinion. It would force everyone to see who they are through the eyes of others, like animals do. The world would then prize actions and not looks. And change would be a process everyone would embrace, not run away from. Imagine how much we could grow if we learned to do away with our vanity."

"When did you learn that?" Pamela asked.

He flipped the baby in his hands gently over and started rubbing its pink belly with his fingers. "After I came back from Iraq, I saw people as they really are. Always living on alert in Iraq taught me to scrutinize faces for the slightest hint of a possible threat. And I started seeing other things in peoples' faces, like their hopes, fears, and frustrations. Before I left I was exactly the same as all the other kids at Harvard. I never looked at the person standing before me. I only judged people based on their clothes, or the type of car they drove. When I came back, I didn't see the material things anymore, only the faces of the people. I couldn't tell you half the names of the people I went to high school with, but I could describe to you every person I've encountered since I came home from the war."

"I can't imagine what it was like for you. I saw so much on the news, but that was the watered down version of the war. I did get a taste of what it must have been like for you after Katrina. Destruction and death were everywhere in the city, but I'm sure nothing like what you encountered."

Daniel stared at the squirrel in his hands. "I lost a lot of good friends over there. Most were guys I would never have associated with prior to Iraq. But fighting side by side with anyone makes you like family." He paused and his eyes seemed to darken slightly. "What haunts me to this day is the smell. I wake up sometimes in the middle of the night, smelling the odor of charred flesh and burning buildings."

"How did you adjust to being back in the states after going through all of that?"

He shook his head and gave a discouraging sigh. "People who have never been there think you get off of the plane and because you're home, everything is fine. But it's not that simple. You walk around in open public places and you're terrified because you feel you're an easy target for a sniper. Every noise makes you jump. Every loud bang makes you want to dive for cover. Hell, I couldn't drive under bridges without having a panic attack for damn near a year after I came back."

"Bridges?"

"Snipers liked firing grenade launchers at us from bridges. You always had to stop and check out a bridge before you went under it. I used to get out of my car and search around every bridge when I first came back to the states."

Pamela took the syringe out of the baby squirrel's mouth and started rubbing its round tummy. "How long before you felt comfortable being home again?"

He placed the baby in his hands back in its container. "I'm still waiting for that day." He snapped the lid closed on the container and then reached for another one. "I sometimes wonder if I will ever feel comfortable again. I don't take anything for granted anymore." He pulled another baby out, placed the nipple into its small mouth, and laughed as the squirrel's impatient little paws wrapped around the syringe like a human baby placing its hands around a bottle.

"Any time you want to feed babies, you are more than welcome, Daniel."

"Thanks, Pamela." His bright smile dimmed a little. "I've got to work for the next few days but after that I'll be able to return. I'll be looking forward to getting back to these guys by then."

Pamela laughed. "You're beginning to sound like me."

Daniel gazed into her gray eyes and grinned. "Maybe that's not such a bad thing after all."

CHAPTER 5

A few days later, a brooding Daniel Phillips returned to Pamela's sanctuary. His Jeep slammed into the gravel driveway, spewing rocks all around when he came to a skidding stop just before the entrance to the cottage. Pamela and Carol watched from the front porch as the tall man climbed out of his Jeep, ignoring her pack of barking dogs.

"Mornin'," he mumbled as he removed his sunglasses and walked directly to the side of the house.

Carol turned to Pamela and raised her mug of coffee to her lips. "Obviously not a morning person."

Pamela put her mug of coffee down on the railing. "I'll be back," she said to Carol and then quickly made her way down the steps and around the side of the house.

"God, I just love a hot mini-drama in the morning," Carol whispered, smiling.

Pamela came up to Daniel, who was banging the ladder around trying to get it positioned right up next to the house. His face looked drawn and there were dark circles under his eyes. His hair was disheveled and he had a thick five o'clock shadow across his square jaw. He looked as if he had just climbed out of bed and headed right over to the sanctuary.

"Coffee?" Pamela offered, figuring he was probably in desperate need of a caffeine boost.

"Yeah," he replied without looking at her. "That would be great, thanks."

"Everything all right?" Pamela inquired.

"Just peachy," Daniel answered, keeping his eyes riveted on the house in front of him.

"Peachy, huh?" Pamela folded her arms across her chest. "You look like shit, Daniel."

He turned to her and his dark eyes ripped her to shreds. "Shit? Thanks. That's just what I needed to hear."

She stood there for several minutes watching him as he gathered up his tools. Finally, he stopped and glowered at her. "Didn't you say something about coffee?" he asked as he raised his dark eyebrows at her.

"After you tell me what your problem is this morning."

Daniel sighed and threw the hammer in his hand to the ground. Lester, in the tree behind him, gave out a sudden hoot of surprise.

Daniel glanced up at the owl. "Great. That's all I need today."

"Tell me what's wrong?" she pleaded.

As he turned to her, a veil of cool indifference descended over his countenance. Pamela felt an uneasy shudder jar her body as her eyes met his.

He drew a deep breath through his lips and then let it out slowly. He surveyed the land around him. "Do you really want to hear this, Pamela, or are you just pretending to give a shit like the rest of the world?" He turned his face back to hers.

"I'm not pretending, Daniel."

His eyes probed hers for what felt like an eternity to Pamela. "All right," he said as he angrily nodded his head. "I got fired last night."

She let her mouth fall open slightly. "Fired? Why?"

"The guy that I slugged a few months back for roughing up his girlfriend; you know, the one who filed charges against me? Well, he showed up at the bar last night and started ranting about why I was still working there. Cursed out the manager and was a general pain in the ass. Security had to come and escort him out of the place. After that, the manager told me to leave and not come back."

"What are you going to do?"

He shrugged, appearing unconcerned about his situation. "Get another job. Won't be as lucrative as Pat O'Brien's, but I'll manage. There are a lot of bars in the Quarter."

"I'm sorry," was all she could think to say.

Daniel gave her a weak attempt at a smile, but his eyes were still cold and menacing. "Now, what about that coffee?"

She nodded. "Coming right up. How do you want it?"

"Black."

Pamela turned to go when his voice stopped her.

"Thank you for not pretending," he whispered.

She looked back at him. "Let's just say I think of you as a very large squirrel."

Daniel laughed, a heartfelt laugh that seemed to break the tension in his face. "I think that is the nicest thing anyone has ever said to me."

Pamela walked away and as she turned the corner to the front of the house, she saw Carol leaning over the porch railing, obviously straining to eavesdrop on her conversation with Daniel.

"Should I send you a transcript?" Pamela quipped as she glared at Carol.

Carol waved a dismissive hand at her. "Nah. Heard plenty enough from my spot here." Carol smiled coyly at her. "So you and the criminal are friends, eh?"

"And you told him I had lupus."

"I also tell everyone that you are mentally unstable and ritually sacrifice small children out in the woods, but no one ever believes me."

"I should sacrifice you out in the woods," Pamela replied under her breath as she climbed the steps to the porch.

"So what's up with you and that fine looking man on your roof?"

"Keep your voice down," Pamela chided. "Stop it, Carol. There is nothing between Daniel and me."

"Yet," Carol slyly added.

"Why do I put up with you and all—?"

But the sound of a car heading down the gravel drive silenced Pamela's remonstrations. She and Carol watched as a bright red Mercedes-Benz SLK 350 roadster pulled up next to Daniel's blue Jeep. The dogs quickly rose from their respective spots on the porch and went clamoring after the car.

"Shit!" Pamela cursed. "This is all I need!"

"Oh, how exciting," Carol squealed as she examined the car. "Imelda has decided to grace us with her presence."

The door of the Mercedes opened and a woman's long, slender leg slid out from the car.

"Pamie!" A high-pitched voice cried out from inside the sleek roadster. "Can you get the dogs away from my car?"

Pamela cursed under her breath one more time as she ran down the steps to the drive. She tried to corral a few of the dogs away from the shiny red car, but for some reason they seemed hesitant to listen to her. Pamela could hear Carol giggling from the porch behind her.

"Go!" she yelled at the dogs and then clapped her hands to try and scare them away. Every dog ran back to the porch except for Tequila, the brown chiweenie. She just sat there staring at the car, wagging her tail, and not paying one bit of attention to Pamela. Finally, Pamela reached down and picked up the dog.

"It's all right, Clarissa," Pamela called out as she carried the small brown dog back to the porch.

Slowly, another leg appeared from inside the car. Then a tall woman, dressed in a form fitting red, silk shirtdress and black Manolo Blahnik pumps, emerged into the morning sunlight. She was slender with long, dark brown hair and bright green eyes. Her face was oval, pale, and looked slightly Asian. Her petite nose, small chin, and almond-shaped eyes only seemed to add to the exotic quality of her face. Clarissa didn't look a day over thirty, but Pamela knew for a fact that she was pushing forty, and attributed her youthful glow to her plastic surgeon's skill rather than a healthy lifestyle.

"Pamie!" Clarissa's slender arms went up to her as if begging for a hug.

"Clarissa," Pamela stated as she walked up to the woman and gave her a friendly embrace. She quickly stepped away, trying to breath with restraint after the first whiff of the woman's heavy perfume. "What are you doing here?" she asked.

Clarissa held up her iPhone in her perfectly manicured little hands. "I came to take some pictures of all of your animals," she replied in her high-pitched voice that reminded Pamela of something akin to mice squealing. "I've got a friend over at the *Times-Picayune* who wants some pictures of your place to put in the Sunday paper. You know, a human interest thing. And since the BP oil spill, everyone has been so worried about all of the animals affected. You never know, it might just help to drum up some donations for you."

"I worked the oil spill, Clarissa, and it involved mostly birds," Pamela clarified in a patronizing tone. "I try to limit myself to small mammals at this facility."

Clarissa laughed, and the dogs on the porch all stood up and looked at her like she was a large squeaky toy. "Honey, no one is gonna' know one way or the other. Mammals, birds, what's the difference? As long as it is cute and fuzzy, everyone will just melt over your little critters. And you can make some money in the process." She slammed the car door shut and walked over to the porch.

"Hello, Mrs. Patrick," Carol said, sounding welcoming.

"Oh, hello." Clarissa stopped halfway up the steps and stared at Carol. "You're Beverly, right?"

"No, I'm Carol." Carol gave her a fake smile. "I handle the books and we see each other at the fundraiser every year."

Clarissa waved her hand in the air. "Oh, yes, silly me. I remember you, dear." She pointed at the coffee mug in Carol's hand. "Ya'll got any more of that inside?"

"I'll get you a mug," Carol offered. "Cream, no sugar, right?"

Clarissa appeared a little shocked. "How clever of you to remember!"

"How could I forget, Mrs. Patrick?" Carol remarked as she headed inside.

Clarissa turned back to Pamela, who was coming up the porch steps behind her. "So, why don't you show me what's new around here and—"

Just then Rodney the raccoon emerged from around the corner of the house. He laid eyes on Clarissa and immediately began to snort and growl at her.

"I see you still haven't gotten rid of that vile creature," Clarissa muttered as her green eyes glared at Rodney. "Shouldn't you put him to sleep or somethin', Pamie? I mean havin' such vermin hangin' around can only bring diseases to your other animals. Don't they carry rabies?"

"Clarissa, you know I don't put animals to sleep unless it's absolutely necessary. Rodney is very friendly with most people, and does not have rabies. He's had his shots. I just don't understand what his problem is with you."

Clarissa shot Pamela a dirty look.

"I simply meant maybe it is your perfume or something you wear that sets him off," Pamela explained. "They have a very acute sense of smell."

"Well, I think he's just—" A sudden round of banging from the roof stifled Clarissa's campaign against the roaming raccoon. "What's that?" she asked.

"I have someone repairing the broken shingles on my roof," Pamela told her.

Clarissa raised her dark brows, questioningly. "Since when can you afford to have any work done on this place?" She narrowed her small eyes on Pamela. "Bob hasn't given you any more money, has he?" she asked in a husky voice.

Pamela could not help but grin as she saw the blush of anger spread across Clarissa's pale face. "No," she said, calmly. "You and Bob have been more than generous over the years."

"Then how can you afford to have your roof fixed?" She walked around to the side of the porch, her Manolo Blahnik's clicking on the wood beneath her feet as she went.

"A volunteer has generously donated the materials to fix up my house," Pamela clarified as she followed Clarissa to the edge of the porch.

"Volunteer!" Clarissa almost laughed. "Pamie, your volunteers are just as poor as you. Now who would pay to have—?"

At that moment, Daniel rounded the corner. He was soaked through and his thin white T-shirt clung to his muscular torso. He stopped dead in his tracks when he saw Clarissa.

"Sorry." He cleared his throat. "I just needed to get something out of my Jeep." His dark eyes volleyed back and forth between Pamela and Clarissa.

"Well, hello there!" Clarissa purred while sticking out her amply enhanced cleavage.

"Clarissa, this is Daniel." Pamela motioned to Daniel. "Daniel has been helping out around here."

"So happy to meet you, Daniel," Clarissa cooed as she leaned over the porch railing and offered him her hand.

Daniel took the woman's extended hand and gave it a brief tug.

"Daniel, Clarissa is a very generous patron of my facility." Pamela gave a fake smile and tried to implore Daniel with her eyes to play nice.

He paused for a second or two, and then Daniel turned back to Clarissa.

"Well, hello," he cheerfully called out, flashing a boyish smile that Pamela swore she had never seen before. "It is very nice to meet someone so interested in Pamela's little organization. You must be a woman of exceptional taste."

Clarissa became like butter in a frying pan. "Oh, I try my best to support all worthy causes," she gushed as she ran her hands through her long hair and showed off her beautiful porcelain smile.

Pamela tried to curtail her grin as she saw Clarissa touch her face and play with the fabric on her dress.

"Clarissa came out to take some pictures of some of the animals for the newspaper," Pamela explained, surprising herself with the chipper inflection in her voice. "She thinks it might be a real help in getting donations for the facility."

"Really? That is so kind of her." Daniel's smile looked so fake that Pamela had to wonder if he was laying it on a bit too thick.

But Clarissa didn't seem to notice. "You know I could use some people in my shots. Perhaps highlight the volunteers who work so hard to keep the place goin'."

"Gee," Carol said, coming up behind the women. "I always wanted to have my picture taken for the newspaper."

Clarissa turned and Carol extended a mug of coffee to her. Clarissa inspected the mug and frowned. "I was actually thinkin' more along the lines of havin' Daniel here…" Clarissa turned back to Daniel, "…pose for a few shots, Beverly."

"It's Carol," Carol corrected.

Clarissa just waved her hand at Carol, never taking her eyes away from Daniel. "What do you think, Daniel? Up for a few pictures to help the cause?"

Daniel glanced over at Pamela and beamed. "Absolutely!"

"Wonderful!" Clarissa clapped her hands together. "Why don't you and I go over to those cages across the way and take some pictures with the animals." She pointed to the man's sweaty T-shirt. "But lose the shirt, darlin'. I think it would be so much more interestin' if you looked like you were workin' really hard."

"And nothing says a man is working hard than when he shows off his naked chest," Carol announced.

Clarissa glanced back at Carol. "I find that to be true, Constance." She took the steps from the porch to the gravel drive one at a time, and by the time her expensive black shoes hit the ground, Daniel was at her side.

Carol and Pamela looked on as the pair walked around the side of the house and toward the back of the facility.

"I hope those heels get stuck in a big old pile of mud," Carol muttered beside Pamela.

"I can't believe the fate of my rehab center rests on the shoulders of a half-naked bartender," Pamela mused as she felt the weight of the world descend upon her.

"Well, those shoulders can definitely handle the burden." Carol shook her head. "I've seen monkeys in heat more subtle than that woman. Now there's a troubled marriage."

Pamela stared at her. "What makes you say that?"

Carol pointed at Clarissa. "If she's on the prowl, so is Bob. A woman never goes after another man unless the man she's got isn't man enough, if you know what I mean," Carol expounded with a wink.

Pamela drew her blond brows together. "I have no idea what you are talking about." Pamela turned and watched as Daniel lifted Clarissa over a large puddle on the ground.

The woman's squeals of joy could have been heard all the way to New Orleans.

"God, I hope I never become that desperate," Carol commented with a sigh.

"I don't care how desperate she is," Pamela said with a frown. "If I knew it would help, I would pay Daniel to sleep with that stupid woman. I will do anything to keep this place going."

"Maybe you could get a two-for-one discount. He could do Clarissa and then you."

Pamela snapped her head around and glared at Carol. "What is that supposed to mean?"

"You two seemed real cozy earlier this morning around the side of the house." She shrugged. "All I'm sayin' is, maybe you and the gigolo should get to know each other. You know, horizontally."

Pamela rolled her eyes. "Carol, all you think about is sex!"

"Yeah, maybe. But at least I'm thinking about it." She nodded her head slightly toward Pamela. "Are you?"

* * * *

It was well into the afternoon when Clarissa's bright red Mercedes pulled out of Pamela's gravel drive and headed back to the city. Soon after she saw Clarissa's tail lights turn on to the main road at the entrance to her property, she heard the hammer start up again on her roof. Pamela stood outside on her porch and fought back the urge to go running to Daniel and ask what happened between him and the insufferable woman. She decided instead to go inside her house and feed her collection of baby gray squirrels. But as she shut the front door to her home, the images of Clarissa and her high-heeled shoes walking off with Daniel to take pictures of her animals, in her facility, irked her. Maybe she should have insisted on tagging along, but the idea of spending any more time than necessary with her ex-husband's wife made her stomach almost heave in revulsion.

After she had settled on the floor and began to feed one of the baby squirrels, a knock came from her front door.

"It's open," she shouted.

The door flew open and Daniel rushed in. Shirtless and out of breath, he hurried toward her with something cupped in his hands.

"I found this when I was up on your roof, by the chimney, sealing up some leaks. It fell into my hands when I moved some of the loose tiles away," he said as he leaned over to her and opened his hands to reveal a tiny creature with bright brown fur.

Pamela put the baby she had been feeding back in its container and analyzed the speck of life cradled in the man's long hands. She tenderly lifted the creature out of his hands and carefully inspected it.

"It's a flying squirrel," Pamela announced. "Don't get many of those unless they are trapped up in people's attics." She smiled up at Daniel.

"Is it hurt or something? It didn't move too much when I brought it down the ladder." He paused and a worried look crossed his face. "Do you think I could have injured it?" he questioned.

She felt a sudden tug at her heart as she caught sight of the man's pained expression. "No, I'm sure you didn't injure it," she reassured him. "Let's find out exactly what is wrong."

Pamela pulled at each of the animal's spindly little legs and ran her fingers over its soft, silky fur. Finally she extended its feather-like tail and pressed gently on its head.

"Nothing appears to be broken. There are no cuts or blood anywhere on the fur," she told him as she turned the creature over in her hand. "Might be sick," she added.

"Can you help it?" Daniel asked, looking more like a little boy than a grown man.

Pamela gazed over at his bare chest and felt her stomach do a few nervous flips. She immediately turned her eyes back to the flying squirrel. "I can start a round of antibiotics and get some good nutrition into her," she informed him.

"Her?" Daniel asked, raising one eyebrow.

"Her," Pamela confirmed. "She's definitely not a him."

Daniel grinned. "I guess she found me irresistible, too."

Pamela just shook her head and got up from the floor. She went to the kitchen cabinet where she kept her medicines.

Daniel followed behind her. He watched as she opened the cabinet and then gave a long whistle.

"Woman, you got a lot of drugs there," he declared, taking in the row upon row of medicine bottles piled high in the cabinet.

"Always stay well stocked on antibiotics, wormers, creams, and lotions for skin irritations and burns. In the next cabinet I have my IV equipment, needles, syringes, different sized nursing nipples, suture sets, splints, plaster of Paris for casts, and my tubing supplies."

"Tubing supplies?"

"I tube baby opossums instead of feeding them through a syringe. I stick a tube down their throats and pump the food gently into their stomachs. They do better that way."

Daniel went to the next cabinet and opened it. He looked over shelf upon shelf of the medical and nursing supplies. "What about going to a vet?" he asked, glancing back at her.

"Vets are expensive and most don't have any experience working with wildlife. If I need x-rays or surgery, I can take the animal to LSU Veterinary School. They work with all the permitted rehabbers in the state."

"Where did you learn about all this stuff?"

She took out a bottle from her cabinet and reached in front of him for a syringe. "You learn some from other rehabbers but most of it is self-taught through books or the Internet. Being an EMT helped tremendously. My medical background gives me a leg up on other rehabbers who are not as well versed in medical emergency protocols."

She pulled out a small scale, put it on the counter, and gently placed the animal in the weighing dish. She read the weight, picked up the animal, and handed it to Daniel.

"Hold her while I draw up her medicine."

"Why did you weigh her?" he asked.

"In order to find out the proper dose of medicine to give her—all medicine is given by weight, for people and for animals."

He shook his head while Pamela withdrew a small amount of pink medicine from a bottle. "I never realized there was so much to rehabbing wildlife. You're really running a hospital and a nursery for animals here, aren't you?"

"Of course," she answered as she took the flying squirrel out of his hands and fed it the contents of the syringe. "Most people think that the pictures on television of people cleaning birds from the BP oil spill depict what rehabbers do. But only rehabbers know what is involved in keeping these animals going."

"Maybe someone should tell people what you do," Daniel suggested in a deep voice.

Pamela found herself becoming acutely aware of the close proximity of his half-naked body. She quickly redirected her attention back to the animal in her hands. "Many people don't care about what we do. I have been called an animal hoarder, anti-naturist, animal abuser...oh, all kinds of things from all kinds of people. What I, and other rehabbers, do doesn't save the world, cure cancer, or make for an interesting mini-series. Our attention-deficit-driven society does not care when you save a life; they are only interested when you destroy one."

Daniel leaned in closer to her. "Well, I care. I care very much."

Pamela stepped back from him. "Yes, I saw just how much you cared with Clarissa today."

Daniel chuckled. "I thought you wanted me to take her around your place and get some pictures for the paper. I had no idea my services involved leasing myself out to entertain lonely and bored housewives."

Pamela turned away from him and walked over to her hallway closet. She pulled out a plastic container with some clean felt strips inside of it. After she had placed the little flying squirrel on top of the felt strips, she snapped the container lid closed.

Pamela kept her eyes on the container in her hands. "Clarissa is a supporter of this facility and she was obviously impressed with you, though for the life of me I can't figure out why. Besides that, she requested you take her around and she wanted you, not me, in the pictures." Pamela then walked over to the kitchen table and placed the flying squirrel's container on top of it.

"You're angry," Daniel surmised, grinning. "You're pissed because that silly woman wanted me in the pictures and not you."

She spun around and faced him. "Well, it is my facility!"

"Then you should have said something!" he shouted, sounding more than a little perturbed.

"I couldn't say anything to her. I have to kiss her ass so she keeps letting her husband give me money!"

Daniel placed his hand on his hip as he considered her comment. "Why does Clarissa have to let her husband give you money? Why can't she just give you the money?"

"Because Clarissa is married to my ex-husband, that's why!" Pamela replied.

His eyes widened and his mouth fell open. "Jesus, what a twisted triangle! You were married to her husband, and not only do you have to kiss your ex-husband's ass, you have to cater to his wife, as well." Daniel started laughing.

"It's not funny, Daniel. I have put up with a lot of shit from that woman. Like the crap she pulled today with you. I had to bite my tongue, otherwise she would have gone running back to Bob and nagged him into cutting off my funding."

Daniel tried to contain his laughter, somewhat. "Pamela, it's very funny. You have to admit."

Pamela threw her hands into the air. "It's no different than women who try to get child support out of ex-husbands who have moved on to greener pastures."

"I wouldn't exactly call Clarissa greener pastures. She's a pretentious bore who made it quite clear today what she wanted from me," Daniel admitted.

Pamela folded her arms over her chest and glared at him. "And what did she want from you?"

He leaned in closer to her. "Do I have to spell it out for you?"

Pamela said nothing. She could feel the seething anger rising beneath her skin.

Daniel shrugged his wide shoulders. "I have been around enough women to know when they want more from me than a handshake."

Pamela marched toward the front door. "I think this conversation has gone far enough," she growled over her shoulder.

Daniel stared dumbfounded at her back. "You're mad at me?" he asked as he followed her to the door. "Because that woman hit on me!" he shouted behind her.

"Yes! You could have jeopardized everything I have worked for!" she yelled back as she opened the front door. "Now get out," she demanded.

Daniel walked up to her and stared into her face. Then his countenance softened and a slow grin replaced the angry grimace on his lips.

"You're not angry about Clarissa." He placed his hands on his hips as his grin grew in size. "You're jealous that I spent the afternoon flirting with her," he challenged.

Pamela's jaw dropped. "Did you flirt with her?"

"I thought I was helping you!"

"Get out!" she shouted, pointing outside.

"No, I won't leave until we have settled this." He slammed the front door closed.

Pamela reached over and placed her hand on the doorknob, but Daniel leaned his body against the door so she could not open it. Pamela stood there for several minutes pulling on the doorknob.

"Are you finished?" he asked, looking thoroughly amused with her ardent determination.

Pamela let go of the doorknob and stood back from him, breathing heavily. "I want you out of here. You're an arrogant, self-centered, conceited bastard."

He smiled at her. "Now, are you finished?"

She stood before him, still breathing hard from her exertions. She was so angry. No one had ever challenged her like this. With wild animals she expected this kind of behavior. Asserting dominance was merely a way to establish their authority. But this was something she had never experienced before. How should she handle this obstinate and difficult man? Her fists curled with frustration and, without thinking, she reached out and punched Daniel as hard as she could in the arm.

"Ow!" he yelled as he grabbed at his arm.

"Get out!" she cried and made a move to punch him again.

But Daniel was too quick for her and reached out and wrapped his arms about her body, pinning her arms beneath his.

"No punching or kicking." He leaned in closer to her face. "Biting and scratching, however, are definitely encouraged," he murmured into her ear.

Pamela stood encased in his long arms, wiggling with all of her might to free herself. She could not stand the feel of his skin against hers, the smell of his body, or the way his breath teased the sensitive skin along the nape of her neck.

"Let me go," she begged, her voice filled with fear.

"Not yet," Daniel whispered as he lowered his head to hers. "There's something I have wanted to do to you for quite some time."

Daniel leaned forward and kissed her, hard on the lips. Pamela tried to scream, but his lips stifled her cries. She wanted to flay him alive, but a forgotten cavern inside of her body began to have other ideas. A vibrant and all-consuming flow of electricity shot out around her body. Her legs felt weak, her heart raced, and her toes began to tingle. This was not like the kisses she had shared with Bob. His ardor had seemed to be fanned only when she played the roll of the submissive housewife and catered to his every whim. And even then, his passion reminded her of something similar to warm milk instead of this forbidden absinthe. Pamela felt her defenses weakening, and her body slowly began responding to his.

Suddenly, he pulled away. He let her go and took a step back from her. Pamela felt her eyes searching his, as if wanting to know what she had done wrong.

"I'm sorry," he softly said.

Pamela studied his face for the slightest hint of what he was thinking, but her own emotions seemed to be clouding her judgment.

She lowered her eyes to the floor and took a frustrated breath.

"I'll go," he blurted out, and then reached for the door.

"Wait, Daniel." She paused and ran her hand along her forehead. "You were right. I was jealous of you spending time with Clarissa today. I've always wondered what she had that I lacked, and then today when I saw her hanging all over you…"

He smiled for her. "So does that mean I can come back and see you again?"

She tried to frown, unsuccessfully. "You can come back and finish fixing up my house, if we happen to run into—"

Daniel's laugh interrupted her. "Pamela, playing hard to get doesn't suit you. Next time, just nod."

She stepped up beside him at the door. He leaned over and kissed her forehead.

"I'll be back in a few days," he assured her as he opened her door.

"I'll be here, Daniel." She watched as he walked out the door and across the porch.

He grabbed his white T-shirt hanging from the porch railing and looked back at her once more. "Take care of my flying squirrel for me. I'm thinking of naming her Pamela," he called out.

Pamela gave him one last smile as he bounded down the steps and climbed into his Jeep.

Daniel tossed his T-shirt on to the passenger's seat, put on his sunglasses, and eyed the woman standing on the porch.

"I'm one lucky son of a bitch," he mumbled to himself as he started his Jeep. "I just hope I don't blow it."

CHAPTER 6

A familiar silver Mercedes-Benz CL 550 coupe made its way slowly down Pamela's long gravel drive from the main road. She had been sitting out on the front porch, enjoying an afternoon break from the animals, when the car pulled up in front of her house.

"Great, this is all I need," she whispered.

The usual welcoming committee of stray dogs surrounded the car, but this time there was no loud demonstration of barking as a man dressed in a tailored gray suit stepped from his Mercedes. He removed a pair of expensive Vuarnet sunglasses and threw them on the seat as he gazed up at the porch. The dogs eagerly gathered around the man with their tails wagging, waiting for their customary pat on the head.

"Hello, Pamela," he said as he looked up from rubbing Quincy's thick neck.

"Hello, Bob. What brings you out on a weekday?"

Bob Patrick was a man of medium-height with a thick body, and perfectly coiffed light brown hair. He had a long nose, round face, and a wide forehead that made his pale green eyes appear to be very intense. It was a feature Pamela knew he used to his advantage in the courtroom every time he cross-examined a witness.

"I had some free time this afternoon and thought I would come out and see how things were going," he told her as he made his way up the steps. "I haven't heard from you in a while," he added as he walked up to her side and tenderly kissed her cheek.

She could smell the woody cologne on his clothes as he approached. Pamela had forgotten how heavy-handed Bob tended to be with the stuff. It used to drive her out of their bedroom every morning when they were married. She felt she had spent half of their marriage running away from the smell of him. She had always been too afraid to tell him how she felt about his liberal use of cologne. At that moment, she realized she had always been too afraid to tell him about a lot of things.

Bob's pale green eyes explored up and down her body. "You've been feeling all right?"

Pamela frowned at her ex-husband's attempt at concern. "I'm fine, Bob."

"You look good." He leered at her. "But then you always look good, no matter how sick you are."

He inspected the property as if searching for something. Pamela followed his eyes and wondered what he could possibly be looking for.

"I ran into Jennifer Barons the other days at Galatoire's," he said as his eyes came back to her. "She asked about you. I said I would pass on her best. She and Elliot divorced last year. Ted Yanosky handled it. Very nasty, according to Ted."

"Well, Jennifer was the one with all of the money," Pamela commented, not really interested in the vacuous lives of forgotten friends in the city. "Elliot told everyone he married her for her money. He wasn't a very subtle man."

Bob nodded in agreement. "His two mistresses didn't think so either. They both testified against him at the divorce hearing, so Jennifer ended up walking away without having to pay him a dime."

Pamela studied his face for a moment. "You didn't drive all the way up here to talk about Jennifer and Elliot. I know you, Bob, and you wouldn't go to this much trouble without a reason."

"I could never pull one over on you, P.A.," he remarked, smiling.

"P.A.? You haven't called me that in years," she responded, referring to Bob's favorite nickname for her when they were married.

"I've always called you P.A. You're the one who hated being called Pamela Anne," he reminded her.

"No, Bob, I didn't hate being called Pamela Anne. I just hated the way you said it. You made my name sound like something you owned and not someone you loved." She sighed as she folded her arms about her body. "Why are you here?" she softly asked.

"Clarissa told me about the handyman you have working around here. In fact, she never shut up about the guy." He rolled his eyes. "She seems to think he's a gigolo, looking for a meal ticket. I immediately became suspicious and decided to come up here and check him out."

"You came all this way to check out a worker?" Pamela cracked a grin. "That's a first. You could have saved yourself the drive because he's not here, Bob."

He focused his intense eyes on her. "You can't just let any bum off the street in here, Pamela. You're a woman living alone and you're vulnerable in this godforsaken place. You need to use your head."

"This is beginning to sound like the conversation we had right after we got married. You pestered me to quit my job as an EMT because you thought it wasn't safe."

"It wasn't safe!" he shouted and then turned away. He stared down the gravel drive for a few moments, and when he turned back, his pale green eyes appeared to be once again in control. "You were a woman working on the streets of New Orleans with drug dealers and pimps."

"I knew what I was dealing with better than you, Bob." She paused and took a deep calming breath. He had always known how to push her buttons. "You need to stop worrying about me. I'm not your concern anymore," she coolly added.

"Pamela, you know I can't just turn off my emotions like that. I still care for you and worry about you out here all alone with only a few stray dogs to protect you. You need to think about getting an alarm system and perhaps taking a few self-defense classes, just in case. You're a long way from the nearest police station and you need to be a little more selective in your choice of workers."

"I'm not your wife anymore, Bob. Please don't lecture me. And the guy was sent by the probation office to do some community service. You're the one who told me to call them and get some free help out here because you were concerned I was doing too much by myself."

He blew a breath out through his clenched teeth. "Yeah, I know that. But the way Clarissa described him made me think I should come and check him out."

Pamela shook her head as a realization came over her. "You came out here looking for a fight, didn't you?"

"No, and that happened a long time ago," he angrily replied. "Why do you persist in bringing up one minor altercation that happened over ten years ago?!"

"There was more than one minor altercation, Bob." She gave him a stern reproach with her eyes. "Why this sudden urge to check out my workers? You never showed an interest in anyone who volunteered out here before. Why is Daniel any different from the fifty other people I have had on the site?" She paused and nodded. "Is it because Clarissa found this one so charming? Is that what's got you worried?"

Bob frowned at her. "You know me better than that. And this isn't about Clarissa, it's about you."

"Yes, I do know you, Bob. Your jealous tirades were the talk of the town when we were married."

"Jesus! Why are you being so hostile about this?" He placed his hands on his hips. "I came up here to make sure you're all right, and all I get is shit for it."

Pamela took another deep calming breath. She couldn't let him get to her, she reminded herself. "I'm sorry. But there is nothing to worry about as far as Daniel is concerned."

"Then just think about it. Call me when you're ready and I will run a background check on the guy. What harm could come of it?"

Pamela said nothing. She nodded and kept the fake smile on her face.

"Oh, the other reason I came out here was to talk to you about this big benefit the Louisiana Bar Association is hosting next weekend for Gulf Oil Spill Relief. It's at the new Roosevelt Hotel in the city. I think it could be a good opportunity for you to network your facility. There will be a lot of wealthy people attending, and I thought maybe you could pick up a few patrons. It's black tie, so you will need a nice dress." He examined her dirty blue jeans and stained T-shirt. "Do you even own a dress?" he asked.

"I'll find something to wear, don't worry."

"It's next Saturday at seven. I'll leave two tickets at the door so you can bring Carol with you."

"She would like that. Thanks, Bob."

He looked around the porch and then nodded his head. "I'm sure you have animals to feed or something else to do." He took a step backwards. "I'll see you next Saturday. And please think about letting me look into this handyman of yours."

Pamela opened her mouth to protest.

Bob raised his hand, silencing her. "I know, but if you won't do it for yourself, then do it for me. I don't want to see anything happen to you, P.A."

She took a step toward him. "I'm not your problem anymore, remember?"

He reached up and took a strand of blond hair that had fallen from her ponytail. "We'll never be completely free of each other, you know that. I sometimes wonder what it would have been like if we had stayed together."

Pamela raised her chin. "You're the one that wanted out, Bob. You couldn't stand the idea of having a sick wife, wondering what people would think of you for marrying a woman with lupus. You always worried about how you would explain my absences from all those political fundraisers you attended. You thought my disease would become more important than your career."

He let her blond hair fall from his fingers. "You haven't changed, have you, Pamela? Still trying to bait me with your cool condescension." He headed down the steps. "I'll see you next Saturday," he added over his shoulder as he walked away.

Pamela turned and went inside her front door, slamming it behind her. She walked over to the large wire cage by the window and took a napping Louis out of his sleeping sack and held him against her chest. The small bundle of brown and gray fur cuddled against her skin, instantly calming the swirling frustration inside of her. All the pain she had experienced during their marriage returned whenever Bob came to visit. It was as if the years apart had vanished into thin air, and she was once again a lonely housewife filled with a desperate desire to escape her troubled existence. Holding Louis against her, she went over and sat down on her couch. Summoning every ounce of control she possessed, she pushed all of her unhappy memories back into the darkest corners of her mind and focused her concentration on the warm little squirrel nestled in her hands.

* * * *

The following morning, Carol sauntered in the front door. She was dressed in a dark blue pantsuit and had applied a light touch of make up to her round face. In her hands were two grande Starbucks coffee cups.

"I got our usual chocolate mocha lattes," she announced as she walked over to Pamela.

Pamela put the last of the baby squirrels she had been feeding back into its little container and got up from the floor. She stretched uncomfortably, feeling the joints in her body ache at the idea of movement.

"You look nice," Pamela commented as she took in Carol's outfit.

"I have to meet with a new client this morning. I thought I would stop by and deliver one of these before heading over to the office." Carol handed Pamela the large coffee cup.

Pamela noticed the bags under Carol's eyes. "Another late night with Ian."

BROKEN WINGS

Carol nodded and held up her grande cup of coffee. "Hence the extra shot of espresso." She took a seat on one of the stools next to the kitchen counter. "God, that man's relentless in bed," she added, smiling.

"Carol!" Pamela shouted, trying to look offended. "I have known you since you were five years old, and to hear you discuss your sex life is rather disturbing."

"Want details?"

"No!" Pamela asserted as she leaned on the counter across from Carol.

"All right," Carol acquiesced. "But I thought you might like to live vicariously through me since you haven't had sex since that weirdo, Walden." She took a sip of her coffee.

"Walden was a nice guy. Just because he was a funeral director, you thought he was a weirdo," Pamela defended. "Anyway, he was just what I needed after the divorce."

"He looked like a gerbil. And that laugh." Carol feigned a shiver. "It reminded me of that peacock you took in three years ago, the one that kept loosing its feathers. That bird always sounded like a woman screaming for her life."

Pamela gave Carol a withering glance and then took a sip from her coffee.

"All right, I'll change the subject. Tell me what happened after I left the other day with the gigolo and the shoe hoarder," Carol demanded.

"Nothing." Pamela looked down into her coffee and prayed she sounded convincing enough to avoid further questioning.

"I find that hard to believe. The slut didn't drag his ass down to the local Motel 6 for a quickie?"

"Visually descriptive, but no." Pamela put her coffee down on the counter in front of her. "Clarissa left after she got her pictures. Then Daniel went back to work on the roof." She turned to the kitchen cabinets behind her.

"So, if nothing happened, why do you look guilty?"

Pamela spun around to face her. "I hate it when you do that!"

Carol raised her dark brows, feigning innocence. "Do what?"

"Interrogate me as though I have something to hide."

Carol snickered. "You always have something to hide. You never tell anyone what you are thinking or feeling. You keep everything bottled up inside of you."

Pamela ran her hand up and down the side of the white coffee cup in front of her. "I don't keep things bottled up inside of me." She picked at the paper rim of the grande Starbucks cup.

"Pamie, one day you're gonna blow and take half the Gulf Coast with you. You keep more bullshit hidden away inside of you than a pregnant nun in a cloister."

"Colorful."

"Thank you." Carol smiled, looking pleased. "So tell me, what is going on between you and Daniel?"

Pamela threw her hands in the air. "Nothing is going on!" she shouted.

Carol leaned over the counter. "You're overreacting. Whenever you overreact, you have something to hide. If nothing were going on between you two, you would just tell me to shut up and go feed something. But you're standing there fidgeting." She grinned. "And you never fidget."

"You've been watching too many detective shows on television," Pamela asserted as she watched Carol's pale blue eyes continue to stare at her. "Oh, all right." She rolled her eyes. "After Clarissa left the other day, Daniel found a flying squirrel under a roof tile, near the chimney, and brought it to me."

"Interesting, but I'm assuming there is more." Carol made a rolling motion with her hand. "Let's hear the rest of it," she directed.

"He told me that Clarissa had hit on him. We had an argument about his brazen attempt at flirting with the woman, and then he left."

"Brazen attempt at flirting? Boy, have you got it bad. What else?"

"Nothing." Pamela's voice cracked. "Nothing else happened. He left and now I have a flying squirrel in the kitchen." She started nervously playing with the cup of coffee in front of her.

Carol continued to stare. "What else?" she pressed.

Pamela shifted back and forth, from one foot to the other, until she could not take Carol's eyes on her any longer. "All right, he kissed me!" Pamela shouted. "There, happy?!"

"Don't ever murder anyone; you'd snap like a dried twig under interrogation," Carol joked as she picked up her coffee.

Pamela watched in astonishment as Carol then reached for an old newspaper on the counter and started gleaning the front page.

"Aren't you going to say anything?" Pamela finally asked, unable to tolerate Carol's continued casual indifference.

"He kissed you." She shrugged, never looking up from the newspaper. "That's all?"

"Isn't that enough?" Pamela responded, surprised by her cool reply.

"Hardly!" Carol rolled her eyes. "Let me know when he rips your clothes off and carries you to bed." She picked up her coffee, got up from the stool, and went over the couch. "So, any other wildlife come in besides the flying squirrel?" she asked as she took a seat on the couch.

The sound of a car coming down the drive made the two women turn their attention to the front door. The dogs outside started barking incessantly.

Carol put her coffee down on the table in front of her, got up from the couch, and quickly made her way to the door. "Maybe it's Imelda back for some of your boyfriend."

Pamela shook her head and immediately regretted ever telling the young woman about Daniel.

When the two stepped outside, they saw Daniel's blue Jeep pulled up next to Carol's green Nissan Sentra.

"I bet he's come to take you to the local Motel 6," Carol mumbled, nudging Pamela with her elbow.

Daniel stood up in the Jeep and threw a handful of dog biscuits to the barking strays gathered around his car. The dogs instantly went for the treats on the ground and let Daniel step away from his car, unscathed.

"Good looking and resourceful," Carol murmured next to Pamela. "I say jump his bones ASAP before that crazy bitch tries to dig those Manolo Blahnik's into him."

The dogs were still crunching away on their biscuits when Daniel came bounding up the steps, grinning like a child on Christmas morning.

"I think I should get going," Carol stated before Daniel had even made it on to the porch.

"Don't feel you have to rush off because of me," Daniel said, half laughing at Carol.

Carol pulled her car keys out from her pocket. "I would love to hang around and watch you two drooling over each other but I have to go into the office today and pretend to be a real accountant for a few hours."

"Carol, wait," Pamela pleaded. "I have some things to discuss with you."

Carol eyed her suspiciously. "You've got two minutes."

Pamela glanced from Carol to Daniel. "Well, for starters, Bob came by yesterday and wants us to go to this big oil spill benefit in New Orleans next Saturday."

Carol shook her head. "Can't make it." She pointed to Daniel. "Take your boyfriend."

Daniel looked from Carol to Pamela. "You told her I was your boyfriend?"

"No," Pamela replied, shaking her head.

"She told me that you found a flying squirrel and then you kissed her," Carol clarified.

"Carol!"

"What?" Carol shrugged. "You did tell me that."

"So does that make me your boyfriend?" Daniel asked, smiling.

"Technically, it makes you interested in becoming her boyfriend," Carol explained. "I don't think it actually becomes official until you two…" She raised her eyebrows and grinded her hips suggestively. "You know?"

"Oh, God," Pamela whispered.

Daniel smiled as he shook his head at Carol. "Perhaps I should take her out on a date first," he proposed.

"Absolutely! A nice dinner at some place that uses real silverware on the table," Carol offered.

"Would you two please stop?" Pamela begged.

"Or I could pick up something and bring it here," Daniel suggested. "Since she probably won't want to leave her babies for an entire evening."

"Ah, bringing food to the lady, nice touch." Carol gave Daniel the thumbs up sign.

"Enough!" Pamela cried out as she ushered Carol off the porch.

"Should I bring flowers and wine with the food?" Daniel asked Carol as Pamela pulled her to her green Sentra.

"Definitely," Carol shouted. "She likes Merlot and daisies!"

Pamela stood in the drive and watched as Carol's car disappeared around the bend in the road. She didn't want to turn and see Daniel standing there, grinning at her. But she knew there was no way around the inevitable conversation, so she took a deep breath and folded her arms across her chest. She finally mustered up the nerve to turn and face the porch, but was surprised to see that Daniel wasn't there. She looked around the cottage but he was nowhere to be found. Relieved, she walked back up the porch steps and inside her cottage door.

She found Daniel standing at her kitchen table with an open container in front of him. He didn't seem to notice as she walked in the room. Instead, he was preoccupied with something cupped in his hands.

"Couldn't wait to see how my girl was doing," he declared.

She stood for a moment and watched, a little mystified, at how the man's muscular body curled around the creature as he pulled his cupped hands close to his chest. His shoulders, back, and neck reflexively encircled the contents of his hand, as if to shield the helpless animal from any further harm.

"Has she been eating?" he asked as he glanced over at Pamela.

"Not as well as I would like. She wasn't too interested in her plate of mealworms and fruit this morning."

Daniel carefully placed the groggy brown and white squirrel back in her container and closed the lid. Putting the container back amid the pile on the table, he then turned and looked at Pamela. He smiled and slowly walked across the room to her side, then reached his hands around her back and pulled her into his arms.

"So now that I'm your boyfriend, I guess I can do this," he whispered as he leaned over and kissed her tenderly on the lips.

Pamela's first instinct was to pull back and slap him across the face, but then another kind of instinct took over. She felt her arms reach up about his neck as her body slid in closer to his.

Daniel responded to her submission by deepening his kiss. He let his hands travel the length of her back.

Pamela quickly pulled away. She took a step back out of his arms, leaving Daniel confused.

"What's wrong?" he asked.

"What are we doing?"

"I think it's called dating," he answered with a grin.

"Dating or mating? I think you have the two confused."

"No, I don't," he affirmed. "Trust me, I know the difference. If we had been mating, we wouldn't be standing in the living room."

She took another step back from him. "Perhaps we shouldn't do this. Neither one of us has a very good track record with the opposite sex, and our becoming involved might make our working relationship difficult."

He placed his hand on his hip and shook his head. "You need to stop analyzing this, Pamela. What we were as individuals is not what we will be as a couple. People change people no matter how short, or how long, a relationship lasts. Why don't we just enjoy what we have now and see what happens?" He paused and smiled at her. "Just consider me a new type of wildlife that you are eager to learn everything about."

Pamela scowled at him. "I don't end up in bed with my wildlife."

Daniel raised his dark brows. "Have you been thinking about how we would be in bed together?"

She felt her cheeks blush over. "Perhaps you should get to work on my roof before this," she motioned to Daniel, "gets out of hand."

"Am I moving too fast for you?" he asked as his eyes probed hers.

Pamela stood for a moment and considered the question. "Daniel, I think at my age moving too fast is more a necessity than a problem."

He laughed. "You're not old, Pamela."

"I'm older than you." She shrugged. "Perhaps too old."

"I don't care about your age." He reached out and pulled her back into his arms. "It's not the age of the wine that matters. It's the taste."

"You can't compare people to wine, Daniel."

"Relationships are not right or wrong because of someone's age. We are both over twenty-one and free to choose who we want to be with."

She looked down at the hardwood floor beneath her feet. "Even if the woman you want to be with is broken?"

He cupped his hands around her beautiful face and brought his lips within inches of hers. "You will never be broken to me."

Her eyes eagerly searched his. "I wish I could believe you," she whispered.

"How can I prove it to you?"

Pamela sighed as she felt that familiar nagging feeling of doubt rise from her gut. No man could ever prove his sincerity as far as she was concerned. Trust was a commodity she had stopped investing in years ago.

She took a step back from Daniel. "The roof is waiting," she said in a firm voice.

Daniel stared into her eyes and Pamela thought she saw a glimmer of hurt linger in his dark orbs. He smiled and the serious mood lifted between them. He nodded to her. "I'll get right on it, boss lady," he cheekily replied.

Daniel turned away and headed out the front door. Pamela felt a flurry of excitement stir beneath her skin. But a rush of apprehension soon replaced her excitement. Her gut screamed that this was a mistake, and no matter how hard her heart fought to quell her doubt, she knew that any romantic relationship between them would never last. She had realized a long time ago that she was never meant for love and she had gotten used to the idea of growing old alone. Life had instantly found a way to interfere with her plans, and the thought of a future with another person suddenly scared the hell out of her. But stirring amidst the doubt was an underlying twinge of desire; a feeling she had not experienced for a very long time.

* * * *

Later that afternoon, Pamela and Daniel were sitting on her back porch, eating sandwiches and taking a break from their work. Daniel had finished the roof and was starting to strip the old paint from the outside of the house. Small flecks of blue and white paint still covered his dark hair, face, chest, and forearms. Even his faded jeans had remnants of the paint on them.

"Sorry I don't have anything heartier than tuna for you," Pamela apologized. "I don't have any red meat in the house, and the chicken I do have, I have to keep for the animals."

Daniel held up his sandwich. "The tuna's fine, Pamela." He paused as he gazed out over the facility. "You know, with a little work this place could really be something," Daniel said, and took another bite of his sandwich.

"Yes, but the kind of work I need done costs money."

He finished chewing on his sandwich and asked, "What else do you need, besides an overhaul of your house and the barn?"

She eyed the large cages next to the barn for a moment. "Well, I need to get a few more exterior cages built. Then I would love to add more outdoor lights so I wouldn't have to carry a flashlight with me when I check on sick animals at night. Then there are the extra faucets needed around the cages."

"I might be able to help out with the outdoor lights," he volunteered. "I can do some basic wiring and run a line out from the barn."

"You're already doing too much. I feel like I'm taking advantage of you and I don't like feeling that way. I prefer to pay people for their services."

"I told you I want to do this," Daniel insisted.

She could not help but smile at him. "I find it's getting harder and harder to get you to accept no."

"Like I said, I rarely listen to women; especially the stubborn kind who don't like to accept help from friends."

Pamela said nothing. She watched in silent amazement as the man gobbled down two tuna sandwiches before she had barely gotten through half of her cheese sandwich. She waited until he had finished the last bite of his second sandwich before she brought up the subject that had been bothering her all morning.

"So how is the job hunting going?"

"Great," Daniel replied as he wiped the crumbs from his hands. "Got another bartending job at the Port of Call on Esplanade. It's not far from my place in the Quarter. The pay isn't as good as it was at Pat O'Brien's, but the tips are probably better. Tourists aren't the greatest tippers."

"Where do you live in the Quarter?"

"I rent a cottage that was converted from a carriage house. It sits across a courtyard from a house that was split up into apartments. It's small, but it's enough for me."

"I'm glad to hear that you found a job. I was worried you wouldn't find anything."

He shook his head as he grinned at her. "I always land on my feet, Pamela."

She gave him a cool going over with her gray eyes. "It's not your feet I worry about."

He looked out over the property. "You don't need to worry about that, either. It's been better lately. I feel less…agitated, I guess. Every time I feel myself getting tense, I remember what holding those baby squirrels feels like. Just holding those little guys really calms me. Then I think about this place." He paused as his eyes found hers. "And about you."

Pamela nervously cast an eye to her cheese sandwich, avoiding his penetrating gaze.

"Thinking about all of this helps me," he continued. "I've been to shrink after shrink and none of them have been able to do in six years what you and your animals have accomplished in a few days."

She kept her eyes peeled on her sandwich. "Animals help many people overcome mental and physical problems. Horses and dolphins have been used to connect with children who are autistic. Dogs and cats visit nursing homes and hospitals to comfort the sick and elderly. A variety of animals are trained to help individuals with chronic diseases, physical handicaps, or mental disorders. There is a long list of animals that have been utilized in some sort of program to help all kinds of people. Maybe my animals have helped you."

"Is that why you got into this?"

"I don't understand," she said, putting the rest of her sandwich back in a plastic bag.

He turned to her and let his dark eyes travel the delicate features of her face. "Do the animals help you? Is that why you surround yourself with them?" he finally asked.

She played with the sandwich bag in her hand. "They help give me something to live for, to get out of bed for. So, yes, I guess they have helped me. They have kept me going and not let me give in to my disease."

"Have you ever thought about when you can't do this anymore? I did some research on lupus after Carol told me about your condition. It seemed pretty daunting to me," he admitted.

"It's only daunting to you. For me, it's just something to live with like a limp or bad teeth. And I have no one to hand this place over to if something were to happen. I have no family to speak of and my biggest fear is that Bob will take over the facility and turn it into an elite petting zoo."

"What about hiring others to run it for you?"

She gave a slight shrug of her shoulders. "I don't have the money for that. I would need a nice sized trust fund for the sanctuary to pay a small staff. Most rehab facilities last only as long as the person who founded them. If anything were to happen to me, this place would not survive."

Daniel reached for his glass of iced tea. "So how do we find the money to make sure your facility keeps going?"

"We?" She rolled her eyes at him. "Are you sure you want to get involved with all of this? It's as nerve wracking as hell. It drives Carol absolutely insane."

"I can handle it. What do we do?"

She thought about the hours of wasted phone calls, sucking up to people she could not stand because she needed the money. The worry over bills, the sleepless nights, and when all was said and done, she still had to care for the animals. At times, the demands of her rehabilitation center seemed overwhelming, and then there were the moments with the animals that made it all worthwhile.

"Well, next Saturday there is that oil spill benefit that I mentioned to Carol. My ex-husband wants me to attend so I can hob-knob with his rich friends and see if I can drum up donations."

He nodded as he lifted his glass to his lips. "Yes, I remember. I'm in." He took a sip from his drink.

She furrowed her brow at him. "It's black tie."

He leaned closer to her. "I do own a tux, Pamela. I'm a bartender, not a bum." He leaned back from her and looked down into his tea. "I'll pick you up at five. We can go have a nice dinner in the city. And after the benefit, I can show you where I live."

She shook her head. "This isn't a date."

"For me it is," he said and took a long sip of tea.

Pamela sighed. "Now I'll need to go shopping for something to wear." She cringed and added, "Ugh!"

"I thought women loved shopping for clothes," he said, a little confused.

"This woman does not like shopping for clothes. I live in jeans and T-shirts. The idea of wasting money on some fancy cocktail dress I'll only wear once is infuriating. I'd rather be spending the money on my animals."

Daniel stood up from the porch. "Fine. I'll take you shopping later on this afternoon and buy you a dress for the benefit. I've got a change of clothes in the car. I can shower here and we can grab some dinner after. How does that sound?"

Pamela scowled at him. "I wasn't asking you to buy me a dress, Daniel. I can afford to buy my own clothes."

"You'll buy something that will cover up your body and make you appear frumpy and unattractive. I'll buy you a dress that will turn heads and have every man at that benefit pulling out his checkbook to win you over." He winked at her. "I know how to dress a woman to look like a woman."

"They teach you that little trick in bartending school?"

"Yeah, in between how to mix daiquiris and martinis." He reached over and pulled Pamela to her feet. "Now, go and take care of everybody so we can make an early start of it. I'll take you to Baton Rouge where they have some decent malls." He handed her his empty glass and headed down the porch steps.

Pamela could not help but smile as Daniel walked away from her. For the first time in a long time, she was actually excited about the prospect of shopping.

CHAPTER 7

"Daniel I can't wear this!" Pamela exclaimed as she looked at her reflection in the department store mirror.

She had on a black silk cocktail dress that was cut high above the knee and draped over one shoulder. The waist and skirt were fitted, accentuating every curve of Pamela's slim figure. There were tiny silver beads sewn intermittently throughout the fabric, making the dress shimmer in the dull fluorescent light of the store.

"Now that will make any man's mouth water," Daniel remarked, standing behind her at the mirror, grinning. "But we have to do something about the scratches on your arms. You look like you have been attacked by wild animals." He waved his hand over the long red scratch marks on her arms and upper chest.

"One of the drawbacks of rehabbing wild animals, I'm afraid," Pamela admitted as she looked at him through the department store mirror. Her eyes traveled once more over her reflection and then she turned around to face him. "I can't wear this. I look like a hooker," she whispered so as not to be heard by the saleswoman standing close by.

Daniel leaned in closer to her. "You don't look like a hooker. You look like a hot wildlife rehabber."

"But I'm supposed to look like a respectable wildlife rehabber. I run a not-for-profit charity, not a brothel."

"Pamela, when are you going to realize that certain types of men don't want to respect you, they want to sleep with you. And wearing a dress like that is how you're going to trick them into giving you money." He spun her around and started to unzip the top portion of the dress for her. "We'll take it," he said, nodding to the older saleswoman with silver hair.

Pamela looked down at the price tag hanging from the dress. "It's a fifteen-hundred-dollar dress!" she whispered in horror. "You can't buy this. It's too much money," she firmly said under her breath.

"I can afford it," he assured her.

"How can you afford a fifteen-hundred-dollar dress?"

"I have a trust fund," Daniel casually answered.

Pamela frowned at him in the mirror. "Very funny."

Daniel turned back to the saleswoman. "Now where can we find her some shoes?"

* * * *

A little over an hour later, Daniel and Pamela were sitting in his Jeep outside of a drive-through burger place in downtown Folsom, a small town in St. Tammany Parish. Daniel was munching on a fried fish sandwich and Pamela was eating french fries. The new dress and a pair of high-heeled black pumps were neatly wrapped in fancy shopping bags in the back seat.

"You shouldn't have spent so much money, Daniel," Pamela scolded in between mouthfuls of french fries.

"You need to look stunning at that party, and to make money you have to spend it," he insisted after he finished the last bite of his sandwich.

"But I feel very guilty that you spent so much." She waved at the bags in the back seat. "That must have cost you two months of tips. I don't know when I will be able to repay you."

He grinned at her. "I don't want you to repay me. It's a gift. And I already told you, I have a trust fund."

Pamela almost choked on a french fry. "I thought you were joking. You're serious?"

"I didn't think it was worth mentioning, but you seem so concerned about my finances."

"Are you..." She stopped herself. "I mean, how does a bartender get a trust fund?"

"The trust fund is actually from my mother's estate. My brother, Josh, and I received it after her death many years ago, but my father retains control. He sends Josh and me monthly allowances, but that's about all we get."

"Your mother left you the money in a trust fund?"

"Yes, she wanted us to have money so we could live comfortably, but didn't want her family fortune squandered on fast cars and loose women. Her family owned sugar cane farms. They were from New Orleans, and that's one of the reasons I came to the city. She died when I was sixteen, and I thought maybe I could get to know more about her by coming to live in the city where she grew up."

"So you're rich?"

"My mother's family was, but not anymore. All that is left of her family's fortune is what is in the trust fund, which is quite sizable. My father is the wealthy one now. He owns an import company in Bridgeport, Connecticut, where I grew up. He imports exotic food items, luxury goods, and clothing, and then sells them to retailers across the country. That's the business he was grooming me to take over when I signed up to go to Iraq."

"And what about your brother? Does he work with your father?"

"Josh is a plastic surgeon in Boston. He's married to a great woman and they have twin girls, May and Emily. He was always the brain in the family, and wanted to be a doctor for as long as I can remember. I was the football star. Dad didn't want him to go into the business because he felt Josh should pursue his dream of becoming a doctor. My father always expected me to take over his company."

"Are you close with your family?"

"Josh and I talk every now and then, but we were never that close growing up. He's a few years older than me and once he left for college, I never saw that much of him. And I haven't spoken to my old man since coming back from Iraq." He paused and his eyes appeared dark and distant for a moment. "He thought once I was back, everything would be as it was before I left. But I wasn't the same; none of us were after that war. He tried to understand but never did, so I left Connecticut soon after I returned home and…well, you know the rest."

Pamela watched the darkness in his eyes fade out like the light from a dying flame. She knew she had not even begun to scratch the surface of all the pain and trauma he had experienced during his time in Iraq, but she wanted to help him; not so much to forget his past, but to rise above it.

She wiped her hands on her napkin. "You could have told me earlier about your trust fund. Then I wouldn't have felt so guilty about your buying all those supplies for my home and my dress." She shook her head. "Begging for money all of the time can be so degrading. I have had people threaten me, call me a leech, and escort me out of their homes or businesses when I was trying to solicit funds for my facility." She sighed. "It's refreshing to finally meet someone who just gives what he has without asking for something in return. True kindness is such a rare quality these days. I guess I'm just not used to it."

"Well, I can't picture any one running you out of this benefit next Saturday." He leaned in closer to her and leered playfully. "Especially not in that dress." He pointed to the dress in the back seat. "And I'm not as kind as you think, Pamela. Perhaps there is something I want in return for my investment."

Pamela eased back from him and felt the blush rise on her cheeks. She looked down at the half-eaten container of french fries still sitting in her lap. Her appetite had suddenly vanished.

He leaned back in his seat, never taking his eyes off her. "I must admit I find it hard to believe a woman like you isn't knee deep in men asking for dates."

Pamela shrugged. "Being out at the facility all day kind of limits my ability to meet people, especially men."

"If you wanted to meet a man, you could have found a way."

She glared at him. "And what is that supposed to mean? If I were desperate enough I could have picked up some farmhand at the local bar?"

"No, it means you like being alone. Most people, men and women, can't stand being alone, and they would have gone down to the local bar and picked up some farmhand, as you put it. I don't know, but I get a sense that you're afraid of becoming romantically involved with any man."

Pamela wrapped up the uneaten french fries in a paper napkin, making sure to avoid Daniel's inquisitive stare. "I'm not afraid of men, if that is what you're implying."

Daniel reached over and placed his hand beneath her chin. He slowly turned her face to his. "I didn't say you were afraid of men. It's more like you are afraid of what a man might make you feel." He leaned in closer to her. "Like the way I make you feel when I kiss you."

Pamela's heart was thudding away inside her chest. A tingle of excitement shot up from her toes, and made her stomach leap upwards. It had been so long since she had felt her body respond to a man.

Daniel traced the outline of her jaw with his finger. "I don't want you to be afraid of me."

She pushed his hand away from her face. "Perhaps you're the one who needs to be afraid, Daniel. You haven't seen me ill and when you do…" Pamela let the words slip from her lips, instantly regretting them.

Daniel eased away from her, took in a long breath, and let his eyes settle on hers. "I don't see illness when I look at you. Your lupus is no different from my PTSD. They're just names in a medical book; they don't define us. I see the real you, Pamela. I will always only see the real you, remember that."

Pamela said nothing. She looked down at her hands and kept her thoughts to herself.

"We'd better go," Daniel said, starting the car. "We've got to get back before all those baby squirrels of yours go hungry."

* * * *

Fifteen minutes later, Daniel pulled his Jeep in front of Pamela's little cottage. It was dark out, but a waxing quarter moon was rising in the sky, blanketing the trees and surrounding property with a soft glow. The dogs seemed not the least bit interested in the car, and continued to snooze on the front porch.

"I thought you were in good hands with that bunch." Daniel nodded to the five sleeping canines. "Maybe I should install an alarm in this place." He glimpsed up at the cottage. "I'll worry about you out here alone at night."

Pamela grabbed her shopping bags from the back seat and climbed out of the car. "I was just as alone and vulnerable before you came along, Daniel. And I will be the same way after you have gone."

Daniel cocked his head to the side as he studied her. "What makes you think I'm leaving?"

She looked over at him and shrugged. "I just don't want you to feel like you're obligated, that's all. Things change and people move on."

"I'm not Bob, Pamela. I don't run out on people I care about when they need me."

Holding her bags close to her chest, Pamela walked around the front of the Jeep to his side of the vehicle. "Is that what you are doing, Daniel? Hanging around, buying me all of these things," she held up the bags, "because you think I need you?"

"No, that's not what I'm doing, Pamela. Bob ran out on you when your lupus got bad. I'm just saying I won't do the same thing." He moved closer to her and rubbed his fingers along her smooth, pale cheek. "You don't have to keep me at a distance because you think I'm going to hightail it out of here as soon as you get sick. I'm not that kind of man."

"That's not the…" Pamela fought back the lump forming in her throat. "I'm not keeping you at a distance," she insisted as she walked to the front porch.

Daniel laughed his warm deep laugh behind her. "Yes, you are. You keep everyone at a distance. Me, Carol, probably even Bob. The only ones you let in under that thick hide of yours are covered with fur and don't have any expectations."

She turned to face him, jutting her chin out defiantly. "Maybe I've been burned once too often by people. Animals are safer to love because they don't lie or let you down," Pamela said, raising her voice.

"You're not the only person on the face of the planet who has been hurt, Pamela," he countered, raising his voice to match hers. "You will not be repeating your past mistakes if you allow yourself to open up to someone."

All the dogs on the porch sat up and nervously observed the quarreling humans.

"And I suppose you're saying I should open myself to you…and then what?" She felt her anger take control. "Sleep with you so you can get a good return on your investment?"

"Now what a minute!" he yelled as he bounded up the steps to her side. "Don't you think for one minute that I have done all of this just to sleep with you." He waved at the bags in her arms.

"No, not all of it," she said, putting a cool tone of disregard into her voice. "I'm sure there was an element of pity mixed in with your plans. Sleep with the poor, sick, repressed wildlife lady. Show her a good time and then you have fulfilled your charitable quota for this lifetime." She backed away from him and placed her hand on the doorknob. "Go back to the bar, Daniel. I'm sure there you can find women who are easier to bed and a lot more interested in your selfish acts of philanthropy," she snapped.

"Jesus!" He ran his hands through his thick hair. "When you push someone away you do it with both hands. Stop trying to sling arrows at me because you don't feel you're worthy of anyone's kindness or regard."

She stood at the door, staring at him, not sure if she should slap him or sic the dogs on his ass.

She sighed and felt the fight inside of her fade away. Suddenly, she was tired; tired of second-guessing people's true intentions, tired of hiding her hurt emotions, and tired of being disappointed. She took in a deep breath and could smell the early traces of white clover in the air. Spring was here and her world was re-awakening. But deep inside, Pamela longed for winter to return. Winter was safe. Expectations, like the tender petals on a flower, were only trampled upon by the violent storms of spring.

She gazed into Daniel's face. "I'm not pushing you away. I just know what you will do in the end, Daniel. It's what everyone has done in my life. They walk away."

He leaned in closer to her and touched his forehead to hers. "I'm not going to do that. Despite what you may think, you and I are a lot alike, Pamela. We are both birds afraid to fly in case we should fall and break our wings. But broken wings heal. And every bird must fly, even if it's only for a brief moment. But in that moment, they get their chance to spread their wings and try to touch the sky."

She gently nodded her head. "I'm sorry. I'm not good at this stuff. I was never very good at dating."

He smiled and wrapped his arm about her shoulders. "No one was ever good at dating. Dating was something you did in high school on weekends and after football games. You were more interested in learning about yourself than someone else. At this stage in our lives, I think it would be safe to call what we have a relationship."

Pamela frowned. "And how is a relationship different from dating?"

He removed his arm from her shoulders and took a step back from her. "Because in a relationship you already know who you are, and are committed to learning more about someone else."

"And you have learned that I'm a repressed, frightened woman who finds animals safer than people, right?"

He held up his hands to her in surrender. "No, we are not going there again. Let's just say I'm still trying to figure you out."

Pamela pulled her keys out of her purse and opened the front door. She then turned to Daniel, who was still standing on the porch behind her. "Aren't you coming in?"

He shook his head. "I think I should head back to the city." He took a step toward her. "I start my new job tomorrow and they have me on a tight schedule for the next few days until I get to know the bar. So it might be a while before I can get back and do some more work on the place." He leaned over and kissed her cheek. "But I will definitely be back next Saturday to pick you up for our date."

"Date?"

"The benefit," he explained. "I plan on making that our first formal date."

Pamela smiled. "All right, Daniel."

He turned to go and she watched as he made his way toward his Jeep in the bright moonlight.

"And take care of my flying squirrel," he shouted from the car. "I expect great things from my little Pamela."

CHAPTER 8

The next several days seemed to drag on like a boring lecture in a room with no exits. Pamela kept busy taking in four baby opossums, a litter of fox kits, and a few more baby squirrels. But the time absorbed with feeding, cleaning, and caring for the animals did not seem to help her restless mind. No matter the hour in the day, her thoughts would find their way back to Daniel. He would call her cell phone in the afternoons before his shift began at work. They would share a few brief exchanges about the monotony of their days and then he would have to go. The short phone calls only seemed to compound her growing anxiety. And as the night of the benefit drew closer, the more anxious Pamela became.

"What is wrong with you?" Carol asked the morning of the benefit. They were going over the end of the month figures at the kitchen counter. "You've been bouncing off the walls since I got here."

Pamela picked up a pencil from the counter and started rhythmically tapping it against the tile. "You know I hate doing accounting, and I have got a lot to do today."

Carol smiled as she watched Pamela's antics. "Could your newfound fidgeting be because of your hot date tonight with the criminal?"

Pamela put the pencil down and said, "It's not a date."

"He is taking you out to dinner before the benefit, and to his place after the benefit. Right?" Carol questioned.

"So?" Pamela reached for the pencil again.

"Honey, I don't care what part of the world you come from, that's a date." Carol took the pencil out of her hand. "So why are you nervous about tonight?"

Pamela ran her hand over her forehead. "I'm not nervous, I'm just a little apprehensive. You know I don't like leaving the place for so long."

"Ian and I will be here to babysit. We will feed everyone and watch over everything while you're gone. Even got my overnight bag waiting in the car, just in case you decide not to come home until morning," Carol added with a smug grin.

"Are you sure you're Scott's daughter?" Pamela asked, shaking her head. "Your father was never like this."

Carol laughed. "Not according to my mother!"

"Well, I'm sure we will be home late, but not that late."

"Pamie, tell me you are not going to be a prude tonight and turn down that man's invitation to join him in between the sheets?" she asked with a hint of disappointment in her voice.

Pamela glared at her. "Jesus, Carol! Tonight is about the facility, not me and Daniel."

Carol sat back on her stool and folded her arms across her chest. "Are you kidding me? Of course tonight is about the two of you. Why do you think he went to all the trouble to buy you that hot dress and shoes that even Imelda would drool over? It's because he wants you. He wants you to be his. Look, men are like animals in the first place. Instead of peeing on you to announce to the world that you are theirs, they have to come up with more creative, and less gross, ways to make that statement. So they buy you things; clothes, shoes, condo's, anything that will show people what you are worth to them and that they have put their mark on you."

Pamela frowned. "I think you're reading way too much into this."

"Excuse me, I've been there when you two are together. I see the way the man looks at you and trust me, tonight he plans on plowing your fields until the till breaks!"

"Oh, God!" Pamela laid her head down on the mound of receipts in front of her. "You need help," she mumbled into the pile of papers.

Carol patted her back. "And you need to get laid."

Pamela sat up and looked over at Carol. "I give up. And what if you are right and he does want to sleep with me, what do I do?"

"Are you asking me what you should do technically, or are we just speaking of the general, should I or shouldn't I scenario?"

"Carol!"

"All right, I know your technique may be rusty, but it's just like riding a bike. Once you've got a naked man beside you, it all comes back. And I definitely vote yes to jumping his bones." She paused and took in Pamela's frantic eyes. "It will be all right. When two people care about each other, it's always all right. Let him in, Pamie. For once, forget the past and embrace the future without reservation." She grinned. "And I want all of the details in the morning."

* * * *

Pamela was standing in front of her bedroom mirror trying to put the last touches on her make up, but her trembling hand was making the mascara wand more of an instrument of torture than something to enhance beauty. Fed up, she put away her make up and gave her reflection a thorough going over. Satisfied with the results, Pamela stepped back and admired her efforts. Her make up was subtle but enhanced her creamy white skin and deep gray eyes. She had even applied some foundation to the scratches on her arms and chest, lessening their appearance. Her shoulder length blond hair was wrapped up in a French twist that Carol had helped her pin. Her dress shimmered in the light of her bedroom as it clung to her figure. Even the high heel of her shoes seemed to add a dash of sexiness to the outfit by accentuating the curve of her slender legs. She patted away the butterflies in her belly and took in a deep breath, then glanced over to her bed and examined the overnight bag she had packed earlier. She had come up with several rationalizations for bringing the bag, but only one reason made sense to her, and it was the only excuse she feared embracing.

The sound of a car coming down the drive made her stomach twist into knots. She walked to her bedroom window and looked past the tree where Lester was perched to see a black limousine making its way to her front door.

"Oh, shit!" she whispered as she walked quickly to her bedroom door.

Carol and a tall, redheaded young man were peering out the living room window when Pamela stepped up behind them.

"Is that what I think it is?" Pamela said in a shaky voice.

Carol turned around and gave a low whistle. "Damn woman. You look good."

The lanky man beside Carol turned, and Pamela could not help but notice how his hazel eyes almost popped out of his head. "Pamela, you look prettier than a blue ribbon at the cattle show," he pronounced in a southern accent.

Pamela stared at Ian for a moment. "Thank you, Ian. I think," she replied.

Ian was a good bit taller than Carol, but Pamela felt his freckled complexion seemed to compliment Carol's pale skin. He had a square face, kind round eyes, a long nose, and a dimple in the center of his chin.

"Looks like your boyfriend went all out," Carol said as she pointed to the window. "He must be a hell of a bartender to be able to shell out for a limo."

"Carol, would you stop calling him my boyfriend?" Pamela asserted.

"Would you prefer I call him your gigolo?"

Ian giggled as Pamela's gray eyes tore into the young woman's round face.

A knock on the door made Pamela almost jump out of her skin. She wasn't ready for this. She couldn't answer the door and see Daniel standing there. She stood glued to her spot on the floor, afraid to move.

Carol quickly went to the door and opened it. There standing in the yellow glow of the setting sun was Daniel. He was dressed in a tailored double-breasted tux. His dark hair was neatly sleeked back and he was carrying a single red rose.

"Aww!" Carol crooned. "He brought you a rose." She turned to Ian. "Look honey, you should do that."

Ian stepped closer to Carol's side, frowning.

Daniel walked in the door and handed Carol the rose. "Actually, it's for you," he clarified. "A thank you for taking over for an evening."

Carol took the rose and then elbowed her boyfriend.

Daniel turned and saw Pamela standing behind him.

Pamela felt her stomach tighten when she saw him in his tuxedo. The smell of his spicy cologne filled the air around her and made her knees go weak. She watched as his dark eyes analyzed the curves of her body. The look on the man's face made every fiber of her being burn with an unfamiliar desire.

Pamela was the first to break the silence in the room. "Daniel, you look very handsome," she said, in a wavering voice.

"I knew that was the right dress," he murmured to her with a devilish grin.

"I feel like I should break out a Polaroid and snap pictures like it's your first prom," Carol teased.

Pamela glared at Carol.

"Daniel," Carol said, ignoring Pamela as she shoved Ian in front of him. "This is my boyfriend, Ian Toujaque."

The two men shook hands as Carol beamed with pride.

Daniel turned to the kitchen table. "Where's my girl?" he asked, eagerly surveying the containers on the table.

Pamela walked over to the table and pulled out the container with the flying squirrel in it.

"How is she doing?" he questioned.

"She's still not eating as I would like," Pamela told him as she lifted the tiny creature out of the container. "She is too docile and still pretty lethargic, but she seems to be holding her own."

"Any idea what is wrong with her?" he asked, examining the small ball of fur in her hands.

"No. I'm still not sure what we are dealing with but I will keep an eye on her and let you know if anything changes."

Daniel took the small flying squirrel from Pamela's hands and raised it to his face. He gave the bundle of fur a careful going over.

"A man after your own heart," Carol remarked to Pamela as she watched Daniel place the flyer back in her container.

Pamela nervously eyed Daniel. "You got a limousine for the evening?"

"I only got it to take us to dinner, and then on to the benefit. I figured after the benefit we could walk to my place in the Quarter. It isn't far from the Roosevelt Hotel."

"An evening stroll in the French Quarter, how romantic," Carol cooed and then elbowed Ian again. "How come we never do that?"

Daniel gave Ian a sympathetic smile. He then took Pamela's elbow. "Perhaps we should go before Ian starts getting bruises."

Pamela nodded, went over to the kitchen table, and picked up her black shawl and purse. She hesitated for a moment as an image of the overnight bag popped into her head. She took a deep breath and decided it might look better to leave the bag on her bed; she did not want it to appear as if she were planning for anything, and definitely did not want to give him any ideas.

She turned to Daniel. "I'm ready."

They walked out the front door and toward the long black limousine waiting in the driveway. Daniel opened the back door and waited as Pamela made her way inside the car. Just as Daniel was about to climb in after her, a shout came from the direction of the front door.

"Wait a minute, you forgot something," Carol yelled as she ran toward the limousine.

When she reached the back door of the limousine, Carol shoved the overnight bag inside.

"You forgot this," she added, winking at Pamela.

Before Pamela could respond, Carol ran quickly back inside of the house.

Daniel slid in next to her and spied the overnight bag. He said nothing but looked from the bag to Pamela with the silliest grin on his face.

"I, ah, just packed some casual clothes and a pair of tennis shoes for after the benefit. I thought I could change at your place and then I would be comfortable on the drive home later tonight. I don't want to drive home dressed like this in your Jeep, right?"

Daniel said nothing and continued to grin at her.

"Don't look at me like that," she protested. "It's nothing. Don't read too much into it. It's just a change of clothes—"

"And a pair of tennis shoes, so you said," he interrupted. He laughed and then leaned over and tenderly kissed her cheek. "You look wonderful," he whispered to her. "And don't look so nervous. We are just two people going out for a pleasant evening in the city. What will be, will be."

That was exactly what terrified Pamela. Because with every passing second in his company, she felt her body hoping for one outcome while her mind was clamoring for another.

* * * *

As the limousine swept past the Louisiana Superdome on its way down Poydras Avenue, Pamela felt as if she had come home. New Orleans had always been home to her. The seventeen years she had spent in the city had left an indelible mark on her soul. She loved coming back to take in the sweet sights, and smells, the Big Easy had to offer. She had gone to EMT school here. She had worked amidst the poorest and in the most dangerous sections of the city, taking people to the city's hallmark of healthcare, Charity Hospital. She had married here, and suffered through the most painful experiences of her life here. Even after the ravages of Katrina had destroyed many of the places she had fondly remembered, the city still captivated her heart.

"I made reservations at Arnaud's," Daniel told her as he reached for her hand.

Pamela grinned at him. "What, no shrimp sandwiches and french fries?"

Daniel shook his head. "Not tonight."

"You really have gone all out. A limo and dinner at Arnaud's... I'm impressed."

"The limo was a necessity. I didn't see you riding around in a Jeep in that outfit. And the dinner is also a necessity. I have been to enough benefits to know that cheap hors d'oeuvres and finger food does not a meal make. I'm always starving halfway through those things and when I get hungry, I get grumpy."

"Thanks for the warning." She looked down at their intertwined hands. "Have you been to a lot of benefits?"

"When I was growing up in Connecticut, benefits and society parties were a staple affair on the weekends. My mother sat on a lot of committees, and my brother and I were forced to attend every single event she ever helped plan."

"Were you close with your mother?"

He sat back in his seat and stretched his legs. "Pretty close, then she got sick. I couldn't stand watching her fade away, so I pulled back." He shook his head. "I've always regretted not being there for her."

"What happened to her?"

"Pancreatitis. My mother loved two things in life, her children and her whiskey. After her third bout of pancreatitis, we weren't too surprised when she started getting worse and not better. Today she would have been called an alcoholic; then she was just the life of the party."

"I'm sorry."

He squeezed her hand. "Hey, tonight is a happy occasion." He smiled for her. "You're going to walk into that benefit and wow them. Tonight you're going to get every penny you need to keep your wildlife facility going forever."

"I'd be happy with enough to just keep it going for the next year."

"Think big, Pamela. And never expect less than what you desire."

Pamela looked into his dark eyes and felt that unsettling twinge wrap around her insides. What she desired had nothing to do with her facility, but she figured she didn't need to share that little tidbit of information with Daniel. Somehow, she suspected, he already knew.

* * * *

When they arrived at Arnaud's Restaurant, the maitre d' greeted Daniel by name and gave him a warm handshake. After introductions and pleasantries had been exchanged, a short, round waiter dressed in a red vest, black pants, and a white starched shirt was instructed by the maitre d' to escort Daniel and Pamela to their table. They were taken off to the side of the main dining room to one of the smaller private dining rooms.

Once seated at their table, the waiter handed Daniel and Pamela their menus.

"I'll just give you two a moment to go over the menu," the waiter said and quickly departed the room.

Pamela took in the charming private dining room. Upon the walls was an extensive collection of pictures of Mardi Gras parades from the past. Some of the photos were old and faded while others looked more modern in origin. Intermixed with the pictures of carnival floats was a decorative collection of large old-fashioned brass keys. The keys shone brightly against the deep red wallpaper.

"How do you know the maitre d'?"

"Ed Rhymes," he said, putting his menu to the side. "I worked here at the front bar when I first came to New Orleans. We used to hang out together after work until I got fired."

"Why did you get fired?" Pamela asked as she put her menu down on the table.

He rubbed his chin. "I, ah, got into a heated discussion with the wine steward, Mike Allen. He complained to the manager and I was let go."

She folded her arms across the table in front of her. "How many times have you been fired because of some fight or argument?" she asked, never taking her eyes off his. "Be honest, Daniel," she added, her voice no higher than a whisper.

"Six, since I have been in New Orleans. You know about my past. When I'm tired or frustrated, which as a bartender comes with the territory, I get anxious. When I get anxious, I look for a fight."

"Does the fighting help?"

He tilted his head slightly to the side. "I don't understand. Help what, exactly?"

"Help you to feel better about yourself." She paused and looked down at the white linen tablecloth before her. "A man who throws punches is either trying to make up for some shortcoming he feels he has, or he is trying to prove something to himself. Either way, it's not the other person he has a problem with."

"And what makes you such an expert on why men fight?"

Pamela played with a fork on the table. "I was married to one for eight years. Every time he fought someone he said it was for my honor, but it was really for his. His insecurities, more than our bad marriage, were the reasons behind his short fuse."

Daniel sat back in his chair. "You weren't happily married?"

She leaned in closer to the table. "In the beginning, I was. But about a year into it, I started to see a side of Bob that I didn't see before our marriage. Once you lose respect for a man it's not long after that your heart leaves him, too. I stayed in that marriage about seven years longer than I should have. I thought I was being a good wife, but in actuality I was just being foolish."

"I watched my parent's bad marriage rip my mother apart—probably the reason she drank. She stayed married to my father for my brother and me. At least you got out and found a life you love," Daniel declared.

Pamela felt her worries come creeping back to the forefront of her thoughts. "But is it a life I can keep?"

The waiter returned to their private room.

"Are you ready to order?" he asked.

Daniel picked up his menu and grinned at Pamela. "Why don't you allow me to order for the both of us?" he asked.

She nodded and then listened in amazement as Daniel ordered a varied selection of appetizers and entrees from the menu.

"And bring us a bottle of your best Pouilly-Fumé with our appetizers and after that we can move on to one of your better selections of a Bâtard-Montrachet Grand Cru with the meal."

Pamela waited until the waiter had left the room, carrying their menus underneath his arm, before she spoke to Daniel.

She reached for her glass of water. "Do all bartenders know so much about wine?" She took a sip of the cool water.

"I've worked in a lot of restaurants and I learned a thing or two about wine and food. I find it impresses the society types I sometimes come in contact with if I can tell the difference between a wine from the Burgundy region of France and one from the Loire Valley."

She laughed slightly as she put her glass back down on the table. "Society types? I just can't see you rubbing elbows with the social set."

Daniel ran his fingers over the white china plate in front of him. "I sometimes moonlight organizing the bar at parties put on by a few of the socially prominent people in town. It pays well and the extra jobs fill in the time between bartending gigs."

"You really do keep busy," Pamela stated as she studied the man across from her. "What do you do when you're not serving alcohol to half of the city?"

He reached across the table for her hand. "Right now, I'm helping this reclusive little old wildlife rehabber woman take care of her baby squirrels."

Pamela smiled. "And before that?"

"I drank a good bit, worked sixty hours a week, got into a lot of fights, and was a general pain in the ass to everyone who knew me."

"Perhaps all of that was your PTSD, and not the real you, coming through. You just couldn't see it before now."

He let go of her hand and sat back in his chair. "Or maybe I didn't want to see it. I never considered myself to be a very patient man before I started working with you and your animals. Now I find my tolerance for everyone has greatly improved. I can't explain it, but I guess I'm not angry anymore. I used to always be so angry, but I didn't know why." He shrugged. "I've learned to stop searching for the why's in my life. Why did this happen to me? Why am I like this? I feel, for the first time in a long time, I can just be me and not wonder why anymore."

Pamela nodded her head as she took in the room around them. "I understand. I used to ask why God gave me lupus, and then I started working with wildlife. As I watched animals carry on, despite their injury or infirmity, I realized we all have something we have to live with. Animals take their misfortune in stride. They never complain or ask for pity; they just go on with their lives. And that is what I decided to do."

"I'm not quite where you are yet," Daniel admitted. "But I'm working on it."

She looked into his dark eyes and smiled. "You'll get there, Daniel. I believe in you."

He leaned in closer to the table. "I know you believe in me, but do you trust me, Pamela?"

Pamela never got a chance to answer him before the waiter returned with their wine. As Pamela watched Daniel inspect the cork and swirl the wine in his glass, she pondered his question about trust. Did she trust him? She desperately wished she knew the answer, but like most mysteries in life, she figured only time would reveal the correct response.

Soon a flurry of waiters brought dish after dish of the house specialties that Daniel had ordered. And with each new course came another glass of wine. Between the souflé potatoes, mushrooms Véronique, asparagus hollandaise, Brabant potatoes, crème brulée, and strawberries Arnaud, Pamela downed glass after glass of the wine. By the time the last plate had been cleared away from the table, her head was swimming.

"God, I think I'm tipsy," she announced as she held her hand against her forehead.

"I told you to slow down during the appetizers," he chided and then turned to the waiter. "Two coffees with chicory, black."

The short, round man in the red vest nodded and quickly exited the private dining room.

"Can't have you slurring your words when you are trying to win over potential sponsors," Daniel reasoned.

Pamela rubbed her hands together. "I guess I'm just a little bit nervous about the party. I never did do well at big functions. Bob was always the one who would work the room and make connections. I would always smile, nod my head, and pray that the evening would soon end."

"Did Bob drag you to a lot of parties?" he asked as he reached for his glass of wine.

"More than I care to remember," she stated, cringing. "If there was an opportunity to meet the politically connected, or just rub elbows with the right people, Bob was there. After I got sick and stopped attending all the parties, people started to talk, and Bob became embarrassed. The last fight we had was on the night of some big party given by one of the maidens of the social set in the city. I was tired and told him I wasn't going. He blew a fuse and told me he needed a wife who would put his interests above her illness. The next morning at breakfast he asked for a divorce."

Daniel took a sip from his wine and then shook his head. "Well, be thankful that you are rid of him. I've met a lot of men like Bob in my life, and none of them are ever interested in helping anyone but themselves."

"Sounds like you have a bit of experience with that sort of man," she said, noting the sudden tension in his voice.

Daniel's eyes focused on the crystal wine glass in his hand. "My father is one. He ignored his wife, his children—hell, everyone who should have mattered to him—all for the sake of his business."

Pamela sat back in her chair as she observed his solemn face. "I understand, Daniel. I know how it feels to be cast aside."

The waiter returned with two cups of coffee on a silver tray, along with the check.

Pamela eagerly grabbed for the coffee cup placed before her. She inwardly scolded herself for saying too much and blamed it on the excess alcohol. But she knew the alcohol was not completely to blame for her ramblings. She had wanted to get to know the handsome man across from her, and despite her growing apprehension about the evening ahead, she still hoped that maybe this time, she had finally found someone who wanted to get to know her, as well.

CHAPTER 9

The limousine made the six-block drive from Arnaud's Restaurant to the Roosevelt Hotel. The Roosevelt Hotel occupied the building previously owned by the Fairmont Hotel on Baronne Street. Destroyed by the floodwaters of Katrina, the space had been taken over and renovated to look like the original Roosevelt Hotel that had operated in New Orleans in the early 1930s.

As Pamela stepped from the car and looked up at the hotel's gray stone facade, she wondered what awaited her inside. She would have preferred an afternoon of general dentistry to an evening of rubbing elbows with the rich and obnoxious.

"We could have just walked from the restaurant," she said to Daniel as they made their way up the front steps to the hotel entrance.

He placed his hand over hers. "It's how you look getting there that matters, Pamela. And we have to look like we mean business."

The benefit for the Gulf Oil Spill Relief Program was being held in one of the grand ballrooms of the hotel. Tickets were collected at the door, where Pamela stopped and checked her wrap and the small overnight bag Daniel had carried in from the limousine. Pamela gave her name to a young brown-eyed girl who was seated behind a table with a clipboard. She collected the two tickets waiting for her and then took Daniel's arm as they made their way into the main ballroom.

Decorated in shades of gold with Greek Doric columns set against the walls, the ballroom had several multi-tiered crystal chandeliers hanging from the ceiling, shining their light on the bright gold and cream-colored carpet below. Along the walls large portraits of wildlife and industries native to the Gulf Coast, and threatened by the oil spill, were hung. Shrimp trawlers and crab fishermen were intermingled among the brown pelican, raccoon, white tailed deer, oyster, and redfish prints. To the left of the entrance, a large buffet service was already in full swing with a long line of people waiting to be served. To the right, a bar built to look like a giant pirogue, complete with crab traps and nets, had another long line of people before it. Dozens of white linen-covered tables were positioned in the middle of the room for the guests to sit and dine. In the back of the room, a ten-piece band played softly in front of a small white dance floor that was cordoned off with gold rope.

Daniel leaned over to her. "See why I wanted to eat before we came," he said as he nodded to the long buffet line.

Pamela scanned the room and tried to find a friendly face, or at least someone she had known from her days with Bob, but no one among the black tie crowd appeared familiar.

Daniel examined the throng of people surrounding them. "What should we do first, casually mingle or go after the first rich looking person we see?" He turned to her. "You brought your business cards, right?" he asked.

She nodded and grabbed at her small black beaded purse. "As many as I could shove into this thing."

"Good," he peered eagerly into the crowd. "Now just follow my lead."

Daniel pulled her along until he stopped beside an older couple. They looked reserved, uptight, and, based on the amount of diamonds the woman displayed on her hands and neck, very wealthy.

"Excuse me, but are you Peter and Esther Robillard?" Daniel asked the couple as he stood before them.

"Why, yes," the older man with a gray beard and dark blue eyes replied. "Have we met?" he asked, extending his hand to Daniel.

"I'm Daniel Phillips of the Arceneaux family from Audubon Trace. My family was in the sugar cane business—"

Esther Robillard's gasp interrupted him. She placed her hand on Daniel's arm. "I went to school with your mother! The last time I saw her was before she married that importer, Edward Phillips, and moved to Connecticut." She clapped a diamond-clad hand to her chest. "My God, you're Elizabeth's boy. I can't believe it."

"I remember my mother mentioning you." Daniel pulled Pamela alongside of him. "I'd like to introduce you to a very good friend, Pamela Wells. She runs a wildlife rehabilitation center outside of the city and has worked extensively in rescuing wildlife affected by the oil disaster."

Esther and Peter Robillard shook their heads in unison.

"Such a tragedy," Esther commented. "It's good to know that there are people like you in the world helping the animals. It is a pleasure to meet you, my dear."

"People like Pamela work tirelessly to help rescue all of these wonderful creatures." Daniel's hand waved to the pictures on the wall. "And they get no financial assistance from the state or federal government. Can you believe that?"

Esther placed a caring hand on Pamela's arm. "How do you manage?"

Pamela put on her best smile. "Well, I'm dependent on the donations of private citizens to help keep my facility going. I take in over three hundred animals a year. Orphaned and injured wildlife require food, formula, housing, and medical care. I have a non-profit organization that holds fundraisers every year, but I'm a one-woman operation and it is so difficult in these economic times to get donations."

"Do you have a card?" Peter Robillard asked.

"Yes, I do," Pamela quickly reached into her handbag, pulled out her card, and handed it to him.

Peter Robillard inspected her card. "I have a few animal-related organizations that I make a part of my annual giving program." He looked up at her with his steely blue eyes. "I prefer to help local, small organizations get on their feet, instead of pumping money into big non-profits that spend half of their donations on salaries for CEOs." He nodded to her. "My accountant is named Steve Mueller with Erickson and Walters. I'm going to give him your information on Monday and have him set you up on our annual donations list."

Pamela felt her heart do a few happy somersaults. "Thank you. That would be...I can't tell you how much this would mean to me and to the animals I help to rehabilitate."

"Thank your young man here," Esther said, patting Daniel's arm. "I heard about Elizabeth's passing a few years back. I'm so sorry. She was a good friend. When we were growing up together, she was always the life of the party."

Daniel nodded. "Yes, that was Mom."

"You keep up the good work, young lady," Esther said to Pamela with a warm smile. "We need more people like you in the world."

Pamela and Daniel said good-bye to the Robillards and headed back out into the crowd.

"I can't believe it," Pamela said, sounding almost giddy. "How did you know those people? And how did you know the woman went to school with your mother?"

Daniel smiled at her excitement. "I told you I have done bartending at a few social parties in the past. Well, I've learned to keep my eyes and ears open and I try to remember everything I hear. Mrs. Esther Robillard is known for wearing her expensive diamond jewelry to every social affair. I have seen them once or twice at events like this. Her husband loves gin and tonics with a twist. I took a shot and it paid off." He shrugged.

"But they knew your mother's family?" Pamela asked surprised.

"My mother's family was very wealthy and very well connected. An older couple like that was bound to have known or at least heard of them. That she went to school with my mother was just blind luck. But then again, this is New Orleans, and a very small town. Everybody knows everybody down here. But I don't have to tell you that." He searched the room once more. "Ah," he said to her. "I think I found another person you need to meet."

Pamela eagerly surveyed the ballroom. "Who?"

"Val Easterling," Daniel announced. "And this ball of fire, I do know."

Daniel took Pamela's hand and pulled her across the room to the side of a round woman dressed in a burgundy gown with short, silver hair, and light blue eyes. She had delicate features and as soon as she spotted Daniel coming her way, she roared with delight.

"Daniel, is that you? Who in the hell let you in here?" she called out and threw her arms about his neck.

Daniel kissed the woman's smooth, pale cheek and stood back from her. "Val Easterling, I want you to meet someone." He gently pulled Pamela to his side. "Pamela Wells is a very dear friend."

Val's blue eyes seemed to take in every inch of Pamela's figure. "Darlin', I hope you know what you're getting into with this boy. He's a handful."

Pamela grinned. "So I'm beginning to notice."

Daniel put a loving arm about Val's waist. "Whenever Val has parties, she always gets me to set up the bar and hire the staff. And she throws the best parties in town."

Val waved a dismissive hand in the air. "I throw much better parties than this sorry affair. Lobster and cream cheese rolls for hors d'oeuvres." She frowned. "It's so eighties. You would think with all the money they sunk into this place after the storm they could have hired a better caterer." She looked over Daniel's face for a moment and then crinkled her brow. "What are you doing here, Daniel? I seem to remember you saying you hated these functions. Don't tell me you have grown a sudden fondness for our local flora and fauna."

"Yes, Val, I'm afraid I have found a soft spot for all the fuzzy little fur balls down here." Daniel smiled at Pamela. "You see, Pamela is a wildlife rehabber and runs a facility outside of the city. She takes in hundreds of animals a year and she needs money to keep her place going."

Pamela felt her jaw drop.

Val placed her hand on her wide hip. "How much are we talking about?"

Pamela felt her stomach knot up. "My budget varies from month to month, depending on the animals I take in, vet bills, and the amount of formula—"

"Just give me a bottom line lump sum, dearie," Val said, cutting off Pamela's marketing speech.

"Five hundred a month?" Pamela said, unsure of how the woman would take her offer.

Val laughed; a deep sounding laugh that matched her boisterous personality. "When asking for money always start out high and bargain your way down. Makes people in this room feel important, or at least that they're in control of the negotiations." She paused and smiled at Daniel. "All right," she nodded and then turned back to Pamela. "Give me your card."

Pamela almost dropped her purse she was shaking so much. She fished the card out and handed it to Val.

Val took the card. "If you're a friend of this boy's," she winked at Daniel, "then you're a good investment. I'll have my accountant call you Monday to set up the details for a monthly deposit. If you ever need more, come to me."

Pamela took Val's hand. "I don't know how to thank you, Mrs. Easterling."

"Call me, Val…everyone does. I need to get you a few more donations for your facility. There's a man here tonight who does nothing with his money but buy wives and gamble." She looked Pamela up and down, "He has got to meet you. We'll make him shell out some dough to help your animals." She turned and explored the crowd. "There he is. Come with me." Val took Pamela's hand and started pulling her across the ballroom.

Pamela let Val Easterling lead her through the crowds with Daniel following right behind. They stopped before a tall man with dark, wavy hair and penetrating green eyes. He was dressed in a designer tuxedo, holding a tall glass filled with some pink concoction and topped with a pink umbrella. Pamela could not help but notice how the man's eyes traveled over every inch of her petite figure.

"I thought you hated these events. And shouldn't you be out on that fancy sailboat Dallas built you?" Val inquired.

"I've been waiting for you to come skinny dipping with me, Valie," the man replied, giving the woman a friendly peck on the cheek.

"That's like inviting a lion to a barbeque. Untold amounts of suffering would be sure to occur." Val turned to Pamela. "We need to help this woman. She takes care of sick wildlife in a facility outside of the city. She needs your money to keep her facility going."

"Does she need a husband, Valie?" he asked, leering at Pamela. "I'm available."

"Did your Viagra just kick in or something? Behave or I'll slip some saltpeter into your…whatever it is you're drinking," Val threatened as she waved at the man's pink drink.

Pamela bit down on her lower lip to keep from laughing.

"I can always count on you to bring me down, Valie," the tall man said with a mischievous grin.

Val smirked. "Pamela Wells, meet Lance Beauvoir, of Beauvoir Scrap Metal," Val said as she turned to Daniel. "This is her boyfriend and my main bartender, Daniel Phillips."

Lance and Daniel shook hands. "I remember you," Lance remarked as he pointed at Daniel. "You do all of Val's parties."

Daniel nodded to Lance's drink. "Yes. I remember you, and your brother as well, Mr. Beauvoir." He turned to Pamela. "The Beauvoir brothers own and operate Beauvoir Scrap Metal," Daniel explained.

"Actually, Billy, my brother, runs everything." Lance shrugged. "I'm just for decoration."

"Kind of like those stuffed heads on the walls of a taxidermist's office," Val declared.

"I wonder if I could do that with ex-wives," Lance contemplated.

"You don't have enough wall space, Lance," Val countered.

"Beauvoir?" Pamela asked as she stared at Lance. "Any relation to the local writer, Nicci Beauvoir?"

Lance dipped his head. "She was my niece," he stated in a soft tone.

Pamela shook her head. "I'm sorry—how thoughtless of me. I didn't realize. I remember reading of her death in the papers. She was so beautiful." She took a breath. "I'm so sorry for your loss."

"That's very kind," Lance replied, smiling reassuringly.

"Look, Lance, I'm giving Pamela five hundred a month for all of her expenses at her wildlife facility. You want to match me?" Val Easterling quickly jumped in, trying to lighten the mood.

Lance held up his drink. "Count me in."

Pamela felt as if she were floating on air. "Thank you, Mr. Beauvoir."

Lance nodded to her and then to Daniel. "I'll let Valie handle all of the details," he said and then took Pamela's hand. "It was a pleasure meeting you, Ms. Wells."

Lance Beauvoir walked out into the crowds and disappeared behind a sea of black tuxedos.

"I know Lance's accountant," Val said beside Pamela. "I'll have him give you a call." She turned and took Pamela's hand. "I'll see you again, Pamela." She nodded to Daniel. "In the meantime, take good care of my boy." Val Easterling gave Daniel a quick peck on the cheek and turned away.

"Oh, my God!" Pamela all but screamed. "Do you know what that money will mean?" She felt like jumping up and down. "I could get out from under Bob's thumb, and add more cages, and fix up the barn the way I always wanted so I could get the babies out of my house. I could even buy a new refrigerator."

"You're happy," Daniel surmised, smiling warmly. "I'm glad."

"I can't believe you knew these people and in just a few minutes you got me connected with more money than I have ever been able to get my hands on." She put her arms about his neck. "Thank you," she murmured against his cheek.

"I think this joyful turn of events deserves a celebration," Daniel whispered into her ear.

Pamela pulled away. "Celebration?" she asked, warily.

Daniel reached for her hand. "Yeah, celebration," he confirmed.

He squeezed her hand and started leading her across the room. He stopped before the roped-off dance area. The band's playing could barely be heard above the din in the crowded room. Daniel walked around the dance floor until he found an opening between the gold ropes. He pulled Pamela out into the middle of the empty white dance floor.

He put his arm about her waist. "I was hoping I would get to do this with you tonight," he said, raising one eyebrow at her. "Among other things," he added, grinning.

She placed her arms about his shoulders as the band began to play a slow jazz tune. "Don't think that just because you have secured some new funding for my facility that I am going to repay you with a night of uninhibited sex."

"Or in your case a night of inhibited sex," he responded with a playful glint in his eye.

Pamela started to pull away from him, but he held her tightly in his arms. "What's that supposed to mean?" she asked, squirming.

"That somewhere beneath that tough exterior I think there is a woman dying to get out and let go. You keep so much pent up inside of you, Pamela, it is a wonder you haven't exploded."

"You're confusing a tough exterior with a woman who is responsible and—"

"You are a woman who desperately needs to be wanted," he interrupted. "Not needed."

"Is there a difference?"

"Yes," Daniel replied. "Need is when you fulfill someone else's requirements. Like what you do for your animals. Want is when you seek to fulfill your desires." He pressed his body into hers. "Like what you want to do with me."

Pamela let her body give in to the rhythm of the sultry beat as the warmth from Daniel's body teased her skin. She felt safe in his arms, protected from the cares of the world that seemed to be hovering just beyond the golden ropes that stood at the end of the dance floor.

"And what makes you so sure I want to do anything with you?" she softly asked as she gazed into his dark eyes.

He leaned forward and let his lips hover inches over hers. "Because I don't see loathing in your eyes when you look at me anymore. I see something else; something that appears to be more…instinctual."

"Instinctual?" Pamela laughed. "Like what? I want to punch you and run away? Because that is the only instinct that comes to mind right now."

"I had a different instinct in mind; something a lot less painful." He paused "Let me show you what I'm talking about." He leaned forward and kissed her lips.

"Pamela, is that you?" a man's voice called out from behind them.

Pamela broke away from Daniel's embrace and turned to see Bob, standing beside the golden rope at the end of the dance floor. He was dressed in a tailored black tuxedo with matching black bow tie. His light brown hair was neatly slicked back and his pale green eyes were staring right at Pamela. Then Bob's eyes shifted to Daniel and instantly flashed with anger.

Bob hurriedly climbed over the gold rope in front of him and walked up to Daniel's side. "What in the hell are you doing here?" he growled at Daniel.

Pamela looked from Bob to Daniel. "Bob, this is my date—"

"This is Bob?" Daniel asked, cutting her off with his raised voice.

"You know each other?" Pamela asked.

"This is the son of a bitch that hit me in the middle of Pat O'Brien's," Bob explained, trying to keep his voice down.

Pamela turned to Daniel. "Wait? You hit Bob? I thought you said you—"

"He's the one who filed charges against me," Daniel whispered, interrupting her.

Pamela turned back to Bob. "Did you start it?"

Bob appeared astonished by her allegation. "Now you think just because of what happened before, I go around starting fights with indiscriminate bartenders for the hell of it?" Bob said in a low voice. He nervously looked around at the other guests gathered about the dance floor.

Clarissa walked up to join them in the middle of the dance floor. She was wearing a form-fitting yellow satin dress with a low neckline and a high slit up the right side. Her dark hair was piled up on top of her head and she had on a matching gold diamond tennis bracelet and necklace. When she stopped right in front of Daniel, it was then that Pamela first noticed her shoes. Yellow and white high heeled sandal creations with yellow straps that went all the way up her ankle. There were even little white butterflies glued on the strap across her toes.

"What's goin' on over here?" she questioned as she grabbed Bob's arm. She turned to Daniel standing before her. "Well, hello there." She nodded to Pamela, "Pamie you look really nice. What a cute dress! Did you borrow that or somethin'?"

"It was a gift," Pamela declared as she glanced over at Daniel.

"You bought it for her? Why are you buying her clothes?" Bob asked, raising his voice.

Clarissa turned back to her husband. "Keep your voice down. You want the whole room to hear you? And I thought you said she was bringin' Carol. What's Daniel doin' here?"

"You're Daniel?" Bob exclaimed. "Why have you been hanging around my ex-wife's place?" he demanded.

Pamela noticed that a few guests mingling about were beginning to take in their floorshow.

"Perhaps we should take this outside," she suggested to the men.

Daniel was standing next to her taking in large amounts of air through his flaring nostrils. His jaw was clenched and his hands were curled into fists. She reached over and placed her hand on his arm.

"Don't let him get to you," she whispered to him. "You are better than he is in so many ways."

Daniel's eyes connected with hers and she could instantly see the anger begin to subside. Bob on the other hand was red-faced and, minus a ring in his nose, looked like a bull ready to charge.

Pamela grabbed Daniel's hand and pulled him off the dance floor. "Please, Daniel, not here," she begged. "Not in front of these people."

Daniel allowed her to lead him across the grand ballroom and out the main entrance. Bob, and a stumbling Clarissa, were not too far behind. Once safely out of earshot, in the corridor outside the grand ballroom, Bob lunged for Daniel. Used to handling Bob in situations like this, Pamela instantly threw herself in between the two men.

"If you throw the first punch, Bob," she growled, "I'll testify that you started it out of jealousy over me."

"What in the hell is goin' on?" Clarissa shouted as she finally caught up to the group. "Bob, why are you goin' after Daniel? So what if he is Pamie's date? She can go out with anyone she likes." She paused and put her hands on her hips. "You're not married to her anymore; you're married to me. It's always about her. I'm always tryin' to keep up with perfect Pamela. Well, I'm your wife now, Bob. I'm your goddamn wife! Not her," she shouted as she pointed to Pamela.

Bob backed away from Pamela and Daniel and stormed over to Clarissa. His face was a deep shade of crimson and the muscles in his jaw were quivering beneath his skin.

Pamela felt Daniel's body flex beneath her hands, but Pamela did not let go of him. She knew Bob's angry tirades better than anyone. He was looking for a fight and she knew she had to keep Daniel as far away from Bob as possible.

"This man hit me when I was with…" Bob stopped screaming at his wife. His expression immediately changed and he cast his eyes down to the floor. The anger in his face had been replaced by an entirely different emotion. "I was out at a bar after work," he began again, sounding calmer than before. "I was entertaining clients, when this man jumped out at me and punched me for no reason," he told her.

Pamela looked from Bob to Daniel. "But, Daniel, you said you hit him because he was roughing up his girlfriend."

Daniel nodded. "Yes, I did." He lowered his voice so only Pamela could hear him. "The woman he was with wasn't Clarissa."

Pamela instantly realized the implications. Clarissa, however, still appeared confused.

"Bobby, what is she talkin' about? I wasn't with you when this happened," Clarissa asked as she stared into her husband's face. "You just said you were with a client, so why did Pamela say you were—"

"Go back inside, Clarissa," Bob ordered, interrupting his wife.

"But Bobby," Clarissa whined.

"Go, now!" He shouted at her.

Clarissa jumped at the sound of Bob's blaring voice. She gazed over at Pamela and Daniel.

The hurt in Clarissa's green eyes made Pamela's insides lurch with disgust. She had never liked Clarissa, but she would never have wished such heartless treatment on her, or any other woman.

Clarissa put her head down and quickly did as her husband demanded. As fast as her high-heeled butterfly shoes could carry her, Clarissa scurried back to the party.

Pamela watched as Clarissa disappeared inside of the ballroom entrance before she turned to confront her ex-husband. He was standing against the far wall. The redness in his face had dissipated slightly, but his pale green eyes were still filled with an intense hatred. It was a look that Pamela was all too familiar with. She let go of Daniel and approached Bob.

"So that's it, Bob. You're screwing around on your wife, and Daniel knew about it. That's why you're angry?"

Bob shook his head and quickly pointed to Daniel. "I didn't know that he was the same guy who has been working for you until tonight. If I had known, I would have—"

"You would have what, Bob?" Pamela questioned. "You would have come to my place and beaten him up?" She paused and stepped back from Bob. "How long has this been going on? How long have you been cheating on Clarissa?"

Bob gave her an indifferent smirk. "That's none of your goddamn business," he hissed.

Pamela shook her head and sank against the wall behind her. Then her body washed over with a sickening wave of realization. She stared at her ex-husband as a disturbing truth permeated her thoughts.

"Did you cheat on me, Bob?" she finally asked, her voice peppered with anger. "Did you lie to me just like you are lying to her?" She waved at the ballroom entrance Clarissa had just retreated into.

But Bob said nothing. He turned away, straightened his tuxedo jacket, and walked back into the ballroom.

Pamela stood motionless in the corridor of the hotel. The past she thought she had neatly packed away came flying out from the deepest reaches of her mind. The few happy memories she had cherished from their marriage were suddenly tainted with doubt.

Pamela wrapped her arms about her body as if overtaken by a sudden chill. "All this time I thought that at least he had never cheated on me. How could I not have seen it? How could I not have known what was going on? All the late nights at the office, the business trips, the dinners with clients. He was lying to me the entire time and I believed him." She shook her head and slammed her fist into the wall behind her. "God, I was so stupid!" she yelled.

Daniel came up beside her and placed his arm around her shoulders. "You never suspected anything?" he asked.

"No, but what really hurts is that I never felt I had reason to doubt him. I must have looked like such a fool." She faced Daniel. "Eight years of marriage, and I suddenly realize I never really knew the man. Who in the hell did I marry?"

Daniel shook his head. "Bob is a man who cares for no one but himself. I'm sorry you had to find out like this. If I'd have known he was going to be here, I would never have come."

He pulled her into his arms. He wanted to squeeze out all of the hurt Bob had inflicted on her. But he knew the only way to forget a painful past was to create a happy future. He prayed to all the powers above that he was the man to give her that future.

She stood back from him. "I thought for a while there you two would end up on the floor, trying to kill each other."

Daniel nodded and gave her a reassuring smile. "I'm fine. I admit I really did want to beat the crap out of him, but then I kept thinking about you. I didn't want you to witness another ugly fight. I wanted to spare you that pain. For the first time since Iraq, I was more concerned about someone else than myself." He shook his head. "Perhaps I'm finally growing up."

She gently placed her hand next to his cheek. "No, you're finally letting go," she whispered.

Daniel looked into her gray eyes and saw a fire there that he had never noticed before. He stood back from her and took her hand. "Come on, let's go home."

CHAPTER 10

Daniel walked hand in hand with Pamela down Dauphine Street, her overnight bag casually slung over his right shoulder. Creepy shadows cast from the tightly packed Creole cottages that filled the French Quarter gave the half-empty street a sinister atmosphere. Known as the playground of ghosts and vampires by night, the French Quarter also held a quaint charm in the moonlight. Without the clamoring footsteps of tourists that filled the streets by day, the Quarter at night regained its cozy atmosphere as a tight-knit community of neighbors, rather than a modern-day vacation destination.

The stillness surrounding them seemed to ease the frustration that had been coursing through Pamela's body. The slow and steady tick of her heels against the sidewalk lulled her throbbing mind into a hypnotic trance. The emotional highs and lows of the evening had left her completely spent. As she felt Daniel's hand in hers, she found an uncanny comfort in his presence. It was almost as if he soothed some inner fire, smothering the flames that had fueled her worry and self-doubt for far too long. With him, she felt as if she could succeed at anything, and that the world was filled with endless possibilities.

As they strolled slowly along the street, they came upon a small crowd of people standing outside of one of the more opulent houses along Dauphine Street.

"Ghost tours," Daniel offered as he nodded to the group of people.

"Which house is that?" Pamela asked as she glanced up at the impressive Greek Revival home with its long rows of romantic cast iron galleries.

"It's the Gardette-Le Pretre House, better known as The Sultan's House," Daniel told her.

Pamela continued to stare up at the long balconies. "What happened there?"

Daniel pulled her over to the crowd of people gathered in front of the home's doorway. "Why don't you listen to the tour guide's explanation?" he suggested as he came to a halt right at the edge of the group of tourists.

"This domicile was owned by Jean Baptiste Le Pretre in the 1870s," a short, dark-haired woman said, standing in the front of the house. "He rented this home to a mysterious middle easterner, a Turk, who was rumored to be the brother of a sultan. He was very wealthy, and his entourage included many servants and a harem of young girls—all thought to have been supplied by the sultan."

Pamela listened to the story as she wrapped her hands around Daniel's left arm and leaned her head against his shoulder.

"Rumors quickly spread throughout the city about the strange foreigner," the tour guide went on. "Soon the home became the scene of lavish parties with guest lists that included the elite of New Orleans society. One night, shrieks were heard coming from inside this house; the next morning, the local police entered and found blood everywhere throughout the home. The floors, windows, and walls were covered with it. All the servants and harem girls had been hacked to pieces. And the wealthy Turk was found in the back garden." She paused dramatically. "He had been buried alive. The murders were never solved, but many believe the foreigner had actually stolen his money, servants, and harem from his rich and powerful brother, the sultan. And for his treachery he had been hunted down and butchered." The woman turned to the house. "Some say when the streets are empty and the night is right you can hear exotic music and screams coming from this house."

Members of the tour group started snapping pictures of the house with their cell phones and cameras. Daniel placed his arm about Pamela's shoulders and gently eased her away from the crowd.

"Creepy," she said as she walked beside him.

"Only about the first ten times you hear it," he said. "I must run into those ghost tours at least two nights a week," he added with a shake of his head.

"Where do you live?" she asked.

He nodded up the street. "Just up on the right, between St. Anne and Dumaine."

Less than half a block later, Daniel stopped in front of a green wooden door. He pulled his keys from his pocket and unlocked it. With one hard shove he forced the door open and waved Pamela inside.

The darkness of the long alley behind the door was illuminated by a single light bulb. Daniel pushed the thick door closed with a thud and drove the bolt home. He then took her hand.

"Follow me," he whispered.

He led her through the dark alley until the pair stepped out into a vast courtyard. The high walls were made of old red brick and covered with green vines. Along the base of the walls were flowerbeds filled with blooming red, white, and pink azaleas. In the center, a wide three-tiered red brick pond filled the courtyard with the soothing music of cascading water.

He led her past the fountain and to the back of the courtyard where a carriage house stood. In the days when horse and buggy were the only mode of transportation, carriage houses were a vital part of any wealthy French Quarter home. But with the modernization of transportation, carriage homes had been converted to apartments. The building was two stories with three sets of french doors situated along the lower floor. The second story had two wide french doors that opened out on to one long balcony. The exterior, like most homes in the French Quarter, was plaster and two gas lamps were positioned on either side of the front door. All around the base of the building was a myriad of potted plants.

"How charming," Pamela commented as she pointed to the plants.

"Yes, my landlady does all of the gardening around here. She keeps putting pots of plants in front of the place for God knows what reason. It's quiet and a haven from the hustle and bustle of the Quarter outside."

Daniel opened the front door to his home and stepped inside. Pamela followed behind and waited as Daniel reached around to the wall and flipped on the lights.

There was one main living room area with a smaller dining area off to the left. The centerpiece of the living room was a massive brick hearth that looked as old as the building. The fireplace portion of the hearth had been closed off with cement and a decorative black grate placed in front of it. A straight, open wooden staircase hugged the far right wall and ascended to a second level. She noticed there was little furniture in the place except for a beige couch, coffee table, television stand, and a desk. On the simple oak desk, a laptop computer and printer were placed next to a small pile of books. She walked over and put her wrap and purse down on the coffee table.

Daniel stepped into the dining room and placed her overnight bag on the dining room table. He then removed his tuxedo jacket and hung it over one of the dining chairs.

"Do you want something to drink?" He disappeared into a room off to the right of the dining room. Suddenly, a light flashed out through the doorway. "I have wine, orange juice, and some vodka," he called out.

Pamela followed the light and found herself in a very small kitchen. There was an oven with a four-burner stovetop, next to a medium-sized refrigerator, next to a sink, and everything was built into a compact array of dark green cabinets along the wall. The beige tiled counter top was filled to capacity by a mini-microwave and a coffee pot.

"This is the tiniest kitchen I have ever seen," she said as Daniel pulled two glasses out of a cabinet high above the sink.

He turned to her. "I believe the term you're looking for is efficiency."

Pamela laughed. "I've read about these," she taunted as he poured two glasses of white wine. "But I never believed they actually existed," she added with a cheeky grin.

"Then you have never lived in New York," Daniel replied. "I once had an efficiency apartment with a bed that folded down from the wall, a hot plate, a miniature refrigerator, and a bathroom smaller than this kitchen with only two outlets in the whole apartment. I would have to unplug appliances to watch television or work on the computer."

"How long did you live in New York?" she asked as she took the glass of wine he offered her.

"A year. I worked some of the big nightclubs in the city. So I slept most of the day, which was a real feat in New York. It's the noisiest place on Earth."

"And after New York?" She took a sip of wine.

He picked up his glass of wine and leaned against the counter. "Oh, let's see. There was Atlanta, Charleston, Chicago, and Miami." He took a sip from his glass of wine. "But I wasn't gay enough for Miami," he added with a frown.

"Do you have to be gay to work as a bartender in Miami?"

Daniel laughed. "Only if you want to make any money."

"And where will you go next?" she asked as she kept her eyes on his.

"To tell you the truth, I'm done with living out of a suitcase. I want to settle down somewhere, get a dog, hang pictures on the wall, and make some roots."

Pamela peered down into her wine. "I think you deserve that," she whispered.

When she looked up again, Daniel was staring at her with the silliest smile on his face.

"What?" she asked.

"And what if I said I want to stay in New Orleans because of you," he told her as he watched for her reaction. "Would I be scaring you away?"

"No, but I would think you might be moving a little fast. We hardly know each other and—"

"You either know or you don't, Pamela," he interjected. "Time won't change how we feel at this moment." He put his glass of wine down on the counter and folded his arms over his chest. "Look, I can't stand here and say I'm not a one-night stand kind of guy, because I have been that kind of guy in the past and one day might be again. But right now with you, I'm not." He took in a deep breath. "Nothing has to happen tonight. I don't want you to think that I brought you here to sleep with you. And I definitely don't want you to think that's all I'm interested in. I want to get to know you. We can go as fast, or as slow, as you want."

Pamela put her glass of wine down on the counter. She smiled at Daniel then turned away and walked out of the kitchen. She went to the dining room table, picked up her overnight bag and slipped it over her shoulder.

Daniel followed her out of the kitchen and found her standing in the middle of the living room. He felt a pang of disappointment blow through him. He nodded his head and went over to pick up his keys from the coffee table.

"I'll bring you home," he said as he moved to the front door.

"But you haven't shown me everything," Pamela called out. "I would very much like to see the upstairs."

Daniel turned to her and suddenly his disappointment faded away. He threw his keys back on the coffee table and walked over to Pamela. He took her hand and led her to the open staircase.

The second floor was nothing more than a bedroom with a small bathroom off to the side. There was a king-sized bed that took up nearly the entire room. It was neatly made with a blue comforter and an array of blue and yellow pillows. There was a single chest of drawers with an antique mahogany amoire beside it. A few books lay piled neatly on top of the chest of drawers next to a yellow porcelain lamp.

Pamela placed the overnight bag on the bed, walked over to the pair of french doors to her left, and opened them. She stepped on to the balcony and took in the view. Below, the courtyard appeared to be filled with more luxuriant foliage than she had noticed when walking through it. The sound of the fountain was blended with the dull noise of the city beyond the garden walls. The hint of music mixed with the laughter of people wafted up to the balcony. The cool night air enveloped her bare arms and she felt her skin tingle with surprise. She reached up and pulled the pins from her hair, letting her golden locks fall freely to her shoulders. She ran her hands through her hair, closed her eyes, and listened to the city.

She felt Daniel's hand on her bare shoulder and leaned her head back as his lips pressed against her skin.

She turned around to face him, and when she looked into his eyes, she lost all of her doubts. For the first time in a very long time, she wanted a man. She wanted to be held and caressed without worrying about what tomorrow would bring.

She leaned forward and hesitantly touched her mouth to his. But her apprehension was quickly replaced by a more urgent need. Her kiss became more demanding and Daniel responded to her desires. He wrapped his arms about her body and pulled her to him. His lips began to explore her face and worked their way down to the nape of her neck. When his teeth sank teasingly into her flesh, Pamela groaned.

Her fingers started hurriedly undoing the buttons on his shirt as her lips tempted his skin. Her movements became more frenzied as she pushed the shirt off his shoulders and let her hands explore the contours of his muscular chest. Daniel reached behind her and started to pull the zipper down the back of her dress. He then slowly eased the material from around her body. She fumbled with the zipper on his tuxedo pants, and soon they joined the dress on the floor.

Daniel wrapped his arms about her waist and picked her up off the ground while kissing her neck. Pamela laughed into his hair as he carried her to the bed. He pushed her back against the cool blue comforter as he lowered his body on top of hers. She reached her hands around to his firm backside and slid his white briefs down his legs. She let her hands travel up and down his back and thighs, and dragged her nails across his naked bottom.

"You'll pay for that," Daniel murmured into her cheek.

Grabbing her body, Daniel flipped her over, placing Pamela on her knees. He kneeled behind her, pulled her hips back to meet his, and pushed her thin cotton panties down. He threw her panties to the floor, then let his hands travel hungrily over her smooth skin and round backside. As he felt her hips grinding against his erection, Daniel leaned over and bit down hard into her shoulder. Pamela threw her head back and gasped. He reached in between her legs and ran his fingers along the tender folds of her flesh.

"Yes," Pamela whispered, as she backed her hips into him in anticipation.

He tried to curtail his need to quickly enter her. Instead, he entered her slowly, eventually driving himself deep inside of her.

Pamela made a guttural moan as he started teasing her with a slow, deep thrusting motion that made her body tremble. Then he began moving faster and faster in and out of her. Pamela's hands gripped the bedspread as she felt the slight tingle at the base of her spine travel up her body. Her muscles tensed, as the tingle became a wave of overwhelming pleasure.

Daniel grabbed her hips firmly in his hands as his body slammed harder and harder into hers. She met every thrust from his hips with her own. Daniel groaned against her skin and wrapped his arms about her as he felt her body coming closer to climax.

Pamela soon lost all sense of the world around her as she was overtaken by the sensations that were pulsating throughout her body. When the final release overtook her, she bent her head back and cried out his name in the darkness.

* * * *

"How long has it been?" Daniel asked as he lay holding Pamela in his arms.

"Was it that obvious?" she said, burying her red face in his chest.

He kissed her forehead. "No, it's just that you never mentioned anyone other than Bob. There must have been someone since him.

"There was a guy right after the divorce, Walden. We went out for a while, but I was just starting my facility and we quickly drifted apart. Since then I haven't wanted to get involved with anyone." She looked up into his face. "What about you? When was your last relationship?"

"Relationship?" He rubbed his chin tenderly against her cheek. "Before I left for Iraq. Her name was Debra and we met in grad school at Harvard. Since Debra, I don't think I've spent as much time with any woman as I have with you."

Pamela sighed. "It's hard opening up to people again, isn't it?"

"I guess the more wounds you have, the deeper the scar tissue you have to cut through. Makes people like you and me impossible to get to know." He paused and let his lips graze her cheek. "But I think we are making progress," he whispered.

"Progress?"

"I think you're beginning to trust me. Tonight you showed me a side of yourself that I suspect not a lot of people have seen."

She rolled over onto her back and took in a deep breath. "Maybe you're confusing passion with trust, Daniel."

He chuckled. "I have had enough experience with women to know the difference."

Pamela sat up and glared at him.

He saw the change in her eyes. The cold look of indifference was back. It was the same way she had looked at him when they first met.

"Perhaps you should take me home," she stated in an icy tone. She turned away from him and started to get up from the bed.

Daniel grabbed her. He pulled her back down on the bed and wrapped his arms about her. She struggled against him.

"Don't you dare think you can run away from me," he whispered into her hair. "You're supposed to be scared, Pamela. But don't you let the fear win this time. Not with me."

"I'm not afraid of you," she mumbled.

"No, you're afraid of what I may do to your well-ordered life. I've had the same fear you're feeling now, Pamela. But running doesn't make the fear go away. It only makes it worse until one day you wake up and you feel nothing." He felt her body relax against his. "Don't run away from what you are feeling. Give us a chance."

She rolled over and faced him. "And what if what we are feeling turns out to be a mistake?"

He brushed a stray lock of hair away from her eyes. "No matter what happens between us, I will never look back on what we have as a mistake."

She fell back against the bed. "I felt the same way with Bob, and look what happened."

He settled in beside her. "I'm not Bob."

"I know that. You don't have Bob's cruelty. He was never around much when we were married, and after I got sick he disappeared completely. Until tonight, I never realized how wrong I had been about him." She paused and let out a long sigh. "The worst part is that, despite what I now know, I'm still stuck with the son of a bitch. I need his monthly allowance to keep my facility going."

"Don't worry. I'll get you enough donations so that you'll never have to be dependent on Bob again," Daniel said as sat up next to her. He traced the long scar down the center of her abdomen. "From the accident?"

She nodded and reached over and touched the three bullet wounds on his right chest. "We make a hell of a pair."

Daniel began teasing her right breast with his fingers. "I think we make a very good team. Like gin and tonic or vodka and orange juice." He leaned over and placed his mouth over her nipple and bit down hard.

Pamela closed her eyes and started running her hands through his thick, dark hair. "You're talking about cocktails and I'm talking about people."

Daniel let his lips work their way to her stomach. "Cocktails are much like people," he murmured against her skin. "They are

BROKEN WINGS

blended with care and a variety of ingredients to create their own unique flavor." He planted tender kisses along her scar as his mouth traveled down her body. "Like one of my personal favorites," he whispered as he knelt in between her legs. "The screaming O."

* * * *

Pamela awoke from a sound sleep to find that Daniel was not next to her. She sat up and gazed about the room until she saw a tall figure standing with his back to her by the french doors overlooking the balcony. She got out of bed and went over to him.

"Can't sleep?" she asked as she wrapped her arms about his waist.

He turned and folded her naked body into his arms. "I was just standing here thinking about things."

"What things?"

"Life things. You know the kind of questions that only seem to come to you in the darkness."

"Mine are more like fears than questions. The 'what ifs' always seem to haunt me at night."

"And what fears keep you up at night?" he murmured against her hair.

"It's usually fears about the future. What will happen to my facility if I get sick, or worse."

"You always have Carol," he ventured.

Pamela stared out beyond the windows into the darkness of the Quarter. Somewhere out in the still night, a ship making its way down the Mississippi River sounded its deep horn.

"I can't ask Carol to give up her dreams for mine. She wants to be made the sole beneficiary in my will, but she's so young and has so many plans for her life. I don't want anyone to suffer because of my shortcomings."

"Being sick is not a shortcoming," he insisted.

"It is to me," she replied.

Daniel sighed against her. "For me it's a liability."

"But you're not sick," she said as she turned to him. "Your PTSD is the result of war and trauma."

He ran his hands up and down her naked back. "So I'm scarred, but not broken. Is that it?"

"That's not what I meant. Your fears are different from mine, that's all."

"Your fears are about the future whereas mine are all wrapped up in the past." He paused and looked down into the dark courtyard. "There are times when I can't let go of the images or the sounds of being in Iraq. My dreams are sometimes filled with the horror of being trapped and shot at again and again until I wake up drenched in sweat."

She pushed away a lock of hair that had fallen over his brow. "Is there anything I can do to help?"

His hands gently caressed her shoulder and neck. "No, you've already done enough. More than you will ever know." He leaned forward and tenderly kissed her on the mouth.

She stepped back from him and took his hand. She pulled him toward the bed. "Well, if you can't sleep, and I can't sleep…" She grinned up at him.

"What did you have in mind?" he asked, raising one eyebrow at her.

"Perhaps you could show me more of those bartending skills of yours," she said in a husky voice as she lay down on the bed, naked before him. "I think it's time for another round."

CHAPTER 11

The bright morning sunlight blazing through the french doors woke Pamela from a deep sleep. At first, she looked curiously about the strange bedroom and didn't know where she was. Then a flood of memories from the night before came rushing back into her mind. She giggled and then stretched lazily in the bed. She looked over at the clock on the dresser and saw that it was already after eight.

"I haven't slept this late in years," she said aloud.

"After last night's exertions, I figured you needed the rest," Daniel spoke up from the bedroom doorway.

Pamela covered her naked body with the bed sheets as she caught sight of Daniel. He was wearing a dark blue robe and carrying a round, red tray with two steaming white cups of what appeared to be coffee. He came over to her side of the bed and carefully sat down, trying not to spill a drop.

"I wanted to make you breakfast but all I had in the house was frozen waffles." He handed her one of the cups. "I thought I would bring you this and then we could walk on over to Café Du Monde and grab some beignets."

She took a sip of the hot coffee. "I should call Carol and check in first."

"I already did that," Daniel told her as he picked up his coffee and put the tray on the floor next to the bed. "Everyone is fine. She fed all of the babies and was chopping up vegetables for the animals in the outside cages."

Pamela felt her insides warm over. "You called Carol." She leaned over and kissed his lips. "Thank you for doing that," she whispered.

"I knew that would be the first thing you wanted to do when you got up, so I did it for you. I didn't want you to worry."

"No one has ever worried about me worrying before. It's a new experience for me."

He stood up. "Get used to it. From now on you share your worries with me."

Pamela stared up at him. "What are you saying?"

He laughed when he saw her astonished face. "I'm not proposing marriage, Pamela. I just don't want you to think you are in this by yourself anymore. Lean on me from now on. Share your burdens with me."

"It works both ways, Daniel. I don't want you to keep things from me, either."

"Deal," he held out his hand to her.

Pamela took his hand and shook it. "Perhaps we should seal it with a kiss," she suggested.

Daniel glimpsed her body hidden beneath the sheets and smiled. He took the cup of coffee from her hand, and then placed both cups back on the tray on the floor.

"I've got a better idea," he said, removing his robe.

Pamela watched as the robe fell to the floor, revealing his naked body. She tossed the sheets aside and went over to the edge of the bed, kneeling before him. She ran her hands over his chest, hips, and thighs. She leaned over and kissed the scars on his chest. Daniel wrapped his arm about her slim waist and eased her back down on the bed beneath him.

"I think I could get used to this arrangement, Mr. Phillips," she murmured against his neck.

"I aim to please, Ms. Wells," he said as he stroked her breasts. "And I plan on making sure you are completely satisfied."

* * * *

Later that morning, they walked over to Café Du Monde, the only place to go in New Orleans for beignets. The open café, located in the French Market on Decatur Street, had been serving the doughy, sugarcoated concoctions to the residents of New Orleans for almost 150 years. Open seven days a week, twenty-four hours a day, the green and white awnings of the cafe were only closed for Christmas and the occasional hurricane.

Daniel and Pamela were sitting by an open table in the far corner of the café facing Decatur Street. Some street musicians were entertaining a handful of tourists right outside the eatery as Daniel and Pamela looked on.

"I wanted to live in the Quarter when I first moved here," she revealed as she sipped her black coffee and chicory.

"I thought you were from New Orleans," Daniel said, sounding surprised. "You seemed like one of the locals."

"I moved here from Dallas when I was twenty, after a spring break trip in college." She wiped some powdered sugar from her jeans. "I was studying pre-med. I fell in love with the place and decided to stay. My father had a fit. He cut me off and left me to make my own way. I got a job waiting tables at an uptown restaurant while I went to EMT school. A couple of years later I met Bob. I quit work to be the full-time wife of a Louisiana attorney."

Daniel placed his cup of coffee down on the table in front of him. "What about your father?"

"He's a plastic surgeon in Dallas. He's on his fourth wife and never had any other children besides me. We never really got along." She paused and peered into her coffee. "I haven't spoken to him in six years. I called him when Bob and I got divorced. He blamed me for Bob's leaving; told me I was a worthless wife, just like my mother." She shrugged and took a sip of her coffee. "After that phone call, I figured we had nothing left to say to each other," she added.

"And you were in pre-med because that was what your father wanted?" Daniel asked as he took in her profile in the midmorning sunshine.

She looked over at him. "He wanted me to join his medical practice and eventually take it over after he retired." She smiled. "So I guess we have that in common, too."

"But my old man has never been as far removed from my life as yours has been. My father has always tried to stay in touch with me. I'm the one who doesn't want to stay in touch with him."

She put her coffee down, reached over, and placed her hand over his. "You should try, Daniel. My father gave up on me. Yours hasn't."

"Does you father know about your lupus?" he asked as he picked up his cup of coffee.

"He knows. He sent me to a few specialists in Dallas. They poked and prodded and gave me pills that made me feel worse than the lupus. They even talked about a T-cell replacement procedure."

"What's that?" he inquired and took a sip from his coffee.

"A special procedure that kills your own naturally occurring T-cells, or immune cells, with chemotherapy, and then implants healthy donor T-cells into your body. It is experimental and controversial, but it has brought remission to some lupus and multiple sclerosis patients."

He placed his cup back on the white saucer before him on the table. "You didn't want to try that?"

Pamela shrugged. "By the time they started discussing that option I was done with doctors and hospitals. They don't really know how to treat a chronic disease like lupus. They just treat you like a lab rat until they find something they think makes you better, but everything they do only makes you feel worse. At least that is how it made me feel." She shook her head as she picked up her coffee again. "So I walked away from the treatments and all of the pills. I found a local rheumatologist here in the city and never went back to Dallas. It was right after I gave up on my treatments that Bob decided he wanted out of our marriage." She took a sip of her coffee.

"But you seem all right now. Is there anything else that can be done?"

She placed her cup down on the table. "I have good and bad days. Today is a good day." She paused and felt the sunshine on her face. "I try to limit my stress, which isn't easy. I eat right, take care of myself, and I go in every six months and get blood work done to check my kidney function. My kidneys aren't as good as they used to be."

"Maybe there are other doctors, other hospitals with better drugs who may be better at treating your disease," he declared, his voice filled with emotion. "There must be something we can do," he implored.

Pamela shook her head. "I've seen some of the top lupus doctors in the country. There is nothing left to be done. I manage with what I have. I'm a lot better off than some patients and, besides, everyone has a cross to bear; even you."

Daniel gazed into her eyes and for the first time since his mother's death, he felt helpless. Here was someone he cared about who was suffering, and he could do nothing to ease her burden.

"There is something that I would like you to do for me, Daniel."

"Name it," he replied with a firm nod of his head.

She gave him a warm smile. "Call your father. You never know how precious family can be until you don't have them anymore."

He sighed and turned to take in the musicians next to the café who were playing a solemn jazz tune. "I promise to think about it," he finally told her.

She picked up her coffee, sat back in her chair, and soaked up the warm rays of the sun on her face.

Daniel watched as her blond hair gleamed in the sunlight and felt something inside of him change. It was not a monumental blow that he felt, but a gentle tug at the deepest reaches of his soul that seemed to instantly shift his entire perspective. She had attached herself to some place deep inside of his heart, a place he had not dared to visit for a very long time. He knew from that moment on his life would never be the same.

* * * *

It was well after twelve when Daniel pulled up in front of Pamela's cottage. The dogs came out to greet them, tails wagging, as they stepped from the Jeep.

"The biscuits must have worked," Daniel speculated as he patted the dogs gathering about his legs.

"They will love anyone who brings them food," Pamela admitted. "They used to attack Bob like crazy until he started bringing them ham bones. Now they greet him as if he is their long lost friend."

"Why didn't you tell me that?" Daniel asked, frowning at Pamela.

She grinned. "Couldn't make it that easy for you, now could I?"

Daniel laughed and took Pamela's hand. They walked hand in hand to the front door.

Before they had even reached the last step, the front door flew open. A panic-stricken Carol came running out the door and grabbed Pamela.

"Thank God, you're back! She started going downhill about an hour ago," she cried out breathlessly as she dragged Pamela inside.

Alarm shot through Pamela's body. "Who? Who started going bad?" she asked.

Pamela and Carol were halfway into the living room when Pamela saw Ian on the couch, clinging to one of the plastic containers on his lap.

"The little flying squirrel," Carol answered.

"She started rollin' around in her container and now she is just lyin' there. She looks like she is havin' some kind of seizure," Ian reported.

Pamela immediately ran over to the couch.

"Is that my flying squirrel?" Daniel asked as he entered the room.

Carol nodded.

BROKEN WINGS

All eyes watched as Pamela took the creature out of her container. She inspected the small face and eyes. Then she felt along the animal's stomach.

"Her belly is tight," she said.

Suddenly, Pamela felt the animal's stomach clench in a hard contraction. She checked between the squirrel's back legs to find that a small pink head was emerging. She immediately replaced the animal back in the container and put the top back on.

She turned to see all of the worried faces staring at her. "It's not a seizure. It's a contraction. Seems little Pamela is in labor."

Daniel let out a relieved breath. Carol smiled, and Ian looked just as confused as the moment Pamela walked into the house.

"Should we boil water or somethin'?" Ian asked.

Pamela tried not to laugh. "No, Ian. We will just let her handle everything. She'll know what to do."

Daniel walked up to Pamela, put his arms around her and lifted her off the floor. "So I'm gonna' be a grandpa!"

"Looks like somebody had a good time last night," Carol commented.

Daniel laughed as he put Pamela down.

"Carol, you would not believe how wonderful Daniel was last night at the party," Pamela happily told her.

"Only at the party?" Carol asked, raising her eyebrows teasingly.

Pamela blushed and looked down at the floor.

Carol nodded to Daniel. "Wow, you rendered her speechless. You must be a real animal in bed."

Daniel smiled at her. "I have my moments."

Pamela punched Daniel in the arm.

"Please tell me there is a videotape," Carol begged.

"Carol!" Pamela yelled.

"And she's back," Carol teased. She folded her arms over her chest and stared at Pamela. "So how wonderful was he at the party?" she asked.

"Well, we have three new monthly patrons, thanks to Daniel. Two of which have committed to five hundred a month."

"A thousand a month!" Carol exclaimed. "That's the same amount Bob gives us now."

"And there's an older couple Daniel introduced me to who will have their accountant contact us on Monday to talk about more funding. Can you believe this? We've been struggling for years and Daniel comes along and in one night does more than you and I could ever have done."

Carol grinned at Daniel. "I, ah, hope she was real grateful."

"I don't kiss and tell, Carol." He walked over to Pamela and took her hand. He led her back to the front door. "I need to get back to the city. I have to work this afternoon."

Pamela opened the door and followed him outside.

"I've been thinking about what you said this morning," he stated as they walked down the porch steps.

"I said a lot this morning," she replied.

He stopped beside his Jeep and glanced back to the dogs resting on the porch. "Maybe I should phone my father and tell him he is a great-grandfather to flying squirrels."

Pamela nodded. "I think he might like hearing from you."

He wrapped his arms about her. "I'll call you later tonight when I'm on break."

She placed her arms about his neck. "Fine."

He kissed her lips. "Now comes the hard part."

"Hard part?" She gave him an awkward glance.

"I've got to cover the next four days to make up for taking off last night," he said to her. "So I won't be able to get up here for a while."

"I'll be here when you come back," she told him. "I'm not going anywhere, Daniel."

He kissed her forehead. "Neither am I."

CHAPTER 12

Over the next four days, the accountants for the Robillards, Val Easterling, and Lance Beauvoir all called with questions and instructions for Pamela. Her small office became inundated with paperwork, and Pamela had to spend a great deal of time faxing forms back and forth and even taking phone calls from other potential patrons Val Easterling had referred to her. The mother flying squirrel and her three new babies were moved from the kitchen to her bedroom to allow them a quiet place away from the constant phone calls and noise of Pamela's busy office. She tried not to notice that none of the calls on her cell phone were from Daniel. He had not called that first night like he promised, but Pamela had been so busy with her animals she had not given the missed phone call much thought. However, when five days had passed, Pamela began to worry when she had not heard a word from him. Almost a week after her night with Daniel, Pamela finally voiced her concern to Carol.

"Maybe he got in a car accident heading home from here and is lying in a hospital bed unconscious," Carol proposed to Pamela as they were feeding animals in the outside cages.

Pamela frowned at Carol as she placed a food bowl inside a cage filled with baby skunks. "How on earth do you think up such things?"

"Soap operas," Carol answered with a shrug. "I watch them all the time at my office."

Pamela nodded. "That would explain a lot."

"Maybe you should just call him," Carol suggested as she moved on to the next cage.

"I did call his cell phone, several times. All I got was his voicemail." She turned away from Carol and walked over to the next cage and opened the door.

Three large opossums scurried to get out of her way.

Carol followed Pamela inside of the cage. "Then you should just go to that bar where he works and ask him what is going on," Carol instructed as she filled a large bowl with a mix of dried cat food and chopped vegetables.

"And what do I say to him? Ask him why he is blowing me off? Tell him I thought our night together meant something?" she questioned as she picked up the water bowl.

"Did it mean something to you?" Carol softly asked.

Pamela took in a deep breath and tried to force back the tears in her eyes. She just nodded to Carol and said nothing.

Carol came up to her side and rubbed her hand encouragingly up and down Pamela's arm. "Don't do this," she begged. "Don't give up on him. I know he cares for you, Pamie. There's got to be a very good explanation for why he hasn't called you."

Pamela felt her resolve strengthening. "Maybe I should go into the city and try to find him."

"Absolutely. Why don't you go today? I've got the whole day off and I can cover everything here for a couple of hours," Carol assured her. "You need to get to the bottom of this."

"You're right. I'll go today," Pamela pronounced as she stepped out of the cage and went to the faucet to refill the water bowl.

Carol closed her eyes and silently prayed for any explanation other than the one she feared Pamela would discover.

* * * *

Two hours later, Pamela stood outside of the entrance to Port of Call. Located on Esplanade Avenue and famous for their pizzas, hamburgers, and a specialty drink called the Monsoon, Port of Call was a familiar hang out for college students across the city. Pamela was well acquainted with the establishment from her days of working as an EMT. She had spent many a night huddled over intoxicated college students who had passed out, or fallen, inside the famous eatery. Getting wasted at Port of Call's was considered a right of passage in New Orleans, like sneaking into Pat O'Brien's with a fake ID, or spending a night sampling the various exotic drinks at Joe's Bar. Pamela never understood many of the bizarre traditions embraced by the inhabitants of this city. But like so many before her, she had learned to love the Big Easy, despite its many decadent faults.

For a Thursday night, the popular eatery was pretty crowded. Pamela had to stop and remind herself that in New Orleans, weekends tended to start on Thursdays. She walked into the small dining area and surveyed the tables filled with young diners eagerly munching on their food. To the right of the dimly lit, paneled room, she saw a small bar with a blond-haired, older man standing behind it.

"Excuse me," she shouted to the bartender to be heard over the mix of conversation and music. "I'm looking for Daniel Phillips. Is he in tonight?"

The older man gave Pamela a stern going over with his blue eyes. "You a friend of his?"

Pamela nodded.

"Well, if you see the son of a bitch, tell him he's fired. I've had to fill in his last four shifts since he stopped showing up for work three days ago."

"What do you mean he didn't show up for work?" Pamela's heart trembled with worry.

"I mean no one has heard from him since he left here late Monday night. I called his cell phone, but he's not answering. You know I got him this gig, and then he goes and shits all over me. If you see him, you tell that son of a bitch never to ask me for another favor again."

Pamela really didn't hear anything else the disgruntled man had to say. She quickly backed away from the bar and raced out the door.

She got back in her old white pick-up truck and headed across the Quarter to Dauphine Street. She drove down the street until she found the green door that she had entered a few nights ago with Daniel, then had to drive around for over thirty minutes until she found an empty parking meter.

By the time she arrived at the entrance, the thick green door was no longer closed to the street, but open. She walked through the doorway and down the dark alleyway until she emerged into the bright courtyard. She felt herself almost running to Daniel's carriage house. When she got to the french doors that served as the main entrance to his home, she started knocking on the glass. At first she softly tapped on the glass, but then her knocking started growing louder and louder.

"Knock any harder on that glass, honey, and you'll break it," a woman's voice said from the side of the patio.

Pamela turned in the direction of the voice to find an older woman wearing blue overalls with a straw hat on her head, gardening gloves on her hands, and a warm smile on her lovely wrinkled face.

"You lookin' for Danny boy?" she asked in a coarse voice that belied her sweet grandmotherly looks.

"Yes, I just came from the bar where he worked and they told me—"

"He's gone, honey," she said, silencing Pamela. "Packed up all his stuff, day before yesterday. He gave me three months' additional rent and left in that blue Jeep of his."

"Gone?" Pamela's heart sank. "Gone where?"

"He never said and I never asked." The woman looked down at a potted pink azalea by her feet. She started to pull at the weeds at the base of the plant.

Pamela remembered something Daniel had told her about the potted plants around his carriage house. "You're his landlady," Pamela said in a soft voice.

The woman looked up at her with a bright pair of gray eyes. "Yes that's me. I own the place. Name's T.J. Powell," she said, holding out her gloved hand.

Pamela shook the woman's dirty glove. "So he never said anything to you about where he was going, Mrs. Powell?" she persisted.

"Call me T.J., and nope he never said nothin' except that he had changed his mind. Last week he said he was goin' to be stayin' on in New Orleans for a while. I figured he had met a girl." She paused and peered into Pamela's face. "Kinda' was hopin' that boy would settle down. I saw the women he had comin' and goin' at all hours of the night around here for a while and then it all stopped." She shrugged. "Until I saw you with him last Saturday."

"You saw us?"

T.J. nodded and pointed back to the main house across the courtyard. "Apartment A is mine. I can see all the happenin's in the courtyard through my windows." She paused for a moment and stared at Pamela. "Was he in some kind of trouble?"

Pamela shook her head. "Why do you ask?"

"There was a man here last Sunday. He was a real fancy dresser. He came knockin' on my door askin' where Daniel lived, so I told him. Next I heard a lot of shoutin' comin' from the courtyard. Daniel and that attorney were having a real—"

"Attorney?" Pamela edged in.

T J. laughed. "Yeah, the guy that has got his face plastered all over town. He's an ambulance chaser; even seen a few of his commercials on television."

"Did this attorney tell you his name?"

"Didn't have to ask him. I recognized him right away. It was Robert Patrick."

* * * *

The R.A. Patrick Law Firm was located in the P&L building on Poydras Avenue in the Central Business District of the city. Bob had moved into his luxury offices right after he and Pamela married. She had thought him crazy for spending so much money on offices for a practice he had barely gotten off the ground. But Bob had considered the opulent accommodations a necessity for attracting high-end clientele. And as the elevator opened on the twentieth floor of the high-rise office building, Pamela couldn't help but think that Bob had been right.

The vast reception area was lined in deep mahogany paneling and decorated with luxurious burgundy leather furniture. The long desk where a perky blond was seated was also made of mahogany and sat atop a plush gold and burgundy Oriental rug. On the walls were assorted posters of famous Louisiana festivals, such as The Jazz and Heritage Festival, the Breaux Bridge Seafood Festival, and the Ponchatoula Strawberry Festival.

Pamela marched right up to the blond at the front desk and smiled sweetly. "I need to see Bob," she said through gritted teeth.

"It's after office hours but I'm sure if you would—"

"Tell him it's Pamela," she barked, cutting the girl off.

"I'm sorry but if you would come back tomorrow—"

"Go get him!" Pamela yelled. "He never leaves the office before six."

The girl frowned and tried to look impervious to Pamela's outburst. "I'm sorry ma'am—"

"Tell him it's his goddamn ex-wife and that I want to see the worthless bastard right now!" she shouted, losing all control.

The girl stood up from her desk and backed away. "I'll go and get him," she said nervously, and then disappeared into the entrance to the back offices.

Less than a minute later, Bob emerged from behind the company doors.

"Jesus, Pamela, I could hear you all the way back in my office. What is it?" Bob asked as he came up to her with a worried expression on his face.

"What did you say to him?" she cried out.

Bob put a concerned hand on her shoulder. "What did I say to who, honey?"

Pamela threw off his hand. "To Daniel. His landlady told me you went to his place and had an argument with him."

"Pamela why don't we go back to my office and discuss this," he urged as he looked around the empty reception area.

"No, Bob. Tell me right now. What did you say to Daniel?" she insisted.

Bob took in a deep breath and cast his eyes to the Oriental rug beneath his feet. "I wasn't going to mention any of this to you, but I had that man checked out after the party. Fortunately, the private investigator I hired was able to get back to me right away. I went over to his house to confront him about what I had found and he started threatening me."

"Oh, please, Bob. You expect me to believe that horse shit!"

"He's a con artist, Pamela. He has been chased out of several other states for swindling people out of money, property, jewelry, anything he could get his hands on. He uses some phony story about serving as a soldier in Iraq to lure people in and then he tells them that he needs money for surgeries or treatments for his PTSD."

"You're lying!" Pamela roared. "He had PTSD. I know the symptoms."

"His name is not even Daniel Phillips, Pamela. It's Alex Weston."

Pamela stared into Bob's pale green eyes. She could never tell when he was lying to her. He had long ago mastered the art of hiding the truth from her.

"I don't believe you," she declared and turned toward the elevator.

"Did he promise to help you get money for your organization? Did he introduce you to some of his rich friends at the party?" Bob asked behind her.

She slowly turned back to him. "Yes, but he asked them for money to help me. He never asked for any money for himself."

Bob walked up to her shaking his head. "You were his ace in the hole, Pamela. Can't you see that? He was going to flaunt you around town and get all of the rich society people to shell out money for your little sanctuary. Then he was probably going to organize everything so that the money came to him and not to you."

"But I have spent the past few days on the phone with a slew of accountants. The people he introduced me to are sending me the money, not Daniel."

"Oh, sure; that's the way he'll start out to make it look legit. But then he would have weeded his way into your life and eventually he would have gotten his hands on your bank accounts. I suspect he first had to lull you into a false sense of security. Did he sleep with you, Pamela, and promise to take care of you?"

She folded her arms across her chest but said nothing.

Bob rolled his eyes with disgust. "That's how these guys operate. First they get into your pants and then into your checkbook."

Pamela reached out to slap him, but Bob was too fast for her and he grabbed her hand. "I know you're angry, but think about it. If he cared so much for you would he have left town?" he whispered.

Pamela anxiously searched Bob's face. She willed herself to believe that this was all a lie. Bob was a manipulative little toad and would do anything to hold on to his control over her.

She pulled her hand away from him. "So that's it?" she asked, trying to remain calm. "You went over to his place to confront him about what this private investigator found."

"It's the truth, P.A.," Bob insisted. "I can give you the investigator's name if you want to call him."

"I might just take you up on that, Bob." She paused and took in a deep breath. "Did he tell you where he was going?"

"You don't want him, Pamela. He was no good."

"Everyone told me the same thing about you," she proclaimed. "But I married you anyway." She headed across the reception area to the elevator.

"I'm sorry, Pamela," he called out. "I really do hope you find a nice guy one day and have a happy life together. But this guy wasn't for you."

She pressed the elevator call button and shouted, "That wasn't for you to decide." She turned and glowered at him. "And if you ever go behind my back again, I'll start talking to all of those snooty friends of yours. I'll tell them the truth about you and our marriage."

Bob gawked at Pamela, the disbelief emanating from his pale green eyes. "I can't believe you would threaten me after everything I have done for you," he hollered.

The elevator doors opened behind her. Pamela stepped inside and hit the button for the lobby. "Don't ever interfere in my affairs again, Bob, or I will ruin you," she warned, right before the elevator doors closed before her.

* * * *

By the time Pamela made it back home it was well after dark. Carol was waiting patiently on the couch inside watching television when Pamela walked in the door.

"Where is he?" Carol asked as she jumped up from the couch.

"Gone," Pamela said as she walked over to the couch and threw her body down on it.

"What do you mean gone?" Carol asked, looking perplexed.

"He left town a few days ago," Pamela explained. "I ran into his landlady when I went to his place to look for him. She told me he had packed up, gave her three months' rent, and never said a word about where he was going."

"That's it?" Carol asked, shouting.

Pamela felt her body begin to ache. She rubbed her hand over the back of her neck. "No, that's not everything. She told me about a man who came to see Daniel Sunday evening. An attorney she recognized from television."

"Bob?" Carol questioned, raising her eyebrows. "That bastard!"

"That's what I thought, and then I went to Bob's office." She paused as Carol came over to the couch and sat down next to her. "Bob told me he had a private investigator check Daniel out. He says Daniel is some kind of con man who was out to use my sanctuary to swindle money out of wealthy, society types. Bob thinks Daniel would have eventually taken the money from our new patrons for himself."

"And you believe him?" Carol cried out. "Bob would make up anything to keep you out of another man's arms. That asshole has always been jealous of you."

Pamela waved her hand at Carol. "I know that. Bob has never told the truth about anything as long as I have known him, but he knew things that Daniel had told me. I can't disregard everything he said, but I can't believe it, either."

"What are you going to do?"

Pamela let her weary body melt into the couch. The whole drive home she had been asking herself that exact question.

"Nothing," she grumbled. "I'm not going to do a damned thing."

"But Daniel cares about you. If you ask me, he is in love with you as much as you are with him!" Carol declared as she jumped from the couch again.

"Carol, he's gone. I don't know where and I'm not about to spend money I do not have to try and find him. If he cared about me, he wouldn't have left. So all I can assume is…" She paused as she felt a lump form in her throat. "All I can assume is that he never really cared for me in the first place."

"So you're going to just let him go?" Carol demanded in a loud voice.

Pamela gave her an exasperated sigh. "He let me go, Carol. He walked away."

Carol did not appear convinced. She shook her head as she stared at Pamela. "None of this makes any sense. There is something else going on here. Something that Bob isn't telling you and until you find out what's going on, Pamie, you'll never be able to just let him go."

Pamela forced herself up from the couch. "Whatever it is, Daniel Phillips is not my problem anymore."

Carol went to the desk and picked up her purse. "I don't believe you. That guy got to you and you're too stubborn to admit it," Carol said as she walked toward the front door. "I have a gut feeling we haven't heard the last of that man. And my gut feelings are never wrong." Carol stepped outside, slamming the door behind her.

Pamela headed to the kitchen to make formula for the babies as Carol's final words repeated in her head. Pamela hoped in fact that she had heard the last of Daniel. The sooner she could put her time with him behind her, the sooner she could get on with her life. The only problem was her life had been dramatically altered. She wasn't the same woman after knowing Daniel. She feared that their short time together had changed her. From this moment forward, she would have to add another broken relationship to the pile that she carried around inside of her tattered heart.

CHAPTER 13

The following morning, Pamela was sitting on her kitchen floor feeding her baby squirrels. She felt every bone in her body ache as she shifted again and again on the floor trying to find a comfortable position. She had slept very little the night before. Her thoughts kept returning to Daniel. In her mind, she replayed every moment they had spent together. She analyzed every word he had spoken, every smile, and every kiss, trying to determine whether or not his affection had actually been genuine. As the sunlight crept into her room at the break of day, she knew she was no closer to figuring out the truth. And as she sat on the floor and reflected on the night they had spent together, the sound of a car coming down the drive broke into her concentration.

As she walked over to the front door, she heard barking erupt from the driveway. When she stepped outside, she saw two pick-up trucks parked in front of her house. On the door of each truck was a logo of a paintbrush and the name "Al's Painting." Pamela examined the trucks, wondering how the two men inside had gotten so lost. She waved the dogs back to the porch and approached the trucks.

"Excuse me, ma'am, but we're looking for Second Chance Wildlife Rehabilitation Center. Is this it?" a dark-skinned man asked from the cab of the first truck.

"Yes, this is Second Chance Wildlife," Pamela replied. "I'm the owner, Pamela Wells. Can I help you guys?"

The dark-skinned man opened his door and climbed out of the cab. In his hand was a clipboard. He was dressed in white overalls, stained with a plethora of paint colors.

"I'm Chip Easton and that there is Miles," he said, pointing to another man getting out of the second truck. "We're from Al's Painting. We came to complete the exterior painting on your house," he told her.

Pamela stared at Chip for a moment before she spoke. "I don't understand. You came out here to paint my house?"

The man glanced down at his clipboard. "That's what is says here," he announced, pointing to the clipboard. "Prime and paint exterior, paint on site, paid in full," he added with a nod to his clipboard.

"Someone has already paid for this?" Pamela felt an uneasy sense of worry slowly climb up from the bottom of her feet. "Who paid for this?" she questioned.

Chip pulled his work order from the clipboard. "I don't know, ma'am. I just get the slip with the address and instructions. If you want, you can call the office and ask Karen, our accountant, who paid the bill," he said as he handed her a slip of white paper.

Pamela took the paper from the man and looked it over.

"So, ah," Chip said, eyeing the house. "Where's the paint?"

"It's around the side of the house." She pointed to her right.

Chip tipped his cap to her. "We'll go ahead and get started then." He walked toward the side of the house as Miles followed behind him.

She was climbing the porch steps reading through the work order again when Chip poked his head around the corner.

"Ma'am, do you know you got an owl in the tree over here?" he calmly said.

Pamela shook her head and smiled. "That's Lester. He won't hurt you."

"All righty then," Chip replied with a nod of his head.

Pamela was instantly struck by the memory of Daniel frozen to the ladder next to her house, afraid Lester would attack him. She thought back to his reaction and how the sweat had poured from his body. How his hands shook as he took the glass of water she had offered him.

"You can't fake things like that," she said out loud.

A twinge of doubt grabbed at her heart. Perhaps Bob was hiding something, but regardless of what had happened between the two men, she couldn't understand why Daniel had not come to her. There had to be another explanation, but no matter the excuse, Pamela was not about to waste her precious resources trying to resolve the situation. She walked inside her house, grabbed her cell phone, and dialed the paint company's office number that was printed at the top of the work order.

"Al's Paintin'," a woman's raspy voice answered after the second ring.

"Ah, yes, this is Pamela Wells at the Second Chance Wildlife Rehabilitation Center in Folsom. Two of your workers just showed up here to finish painting my house and—"

"Is there a problem, Ms. Wells?' the woman hastily asked.

"Well," Pamela paused. "I was wondering if I could find out who paid for this work to be done. I mean I didn't hire the men and I—"

"I'll transfer you to Karen, Ms. Wells. She handles the books," the woman reported, cutting her off again.

Within seconds there was ringing on the other end of the line.

"This is Karen," a woman said in a frail voice.

"Karen, my name is Pamela Wells and I was—"

"Did the men show up at your place, Ms. Wells?" Karen asked, sounding concerned.

"Yes, they're here, but I was just wondering…who paid for this work? I didn't pay for it and I want to know who did."

"Yes, ma'am, I understand. Kind of a weird request anyway, if you ask me. Most people have us come out and get an estimate. This guy just called up, told us where to go, and paid over the phone by credit card for the entire job. No payment plan, no pay half now, half at the end. Just paid up front for the whole thing, no questions asked," Karen admitted.

"Who paid?"

"I got the slip right here," Karen said as Pamela heard her shuffling some papers around. "Daniel Phillips was the name on the credit card," she reported.

"Did he say anything else about the job? Did he say why he was doing this for me?" Pamela anxiously asked. "Did he happen to say where he was or leave a phone number?"

"No, Ms. Wells, he never said nothin' else to me. And I only got a business address from the man. A Phillips Exotic Imports in Bridgeport, Connecticut."

Pamela stood for a moment, stunned, as she looked down at her cell phone.

"Can I do anything else for you, Ms. Wells?" Karen's voice called out from the cell phone speaker.

"No," Pamela answered, coming out of her stupor. "Thank you, Karen. You've been a great help."

As she hung up with the painting company, someone knocked on Pamela's door.

When she opened it, she found Chip standing there, paintbrush in hand. "Does this belong to you?" he asked as he looked down at his leg.

There, clinging to his leg like a child wanting attention was Rodney the raccoon.

Pamela pried the raccoon's legs from around Chip's calf. She picked Rodney up in her arms. "He's very friendly," she assured him.

"So I noticed," Chip said with a smile. "Had a pet raccoon as a kid. They don't bother me."

"I'll get him something to eat and then he should leave you guys alone," she stated.

Chip nodded and turned away as Pamela shut the front door.

She placed a bowl of cereal on the floor in the kitchen and watched as Rodney sat down next to the bowl. He delicately picked up each and every piece of the sweet puffed corn and placed it in his mouth. After he was finished, he proceeded to tip the bowl over and push it around on the kitchen floor like a hockey puck.

"I thought we got rid of that one," Carol commented as she walked in the front door. She was carrying two tall Starbucks cups in her hands. Rodney made a hasty retreat out the open front door before it shut closed. Carol looked over at Pamela. "You said you were going to stop feeding him," she scolded.

"He started molesting one of the painters, so I had to feed him. Otherwise he'll never leave them alone."

"And why are there painters here?" Carol inquired. "I know you're all gung ho about getting that extra money, but don't you think you should consult with me before hiring painters?" Carol advised as she plopped the cups on the counter next to the sink.

"It's wasn't me," Pamela confessed as she picked up Rodney's empty bowl from the floor and carried it over to the sink. "Daniel sent the painters."

Carol clapped her hands and shouted with glee. "I was right!"

Pamela turned to her and frowned. "I called the company this morning and wanted to know who had sent painters to my house. They told me it had been paid by credit card over the phone by one Daniel Phillips. I even asked the woman if he had said anything to her about me." Pamela rolled her eyes. "You should have heard me. I sounded like a sixteen-year-old little twit."

Carol's face lit up. "That's great!" she exclaimed.

"Which part? Me acting like a flustered teenager or Daniel paying for it all," Pamela scoffed.

"See, he does care about you. Why would he go to such trouble to hire painters to come out and finish the job he started if he didn't care about you?"

"I wouldn't say he cared," Pamela suggested as she finished rinsing off some dishes. "I think he felt guilty. That's why he hired the painters."

"Guilt is good," Carol added with a nod of her head. "Guilt implies emotional connection and that means he can't be a con man like Bob is asserting. If he were, he wouldn't be shelling out money to fix up your house."

"I've been thinking about that." Pamela leaned her hip against the counter. "And there are a lot of things Daniel said and did that make me suspicious of Bob's story."

Carol picked up her Starbucks cup from the counter. "So, are we going to do anything about it?"

"No," Pamela said firmly as she turned her attention back to the sink. "It's over, Carol. I was up all night wondering why he didn't come to me and tell me about his altercation with Bob, or why he felt he had to leave. I can't spend the rest of my life wondering, so the only way to get on with my life is to forget about Daniel."

Carol shook her head. "Can you really toss people out of your life that easily, Pamie? He's not some random guy that you had a one-night stand with. You had feelings for him. You opened up to him. You just don't delete someone like Daniel off your hard drive with a press of a button."

"It's simply a question of making myself forget about him," Pamela argued. "I can choose to forget by never allowing myself to remember."

Carol laughed. "Let me know how that works out for you, because if you ask my opinion, you're an idiot."

* * * *

But it wasn't that easy for Pamela to forget about Daniel, because over the course of the next three weeks more workers showed up on her doorstep. An electrician came to the facility to wire new outdoor lights for the cages, barn, and back porch of Pamela's home. A plumber showed up to add new faucets to the four new outdoor cages that the carpenter had been hired to build. A construction crew came in and built walls, installed sheetrock, and added a new air conditioner and heating system in the barn. An appliance company delivered two new refrigerators for Pamela to place in the finished barn. Even an alarm company and a locksmith showed up to improve security in, and around, Pamela's home.

And with every new hired worker who showed up on the property, Carol would give Pamela a roll of her eyes and walk away. By the time the workmen had finished, the place looked better than Pamela had ever dreamed possible. With the new cages and amenities, Pamela could take in even more animals than before.

She felt exhilarated and at the same time devastated. She wanted someone with whom she could share her newfound fortune, someone to plan with and someone to partake in her joy. But at the end of the day, she only had Louis to share her thoughts with; Louis and the flying squirrel with her three babies. She decided not to relocate the mother flyer and her babies to the barn with the rest of the baby squirrels. She wanted to keep them close by so she could look in on them often, but that wasn't the real reason she held on to the little flyer family. She wanted to hold on to something of Daniel's; something he had cared about and, she hoped, had not forgotten.

ALEXANDREA WEIS

CHAPTER 14

It was a few days after the last of the workmen had finally left when Bob arrived. His silver Mercedes-Benz 550CL coupe pulled up in front of the house as Pamela watched from outside of the newly renovated barn. She opened the barn door and called to her new volunteer.

"Mattie, why don't you finish up with feeding all of the babies," Pamela said as she observed the young blue-eyed girl clutching a baby squirrel lovingly to her chest.

Mattie and three other volunteers had shown up with the rest of the workers. They had been sent by Delgado Veterinary Technician Program after Daniel Phillips had phoned the college looking for volunteers to come to the facility and lend a hand. The volunteers had arrived right in time for the brunt of the spring baby season. As the workers had been finishing up around the place, more and more calls began pouring in from people who had found baby animals and read about her facility in the *Times-Picayune*. She had learned from the journalist who had written the article that Daniel's pictures, and the story about Pamela's facility, had been published by the *Times-Picayune* at the behest of one Clarissa Patrick.

As Pamela walked over to Bob's car, she watched as Rodney scurried out from underneath the house and ran to her side. When she went up to greet Bob, Rodney decided to tag along.

His venomous words from their previous encounter were still ringing in her head as she approached him. She nodded to him as she fought to keep her voice calm. "What are you doing here, Bob?" she asked.

Bob removed his expensive sunglasses and inspected the facility. "You've been having a lot of work done around here. I can't believe this is the same place," he said, sounding surprised. "It really looks good, P.A." He glanced over at her and frowned. "I guess this is because of all your new patrons, huh? I heard that Val Easterling and Lance Beauvoir have been singing your praises all over town. Must feel pretty good to have all those high-class connections."

"The renovations were made by one sponsor. Daniel hired all of the workers to come out and fix up the place. He even got me a few volunteers from the Delgado Vet Tech School in the city. Not something one would expect of a con man out to use me to swindle rich people, is it, Bob?"

He shook his head and placed his hand on his hip. "I know you're mad at me, and you were right, I did interfere in your affairs, but…I wanted to come out and tell you that I'm sorry. I was hoping you would let me explain about what happened with Daniel and me."

She folded her arms over her chest. "All right, I'm listening."

He sighed and took a moment before he finally spoke. "I did have Daniel investigated and he does have a past, Pamela, there's no denying that. But he has only had one previous arrest for assault and those charges were eventually dropped. Apparently, the man does have some issues."

"He's not the only one," she snarled. "So why lie to me? Why hurt me like that?"

"I was jealous. Can you blame me? You know I have always cared about you and to see you with that guy holding hands and…well, I just couldn't take it."

She rubbed her hand across her forehead as the disgust rose inside of her. "And the incident in the bar?"

"A misunderstanding. He thought I was shoving Kay around but—"

"Kay?" she interrupted.

"My receptionist. You met her that day you came to the office."

Pamela snickered as she thought of the perky blond she had seen at his office. "She's a little young for you, Bob."

Bob grinned and lowered his gaze to the ground. "We were having a drink after work. We got a little hammered and got into an argument. Daniel jumped in and then he hit me."

"What was the argument about?"

He shook his head. "You don't want to know."

"But I can guess," Pamela admitted as she stared at him. "She wants you to leave Clarissa, right?"

Bob said nothing, but Pamela knew he didn't have to. She had already figured it all out on her own.

"What really happened the night you went to his place?" Pamela asked, still leery of her ex-husband's intentions.

"I got his address from the police report filed after I pressed assault charges against him. I went over to his place and told him to stay away from you. I threatened him and said I would take away your facility if he ever went back to you again. Said I would pull out on the mortgage and cause you to default on the loan. Then the bank would be forced to repossess the property. I told him if he cared about you, he wouldn't want you to lose everything." He gave her a weak smile. "I wanted to protect you. I thought I was doing the right thing."

"So why are you telling me all of this now?" she asked, more than a little confused by his confessions.

"Clarissa left me right after the party," he mumbled as he turned away from her. "She wanted me to end my relationship with Kay, but I refused. It hadn't been working out between me and Clarissa anyway." He paused and turned back to Pamela. "She was always jealous of you, you know. Every time I would bring up your name she'd go ballistic, but after the party she changed. She told me when she was packing her bags that she thought you were a better person than me. She said she had been wrong about you."

"Is that why she had the article placed in the newspaper?"

Bob nodded. "She wanted to make it up to you. She thought some press would help you."

Pamela put her hands on her hips and shook her head. "I still don't understand, Bob. Why are you here?"

He let out a long breath as his eyes explored her face. "I want us to start over, Pamela," he softly said. "When I saw you with that guy at the party, I knew I had lost you. I never really stopped loving you, I just got distracted."

"Distracted?" Pamela tried not to laugh. "You've got to be kidding me. All the years of crap you put me through when we were married, and now you stand there and say you want me back? Why? Because you saw me with another man, and finally realized I don't need you anymore? Is that why you want me back Bob?"

"Pamela, don't do this," his voice instantly filled with anger. "Don't make me beg you to come back to me."

"You don't need to beg, Bob. The answer is no. I don't want you back now or ever. Do you think I could go back to a selfish bastard who ran around on me and then dumped me when I needed him most?"

"You still need me, Pamela," he said in a harsh tone. "My name is on the mortgage to this property and all it would take is one call to the bank to shut your facility down."

She took a step back from him. Her stomach recoiled at the sight of the man. "What are you saying, if I don't go back to you, you'll take away my facility?"

He put his sunglasses back on and smiled at Pamela. "Think about it, P.A.," he said, his voice suddenly cheerful. "I can give you what you want and you can give me what I want."

"I'm still sick, Bob. What do you want me around for? Sympathy?"

"I need a wife who will look good and keep quiet. I don't need another Clarissa in my life. I can't take a chance on ending up with a woman who stands out in a crowd and embarrasses me with her stupidity and tantrums. I need people to see me with a refined and educated woman. You always made me look good, P.A."

She closed her eyes and tried to calm the flood of revulsion surging inside of her veins. "And if I don't agree?"

"I tell the bank to remove me from your loan, and all of this," he waved his hand at her house, "will disappear." He leaned over and kissed her cheek.

Pamela reflexively curled her hands into fists but did nothing.

Bob turned back to his car. "Don't take too long to think about it, Pamela. I'd like to put out the word that we're getting back together before Clarissa files for divorce," he added over his shoulder. "That will really give all of those society friends of hers something to talk about."

Pamela watched as Bob's silver Mercedes headed down her gravel drive. All the joy she had been experiencing over the past few weeks with the re-birth of her facility instantly fizzled out of her. She felt sick to her stomach at the prospect of becoming Bob's trophy wife. She would be the first wife coming back to him to hide the shame and gossip his divorce from Clarissa would inevitably bring. But who would blame him for a divorce when the object of his desire was really the only woman he had ever loved? Even the hard-hearted society set he ran with would melt when they heard his tale of reunited lovers.

Her stomach lurched upward at the thought of being with Bob again. Suddenly, she had to run to the side of the house to vomit. Just as she was steadying herself against the house, Carol's green Nissan Sentra made its way down the drive.

When Carol saw Pamela leaning against the house, she ran from her car to her friend's side.

"Are you all right?" Carol asked, sounding slightly panicked.

Pamela pushed herself away from the house and stood up straight. "I'm fine. I just felt sick all of a sudden." She placed her hand against her forehead and closed her eyes.

"You don't look good. You're awfully pale." Carol placed her arm about her waist.

"I think I must be coming down with something," Pamela admitted as she let Carol help her to the front porch.

"Would this spewing response be a result of Bob's visit?" Carol asked as she eased Pamela down on the steps. "I saw his fancy car pulling onto the road when I turned into the drive."

Pamela placed her head between her knees and took a few deep breaths. When she looked up, Carol was still hovering over her.

"Bob came over to tell me that he and Clarissa have split up. Clarissa found some kind of new respect for me after the party and that's why she made sure the article about my facility appeared in the newspaper. She wanted to help me."

"And that made you sick?"

"No." She paused and shook her head. "Bob told me he wants me back."

Carol frowned. "Now that would make me sick."

"And he said if I didn't come back he would call the bank and have his name removed from my mortgage."

"Jesus, then the bank would call the loan," Carol hissed. "What a prick!" She paused and stared at Pamela. "So what did you say?"

"No, of course!" she shouted. "What in the hell did you think I would say?"

"I was just checking. That man has always had a strange hold on you."

"Well, not anymore!" Pamela hollered.

Carol watched as some of the color returned to Pamela's angry face. "We're going to have to find some way to get Bob's name off that mortgage."

"I could apply to refinance," Pamela said, thinking out loud.

Carol rolled her eyes. "You have no sustainable income. Annual donations are not income and you have no assets to speak of. With this economy, banks are making getting loans very tough. You wouldn't stand a prayer."

Pamela placed her head in her hands. "I've got to find some way of making a lot of money quickly so I can rid myself of Bob permanently."

"What's the rush?"

Pamela looked up into Carol's pale blue eyes. "Bob didn't exactly take no for an answer. Either I agree to go back to him or he will shut Second Chance Wildlife Rehabilitation Center down." Pamela felt a wave of dizziness overtake her and grabbed at the porch railing.

Carol became alarmed when she saw Pamela quickly turn a pale shade of gray. "All right, enough of this," she ordered as she helped Pamela to her feet. "I'm putting you to bed," she insisted as she pulled Pamela to a standing position and wrapped an arm about her waist. "And then I am calling Dr. Derbois," she added with a scowl.

"I'm not going to bother my rheumatologist with the flu," Pamela protested as she let Carol help her up the porch steps.

"You've been doing too much around here with all these renovations and taking in new animals. I know when you are getting run down, and trust me, you look run down," Carol said, practically carrying Pamela in through the front door. "I can sleep in the guest room for a few nights, until you are better," she asserted, placing Pamela on the couch.

"What about your job?"

"I can work out of here for a day or two. All I need is my laptop and phone line to handle my accounts."

"And Ian?" Pamela worriedly asked.

"He can come over and see me here just as easily as he can see me at my place," she replied, shrugging. "Besides, Ian likes it here. He likes playing with all of the babies."

Carol fussed around Pamela as she pushed pillows behind her head and covered her with a blanket. And as Pamela half-listened to Carol's worried clucking, she thought of another man who had also loved playing with the baby animals. And within minutes, the pain that had been plaguing her joints all day disappeared, only to be replaced by a more uncomfortable ache deep inside of Pamela's heart.

* * * *

Two days later, Pamela was driving her old white Ford pickup into New Orleans to meet with her doctor. The pains in her body had not eased and the nausea would come and go. Fearing something worse than her usual discomforts, Carol had called Pamela's doctor to ask for an immediate appointment. Pamela had refused at first to go, but Carol had been very insistent.

"What if it is your kidneys again?" Carol had questioned the day before. "You felt nauseous and achy then, too. You know Dr. Derbois told you to call him the moment those symptoms returned. He said you cannot afford to take any more chances with your kidneys or you will end up on dialysis."

Pamela had waved off Carol's concerns. "It wasn't that bad. I had some problems with my kidney function but after a few weeks of medicine, everything was fine. I'm sure that's all there is to this."

"Just go and see the man," Carol had demanded. "Please do it for me."

And that was why Pamela was driving the sixty miles to Touro Infirmary in uptown New Orleans. She loved Carol and did not want to see her worry. She also secretly wanted Carol out of her house. She thought it funny that she could share her home with so many animals and not feel the slightest bit of intrusion, but have one close friend move in and it was as if she were living in a college dorm again.

Dr. Martin Derbois' office was located across the street from Touro Infirmary and he had been Pamela's physician for several years. As she waited in the austere exam room for Dr. Derbois, Pamela felt that uneasy sense of dread most people feel when visiting a doctor's office. There were always other places people would prefer to be, but as her good friend and former EMT partner, Scott Corbin, had always told her, the human body does not come with any warranties, so regular maintenance is mandatory.

"Hello, Pamela," Dr. Derbois said as he walked into the exam room, carrying Pamela's thick chart.

He was a slender man with a receding head of gray hair, thick glasses, and small brown eyes. He was dressed in a simple pair of slacks, dress shirt, and tie. Never one to wear white coats, Pamela always thought the man looked more like someone who should be teaching schoolchildren rather than a physician. He took a seat on the chair in front of the exam table and gazed up into Pamela's face.

"So what's going on?" he asked in a mild-mannered tone.

Pamela began a short description of her symptoms and added a brief discussion about the stress of the renovations going on around her facility. She had made a mental note earlier to skip any reference to Daniel. She figured the stress of Daniel's hasty departure was probably better suited to a discussion with a psychiatrist rather than her rheumatologist.

"Well," Dr. Derbois began after reviewing all of her symptoms. "Let's get some blood work and a urine test and see what we find." He examined her face. "You do look pale and may be anemic, as well. That could be causing some of your fatigue and dizziness, and it is pretty common with lupus. Any fever, night sweats, or chills?"

Pamela shook her head. "Just the weakness and nausea."

"Back pain or pain with urination?" he questioned.

Pamela shook her head again. "No, not this time. I had the back pain last time when my kidneys bothered me, but I haven't noticed anything other than the usual aches and pains."

Dr. Derbois stood up and felt the lymph nodes in her neck, checked her throat, and listened to her heart. He then tapped on her back looking for tenderness near her kidneys, but Pamela reported no pain with his examination. He sat down in his chair, picked up her chart again, and made some more notes.

"And when was your last period?" he inquired.

Suddenly an unexpected dread grabbed at Pamela's insides. "What does that have to do with anything? This is my kidneys right?"

Dr. Derbois gave a nonchalant nod of his head. "With your history I would suspect so, but I just want to cover all of my bases. Do you remember when you had your last period?"

Pamela remembered perfectly. "March 5th," she said doing the math in her head.

"You're four weeks late," Dr. Derbois said. "Is there a reason to suspect this may be something other than your kidneys, Pamela?" He asked with a hint of concern.

Pamela's heart started bounding in her chest. She had never considered that possibility. "There was only this one time. But it can't be that," she argued as she raised her eyebrows.

"You and I both know it only takes one time, Pamela. I'll just go ahead and add a pregnancy test to your lab work to make sure that is not what we are dealing with." He paused and gave her a worried glance. "But if you are pregnant, you're going to have to figure out some options here."

"Options?"

"Pamela, you have lupus and that immediately puts you into a high-risk category as far as pregnancy is concerned. You are forty-one and have compromised kidneys. Your body would be very stressed if you were to carry a child to term. I'm not an obstetrician, and if you are pregnant, we're going to have to get you in to see a physician who deals with high-risk pregnancies very soon." He paused and frowned slightly. "That is if you would want to keep it?"

Pamela's jaw fell. Her body slumped forward on the exam table. "I haven't considered being pregnant, much less whether or not I would have an abortion," she said as shook her head. "I don't put animals to sleep, Dr. Derbois, so I cannot even fathom doing that to a child."

He nodded his head slightly. "Then you need to be aware there are significant risks with someone with your history. You could miscarry, or you could deliver a premature baby, or even a sick child who would need to stay for an extended period in a neo natal intensive care unit. Then there are the problems you may encounter because of your pregnancy. You may need help with household chores, activities of daily living, and caring for your animal sanctuary. And after the baby is born, you may still not be well enough to care for your infant. Women with lupus do deliver healthy children, but your body has been through a great deal, Pamela, and a pregnancy may just push it over the edge."

Pamela felt her world suddenly shrinking around her. A baby? How would she manage her facility and a child?

"I'd like to go ahead and put a rush on that pregnancy test so we can either rule it out or begin to deal with it right away," he told her as he patted her knee. "Why don't you go upstairs to the lab and get your blood work done. Then go get a bite to eat, and come back to see me in about two hours. I'll have the results back by then."

* * * *

Three hours later, Pamela was in an elevator climbing to the twentieth floor of the P&L building. As her head swarmed with scenario after scenario presented by her physician, Pamela knew the rest of her life had been irrevocably changed. She realized she could not have this child on her own; she needed help. And there was only one person she could turn to.

"I'd like to see Robert Patrick, please," Pamela said to a very young, redheaded girl seated behind the desk in Bob's reception area.

"Your name please, hon?" the girl asked in a thick New Orleans accent.

"Tell him Pamela is here," she said, trying to control her anxious voice.

"Ya' gotta' last name, sweetheart?"

"Just tell him Pamela. He's expecting me."

Less than two minutes later, Bob appeared, bounding through the main doors that led to the attorney's private offices. He looked Pamela over and his face filled with apprehension. "What is it?" he asked.

She walked up to his side. "We need to talk," she calmly stated.

Bob turned back to the girl at the front desk. "Maureen, tell Edna to hold all of my calls," he directed and placed his arm about Pamela's waist.

He walked her through the main doors and down the hall to his expansive office. Once Pamela stepped into the room she felt a fleck of disappointment that the lovely shades of yellow and white she had painstakingly decorated his office in had been replaced by bold brown and taupe tones. She took in the pictures and assorted comic book memorabilia on the walls. An avid collector of comic books since his grade school days, Bob had mounted and framed many of his prized pieces for display in his office. The plain square walnut desk and dark brown chairs standing in front of it sharply contrasted with the colorful comic books hanging on the walls. It reminded Pamela of Bob in a way, a cold businessman on the outside and a selfish child on the inside.

Bob saw her taking in the décor as he shut the door behind them. "Clarissa redecorated my office soon after we got married," he explained as he waved his hand about the large room. "The comic books I just recently added to get rid of her paintings of horses. She has a thing for horses. Even had them painted all over the walls of our dining room." He walked across the room to her side. "I felt like I was in a bad Western movie every time we had to eat in that room." He took her hand. "Jesus, you're shaking," he whispered as he looked into her face. "What is it, Pamela?" he asked.

Pamela swallowed her pride and raised her head to him. "Does your offer still stand?" she inquired in a firm tone.

Bob gave a slow, victorious smile. "Now you want my help," he mused as he left her side and went over to his desk. He stopped and rested his hip against the dark wood. "Yes, my offers still stands," he answered as he folded his arms over his chest. "Marry me and I will take care of your little sanctuary forever. I will let you live your life as long as you let me live mine. We will be seen at parties together and will present a happy home front. I need a wife who is intelligent and can improve my social standing. I have political aspirations and Clarissa was a bit of a liability."

Pamela nodded. "All right. But there is one other thing."

Bob clapped his hands triumphantly. "Whatever you want, it's yours."

"I'm pregnant. It's Daniel's and I have no intention of getting rid of it." She watched as Bob's smile fell. "I want to know that if anything happens to me that you will raise this child and give it everything it deserves."

"Jesus Christ, Pamela!" Bob shouted, standing from his desk. "You were warned by all those doctors in Dallas about getting pregnant when you were first diagnosed. They told us it could be dangerous."

"I didn't plan this, Bob. But now that I'm faced with the prospect of a child I will have to make some compromises. This child will need a father and I want your word that you will raise it as your own."

Bob reflected for a moment. "And what about the biological father? Are you going to tell him?"

"Daniel left and I don't know where he has gone. He obviously doesn't want me to find him and I will abide by his wishes. If you agree, I will tell everyone the child is yours."

"I never wanted a kid, Pamela, but now that I'm considering running for office, a kid might just be the thing I need to look like a legitimate family man to voters. And it would help to convince all the gossips out there that our marriage is legit. We got back together because of your impending delivery." He clapped his hands. "This actually might turn out better than I had hoped," he happily confessed.

Pamela stood as stiff as a board in front of him. Her life was crumbling around her and there was nothing she could do to save it. She fought to keep the tears from her eyes. She could never let Bob see how much this was ripping her apart.

"You know you won't be able to take care of the wildlife while pregnant," Bob told her.

She gave a curt nod of her head. "Dr. Derbois has already informed me of that. If you agree, I'll need money to hire someone to oversee the place, at least until after the baby comes," she stated, trying not to let her voice sound strained by her emotions.

"I'll foot the bill for whatever you need," he agreed as he walked over to her side. "In the meantime, get things settled at the facility, and then you'll have to come and live with me. I'll get you an engagement ring before you move in to make it look good."

"I don't need—"

"We need to make this look convincing, Pamela," Bob interrupted. "Just leave all of the arrangements to me," he insisted with a smile.

She bit down on her lower lip and turned to go.

"This must be killing you," he said behind her. "I know just how much you want to tell me to shove this deal up my ass, but you can't now, can you?"

She stopped at the door to his office but did not turn to look at him "Dr. Derbois made it very clear that this pregnancy is not a good idea. And no matter how much it hurts to ask, I'm going to need help. I have no one else to turn to, Bob. And despite what I may think of you, my feelings aren't important anymore. I have someone else's needs to consider now." She reached for the door handle.

"Did you love him?" Bob asked from across the room.

Pamela wiped away the tears from her eyes. She had never used that word before to describe her feelings for Daniel, and hearing them coming from the man she had just sold her soul to made her feel like dirt.

She turned and faced Bob, keeping her head held high. "Never mention him to me again, Bob. You keep your secrets, and I'll keep mine." She opened the door and quickly marched out of his office.

* * * *

Carol was waiting on the porch with Ian when Pamela pulled up right before dark. Carol came flying down the steps to her side.

"I've called your cell phone about five times in the past hour," she frantically declared. "Where have you been?"

"Is everything all right?" Pamela asked.

"Everything's fine. I wanted to know what Dr. Derbois said," Carol admitted.

Pamela stared into her friend's face and could not summon the courage to tell her the truth just yet. Carol would fight tooth and nail to keep Pamela from selling herself to Bob. All of her life, Carol had admired Pamela like a big sister. Pamela had been there when Carol had gone on her first date, gotten her driver's license, graduated high school, graduated college, and started her first job. All the milestones in life that define one's progress into adulthood, Pamela had shared with Carol. But how could she explain to her that compromise and giving up one's dreams for the benefit of another were life lessons that she may come to know with time? Carol was young and still viewed life as a vast ocean of possibilities. She had not yet learned that some mistakes could sink you below the waves of that ocean and strand you beneath the cold, dark, depths of despair.

"He thinks it's the flu," Pamela said coolly to Carol. "He said it should pass in a few days," she reassured her.

"Whew!" she waved an overly dramatic hand across her brow. "Had me scared there for a moment. I was so worried I called Ian to come over after work and wait with me."

"She's been pacin' around here like an alley cat outside a chicken coop," Ian told her.

"Why don't you and Ian go on home," Pamela insisted as she patted Carol's arm. "I'm feeling better and I'm sure you guys want to get out of here."

Carol's face filled with delight. "All right," Carol called out. She turned to Ian. "Why don't we go grab a bite to eat, then you can take me back to your place and ravish me."

Pamela could not help but laugh as she watched Ian turn three different shades of red.

Carol went running up the steps into Ian's arms, laughing like a schoolgirl at recess. Pamela knew she had made the right decision not to say anything to Carol. It was her burden and passing her worry to someone else's shoulders would not have alleviated her despair; it would have only compounded it.

Pamela watched as Ian's red pick-up truck and Carol's green Sentra sped down her drive to the main road. She wrapped her arms about her body as if to stave off a chill in the air, despite the warm and muggy feel of the coming night. She turned back to her house and studied the place she had called home for the past six years. Her heart plummeted with the heaviness of a soldier about to set off for battle. But this battle would not be waged on the open fields of some foreign land. It would take place inside of her. She knew that from this moment on every day would be a constant battle to quell her wants, her needs, her dreams, all for the sake of her unborn child.

* * * *

Two days later, Bob showed up at her doorstep, carrying an assortment of shopping bags filled to the brim with books on pregnancy, swatches of decorative wallpaper, vitamins, and bottles of fresh fruit juices. He carried bag after bag into the house, smiling and laughing all the while.

"I've been on the phone with doctors and decorators for the past two days," he chirped happily as he set some of the books down on her coffee table. "I got several books on pregnancy for you to start reading." He picked up the different colored fabric swatches and held them out to her. "I've got the baby's room picked out at my house and I called Linda, my decorator. She sent over these swatches of wallpaper to choose from for the nursery. We can either wait until we know the sex of the baby and pick out the corresponding color, or Linda said we might want to go with a generic color and not be tied down by pink or blue. I already found you the best high-risk obstetrician in the city," he went on as he pulled a slip of paper out of his trouser pocket. "I made an appointment for Friday at eleven and I can take you there, if you want," he offered as he handed her the paper.

Pamela felt her eyes grow wide with surprise. "You'd want to go to the doctor's office with me?"

"I thought it might be something we should do together," he told her as he turned from her and back to the shopping bags. "I bought prenatal vitamins, lots of fruit juice—the books say that's good for you—and I got a surprise." He went over to one of the bags and pulled out a small stuffed white lamb. "What do you think? I figured we could start collecting toys for the baby," he added, handing her the little lamb.

Pamela stared at Bob for several seconds before she regained her composure. "I…I can't believe this," she said, stumbling over her words as she looked from Bob to the shopping bags filling her coffee table and couch. "You did all of this? It's almost as if you're excited about this baby."

"I am!" Bob yelled. He walked over to her side. "I never thought I would be, but after you left the other day, I began to think about you and me and a baby and suddenly, I was happy." He paused and smiled, beaming with pride. "I figured that maybe a baby would be pretty damn great for both of us."

"I can't believe this, Bob." She gazed at him with a newfound wonder. "I've never seen this side of you. I always thought you never wanted children."

"I didn't." He shrugged. "And I have to admit after you left my office I was mad. I was absolutely furious over the thought of raising another man's child, but then I thought about it. I remembered when my sister, Vannie, adopted her little girl from China a few years ago. She was so excited, and loves that little girl so much. Vannie once told me that genes don't make a child yours, you do. So I called her that night after you left my office and we had a long talk about you and the baby. My big sister made me realize that I've been given a wonderful opportunity and I would be a fool not to embrace it."

Pamela felt a small shudder of relief pass through her body. That Bob was willing to accept and love her child seemed to lighten her burden. At least she knew that the child would always be cared for, no matter what happened to her.

"Vannie told me what books to get, and what doctor to call and," he waved a hand over the coffee table, "all the rest." He reached into his trouser pocket and pulled out a small blue velvet box. "And I got this today," he announced as he handed her the box. "I want to make it official as soon as possible."

Pamela took the box from his hand and opened it. Inside was a very large emerald cut diamond solitaire set in gold and surrounded on either side by two smaller similarly cut green emeralds. Pamela's heart fell to her knees when she saw the ring. She recalled the first time Bob had given her an engagement ring and how excited she had been. This time the emotions that clouded her mind were not happy ones. Instead, she felt a numbing chill permeate her body. The cold winter of reality settled over her like an impenetrable fog. Resigning herself to her fate, Pamela took the ring from the box and placed it on the third finger of her left hand.

"I remembered your size," Bob said as he admired the ring. "And I remembered how much you always loved emeralds," he added with a smile.

Like a building snowdrift covering the last red rose of fall, Pamela felt her doubt being forever silenced by the steady heartbeat of the child growing inside of her.

CHAPTER 15

"You have got to be kidding me!" Carol screamed.

She was standing in the middle of Pamela's renovated barn, glaring at the engagement ring on Pamela's hand. Pamela had kept the ring in its blue box tucked away in her dresser drawer for the past two weeks. But as the deadline for leaving her little sanctuary for Bob's sprawling mansion loomed ahead of her, she knew that eventually she would have to break the news to Carol. Today had seemed like the right day.

"Bob!" Carol yelled. "Asshole Bob. You're gonna' marry asshole Bob?"

"Maybe you shouldn't call him that anymore," Pamela suggested as she pulled her hand away from Carol.

"I don't understand. Why are you doing this? So what if Imelda packed up all her shoes and left the son of a bitch! You told me before that you turned him down and now you're going to marry him? You don't have to marry him just to save this wildlife facility," Carol argued. "We can still find the money to get Bob off the note. I can sell my place and move in here with you, that way you could take the money and pay off—"

Pamela silenced her with a wave of her hand. "I could never allow you to do that. I told you before I'll never make this place your burden. Besides that house was left to you by your mother when she died, and I loved both your parents way too much to even consider having you do that."

"Oh, but you can go off and marry a man you detest to save your sanctuary," Carol balked. "Do you think I can honestly stand by and let you give yourself to that…that…asshole?"

Pamela sighed and placed a tender hand upon Carol's shoulder. "It's not about saving this place Carol," she said as she turned away. "There are other things I need to consider now."

"What other things?" Carol asked behind her.

Pamela took in the freshly painted white walls of her renovated barn. "My health for one. I can't go on running this facility on my own, and I need to make sure there will be someone to take over for me should the day come when I can't, or won't, be here to run it."

Carol came up alongside of her. "But you've always said you never wanted to have Bob get control of this place. You told me you were afraid of what he would turn it into."

Pamela nodded. "I know, and he and I discussed it and we are going to draw up papers to protect—"

"You're lying," Carol loudly asserted with a smirk on her face. "You would never just settle with Bob over this. You're a fighter, Pamie. You've been fighting for years. Why suddenly give up now?"

"Maybe I'm tired of fighting, Carol," she tried to explain. "You know I haven't been feeling well for a while and I have to face the reality of my situation. We both do."

Carol placed her hands defiantly on her hips as she stared Pamela down. "I know. You haven't been well at all lately and despite what Dr. Derbois says I don't think this is the flu. You're tired and puking all the time. You're so damned pale, and you're losing weight too. I think you should get another opinion."

Pamela laughed. "I don't need another opinion. I'm sure I'll be fine in a few months."

"A few months?" Carol gave her a questioning stare. "How do you know…" She grew quiet. "Oh, my God," Carol whispered. She inspected Pamela up and down. "That's why you're running back to asshole Bob. You're pregnant."

Pamela smiled and nodded her head.

"The baby is Daniel's, isn't it, Pamie?" Carol anxiously asked. "And Bob knows?"

Pamela shrugged. "Knows and is suddenly excited at the prospect of becoming a father. He said he would love and raise the child as his own. Now do you understand why I have to marry him?"

"No!" Carol yelled. "I could imagine a shotgun wedding with Daniel a lot easier than I could see you settling for Bob. Just because you're pregnant doesn't mean you have to go running off and marrying the first idiot you see."

"I have to marry Bob. If I get sick, or if something happens to me, this child will need someone to raise it."

"I'll raise it!" Carol shouted. "I'll move in, and we can tell everyone we're lesbians raising our sperm donor kid."

Pamela laughed, a cheerful, genuine laugh that for a moment lifted her sinking spirits. "I can't ask that of you. You're young and have your life ahead of you. I won't saddle you with my baby just like I won't burden you with my facility. These are my choices, not yours. Go out and make your own life, Carol. You don't need to live with my mistakes."

"And you don't need to live with Bob to raise a kid," Carol replied. "We can find him. I could hire someone to track him down. I think he would want to know about the baby, Pamie."

"Perhaps, but he left without wanting to be found. You know, despite everything he has done around here," she waved her hands about the newly renovated barn, "he didn't leave any forwarding information with any of the companies he hired. I never got a note, a text, an e-mail, or even a phone call. He's gone and I have to accept it." She nodded at Carol. "And so do you."

* * * *

Later that day, they were both sitting on the front porch taking a break from the animals and sipping iced tea when the sound of a car heading down the drive distracted them.

"You expecting a delivery?" Carol asked as she glanced over at Pamela.

Pamela shook her head and put her glass down on the porch step beside her. She stood up and walked toward the driveway as Carol followed close behind.

Rounding the bend at the end of the drive was a black limousine. Carol started immediately jumping up and down.

"He's back!" Carol screamed as she grabbed Pamela's arm. "He's come back to you. I knew it!" she shouted with the exuberance of a child about to enter the gates of Disney World.

Pamela turned to Carol and frowned. "Shhh!" She waved a hand at her. "It could be one of my investors coming to check out the facility and you're acting like a five-year-old."

Carol regained her pseudo-adult-like composure. But then she elbowed Pamela in the side. "I bet it's him," she whispered, still sounding excessively jubilant.

The car pulled up right in front of the two women. A driver, dressed in a black suit, jumped out and went to the rear door. He opened the back door and Pamela's heart flew to her throat as she watched a pair of men's leather shoes emerge from the car. She followed the curve of the man's lower leg up to his hips, then his waist, and then finally up to his face. Her heart sank when she saw an older man with gray hair standing before her. But as she inspected the man's features, she felt there was something oddly familiar about him.

"I'm looking for Pamela Wells?" he inquired in a deep voice as he looked from Pamela to Carol.

Pamela stepped forward, extending her hand. "I'm Pamela Wells, owner and operator of Second Chance Wildlife Rehabilitation Center. How can I help you?"

The man walked over and, instead of taking her hand, shoved a large, brown envelope toward Pamela.

"I was supposed to send this via FedEx, but I wanted to meet you," he curtly replied as he examined her with his dark eyes.

"I'm sorry, I don't understand." She stared into the man's face and thought she saw an older version of Daniel. "Have we met?" she asked.

"I'm Edward Phillips. You know my son, Daniel," he told her.

Pamela's heart stopped. "Daniel," she said softly. "How is he? Is he all right?"

"Where is he?" Carol questioned as she came up to Pamela's side. "He keeps sending workers out here, and we keep wondering when we're going to see him," Carol paused and nodded to Pamela. "Well, actually she's the one who wants to see him."

"Carol, why don't you go and pester the skunks?" Pamela growled through her teeth.

"Ah, you're Carol." Edward Phillips smiled. "He mentioned you, as well."

"Mr. Phillips," Pamela said, waving to the house. "Why don't you come inside and we can talk."

"No. I just came to deliver this." He nodded to the large envelope. "And I wanted to thank you for helping my son."

Pamela glanced down at the envelope in her hands. "What's this?"

"The paperwork transferring the balance of Daniel's trust fund to you," Mr. Phillips answered. "Ten million dollars and change."

Carol started screaming and jumping up and down.

Pamela turned to her. "Carol, go inside. Now!"

"But Pamie, I don't understand," she whimpered.

"Go," Pamela ordered. "I have to talk to Mr. Phillips, alone."

Pamela waited as Carol reluctantly made her way up the porch steps and into the house. After she shut the door behind her, Pamela turned back to Edward Phillips.

"I can't accept this," she admitted, handing the envelope back to him. "Tell Daniel I appreciate his concern but—"

"I'm afraid I'm not taking the money back, Ms. Wells," Edward Phillips interrupted. "The transfer of funds is already complete and inside that envelope is a cashier's check made out to you for the balance. Daniel gave me strict instructions to send it FedEx to you, but I wanted to see you, just once," he explained.

"Where is he?" Pamela felt her lower lip tremble and then she quickly got a hold of herself. "He disappeared without so much as a good-bye or a note explaining what happened. I think I deserve an explanation, Mr. Phillips."

The older gentleman sighed. "All I know is that when he first contacted me, he wanted me to make these arrangements for you." Edward Phillips paused. "Just know that he will never forget you."

Pamela moved in closer to him. "Is he all right?" she whispered. "Is he well?"

The older man shook his head. "I should go." He took a step back from her. "I promised him I would never contact you, never whisper a word of him to you, but I am his father. And a father always wants to lay eyes on the woman who…" He let his voice fade and then Edward Phillips gave a quick nod of his head. "Good-bye, Ms. Wells."

He got back in the car and shut the door. The driver returned to his seat behind the wheel and started the engine. Pamela stood on her gravel drive and agonizingly watched as Edward Phillips drove away, taking all of his secrets with him.

As the taillights of the limousine headed toward the main road, she clutched the envelope to her chest. How she wished that Daniel, and not his money, was wrapped in her arms.

"So what did he say?" Carol screamed as she came running out of the house and up to Pamela's side.

Pamela quickly wiped away the tears in her eyes before she turned to Carol.

"He didn't say anything," Pamela reported. "He just gave me the money and said he wanted to meet me because Daniel had…spoken so fondly of me."

"What a load of crap! You mean to tell me the guy came all the way out here to hand you an envelope and check out your measurements."

Pamela nodded. "Perhaps that is putting it crudely, but yes."

"And the money?" Carol continued. "Tell me you kept the money."

Pamela held up the envelope to Carol.

"Now at least you can tell Bob to kiss your ass. Ten million dollars can set you free of the asshole for the rest of your life."

"It's not that easy, Carol. I may be free of Bob financially, but my baby still needs a father. If anything happens to me, my child will have at least one parent left to care for him, or her." She sighed. "So you see, I will never be free of Bob." She looked down at the envelope. "But at least Daniel has made sure my facility will always be free of Bob. With this money I can set up a trust to fund the wildlife sanctuary and hire a legal representative to oversee the management of that fund."

"And what about Daniel?" Carol asked. "Did his father tell you where he is?"

Pamela shook her head. "Perhaps it's for the best," she reasoned as she ran her hand over her belly. "I don't know what kind of chance we would have had starting out like this. Daniel is a runner. The responsibility of a baby would probably have scared him back on the road."

"Wondering 'what if' is worse than knowing for certain, Pamie. If Daniel knew that you were carrying his child, he would be right by your side and never leave you."

"And after the baby is born? Then what?" Pamela questioned.

Carol shook her head. "He would have stayed until death do you part."

Pamela gazed up at the blue sky above. "But we would not have ended there, Carol. I need to know that if something were to happen to me, someone will be there and be committed to care for the part of me I leave behind."

Carol folded her arms over her chest. "And you think Bob is a better man for that job than Daniel?"

"Bob is here, Carol," Pamela stated as she glanced back at Carol. "Where's Daniel?"

* * * *

The following week, Pamela met Bob at his uptown mansion to make their first visit with the obstetrician. The house was located off St. Charles Avenue in the heart of the New Orleans Garden District. Bob's home was one of the larger mansions on the block and was a classic representation of Greek Revival architecture seen throughout the older parts of the city. The facade had four white Corinthian columns that rose from the first to the third floor of the dwelling. There was a double stained-glass front door with another arched stained glass window above it. Balconies were located outside of french doors on the second and third floors. The well-manicured gardens along the entrance were filled with fruit trees and red cameilia bushes.

After she rang the doorbell, Pamela gazed about the front porch at the white rocking chairs located on either side of her and yearned to relax her tired body for a spell in the comfy rockers.

"You look terrible," Bob said after he opened the front door and saw her standing before him. "You look like you're not sleeping enough." Bob frowned as he noted the dark circles under her eyes. Sleep had become something of a challenge ever since Edward Phillips had come to see her. Pamela wished she could blame her insomnia on hormonal fluctuations, but it was her mind, rather than her body, that was keeping her awake at night.

"Thanks for the concern, Bob," she said sarcastically as she walked in the door.

"I know the first trimester is supposedly the toughest, but you look like you've been to hell and back."

"I get the picture," Pamela grumbled. "And since when have you become an authority on such things?"

"I've been reading a few of those books on pregnancy I bought for you."

She stepped inside an elegant yellow and white wallpapered entrance and out into the foyer. Oak stairways on the left and right of the foyer curved upward from a white marble tiled floor to the second story balcony. Along the stairwell Bob had hung art deco paintings that clashed with the refined southern elegance of the grand foyer. The cold and pretentious home made Pamela long for her cluttered little Acadian cottage.

"Bob, are you sure you want to go with me today? You know how you are about doctors and hospitals."

"I'll be fine," he said, waving off her concern. "Come on, I want to show you the baby's room," Bob stated as he moved over to the stairs. "I decided to put it next to our bedroom."

Pamela stopped in mid-stride. "Our bedroom?"

Bob grinned. "Actually, it's a double master bedroom. Two master bedrooms adjoined by a single master bath, if that makes you feel any better. Clarissa read about it in a magazine when we were renovating the house."

"You and Clarissa didn't share a bedroom?" she asked, itching with curiosity.

"Clarissa liked to stay up late and watch television, and you know how much I hate that. And she always complained about my late hours, so the room was supposed to be a compromise to help our marriage."

"Are there locks on the bedroom doors?"

Bob raised his eyebrows to her. "For the time being," he conceded as he stared into her eyes. "I'm hoping one day we can do away with the locks," he added as he gently ran his fingers up and down her arm.

She pulled her arm away from his touch. "Bob, I think you should know something about me before we go any further with this," Pamela said in a menacing tone.

He gave a curt laugh. "I already know so much about you, P.A. What else could you possibly tell me?"

She looked him in the eye. "I sleep with a gun. Come anywhere near my bedroom door and I'll use it on you." She smiled slyly at him. "And I can make it look like an accident. Remember, you taught me how to do that."

He raised his head as he placed his hands behind his back. "You haven't changed, Pamela," he murmured, his voice dark and angry.

"This is an arrangement, Bob. You need an upstanding wife who will look the other way when you sleep with your office staff, and I need a father for my child. Having sex with you is not part of our deal."

"And what if I want to make it part of our deal?"

Her stomached clenched at the thought of having Bob in her bed. "You already have my soul, Bob. What good would my body do you?" she coolly replied.

"You'll never change." He started up the stairs. "Maybe one day I can make you fall in love with me again," he remarked over his shoulder as he trotted up the oak staircase.

"Not even if you started eating nuts and grew a big fuzzy tail," Pamela whispered as she followed behind him.

The room Bob had chosen for the nursery was a former guest bedroom, next to one of the master bedrooms. The room had been emptied of furniture, and scattered on one wall were several swatches of wallpaper.

"I figured we could take out this carpet," he said, pointing to the beige carpet beneath his feet. "Linda selected these swatches for the baby's room." He waved at the selection of fabrics taped to the wall. "She'll be here Monday afternoon to go over some ideas for furniture and color schemes." He nodded at her. "You should be here to pick out what you want."

Pamela walked over to the french windows overlooking the balcony outside. "I'll be here." She gazed out the window and spotted a towering oak next to the house. Two squirrels were running about the trunk of the tree, chasing each other.

"And we should probably plan an announcement party. Let everyone know we are back together and about the baby," he suggested behind her.

"Maybe we should wait until I'm a little farther along to make baby announcements." She kept her eyes on the frolicking squirrels as she spoke.

"You're probably right," he agreed. "Then we'll just have a party to let everyone know we are a couple again."

Pamela smiled as the squirrels ran down the tree and across the lawn. She turned back to Bob. "What about Clarissa? Shouldn't we wait for your divorce to be final before you start planning parties?"

Bob grinned. "Clarissa and I had a pre-nuptial agreement. If she gives me any shit in the divorce, or discredits my reputation in any way, she loses any claims to her settlement. Trust me, that pre-nup is iron clad." He looked at his watch. "We'd better get going. I don't want you to be late for your first appointment with Dr. Holdford."

* * * *

Carl Holdford was a robust, round man with bright blue eyes, had a long scar over the top of his bald head, and walked with a limp as he stepped into the exam room. When he spotted Pamela and Bob seated in two chairs next to the exam table, he smiled.

"I got your old charts and your most recent labs from Dr. Derbois, Pamela," Dr. Holdford said, opening her chart and taking a stool across from the couple. "And I'm concerned about your kidney function, as well as your blood pressure." He looked down at the paperwork. "My nurse got one fifty over ninety-eight a few minutes ago, and I see your blood pressure has always run a little high on your visits to Dr. Derbois," he added.

Bob turned to her, his eyes flecked with concern. "Since when did you have pressure problems?"

Pamela shrugged. "Started about two years ago," she replied.

"I want to find out if it is your kidneys, or if we are dealing with another issue here," Dr. Holdford clarified, sounding a little more serious than before.

"What other issues?" Bob quickly asked.

"Your fiancée could have a compromised vascular system, making it harder for her heart to pump the extra blood and fluid a pregnancy can introduce into the body. We already know her kidneys are not functioning as well as I would like for someone about to embark on a pregnancy. We can control her blood pressure with medication that won't affect the baby in any way." He turned to Pamela. "You need to be aware, Pamela, that my goal for this pregnancy is to get you to eight months with as few problems as possible. At that time, we'll take the baby via c-section. I don't think going to full term for a woman in your condition is advisable. You also need to be prepared to spend part of this pregnancy in bed, if necessary."

"I'm in the process of hiring someone to take over my facility. I rehab wildlife," she explained. "I have applicants coming in this afternoon, in fact, to interview for the position."

Dr. Holdford nodded. "Your fiancé told me about what you do, and I have to agree with him that you need to have as little contact with wildlife as possible now. If you were to get an infection from a scratch or bite it could prove deadly to the baby."

"And she's going to be moving in with me," Bob disclosed. "I want her in the city and close to you and the local hospitals."

"Glad to hear it." Dr. Holdford closed the chart in his hands. "I know that both of you are aware that this could be a difficult pregnancy, and you need to be prepared. As time goes on and the baby grows, Pamela, your level of fatigue will increase. And that fatigue could continue until well after the baby is born, so you will need to make plans for additional assistance in caring for the child. I have had several lupus patients, and they usually report increased joint pain during, and after, their pregnancy. But every woman is different and your complaints may not be the same as theirs, so we will deal with issues as they come up." He stood from his stool. "So let's take a look at you and see where we are."

When Dr. Holdford waved Pamela up onto the exam table, the color drained from Bob's face.

"Bob, why don't you go back into the waiting room?" Pamela suggested as she stood from her chair.

Bob just nodded and bolted for the door.

Dr. Holdford watched as Bob shut the exam room door closed behind him. "Is he okay?" he asked.

"He has a phobia about doctors and hospitals. I'm surprised he lasted this long," she admitted.

Dr. Holdford gave her a worried glance. "And what do you think he will do in the delivery room?"

Pamela shook her head, already knowing the answer to that question. "I'm sure he won't be in the delivery room, Dr. Holdford," she told him.

"Is he going to be able to help you through this, Pamela?" he asked, looking even more troubled.

"I've got no one else. Bob's all there is."

CHAPTER 16

Two hours later, Pamela pulled up in front of her cottage feeling worn out. She still had an afternoon of interviews to get through to find her replacement, and the prospect of selecting someone to take over her beloved sanctuary felt overwhelming.

She got out of the truck and greeted each of the dogs. As she made her way to the porch steps, Rodney came out from some bushes near the side of the house and said hello. She scratched behind his silver-tipped ears and gave his back a long rub. The sunlight shimmered off the diamond in Pamela's engagement ring and Rodney reached out with his front paws to grab at the shiny object.

"Oh, no, buddy," Pamela chastised as she removed the ring from her finger and slipped it into her purse. "I can just see me explaining to Bob how a raccoon ate my ring."

Satisfied with his moment of attention, Rodney waddled back into the bushes. Pamela climbed the steps to her front door and went inside.

She had just retrieved a cup of tea from the microwave and was going to have five minutes of peace with her feet curled up on the couch when the dogs started barking. A few seconds later, she heard a car pulling up to her house.

Pamela looked over at the clock on the microwave and silently cursed. The first of her interviews was over half an hour early. She put the tea down on the coffee table and went to the front door. Then she noticed the silence.

"That's odd," she said to herself as she reached for the doorknob. "This one must be really good with animals."

She opened the door and saw a tall man hunched over in her driveway with his back to her, petting each of the dogs.

"You're pretty good with animals," she called out.

At the sound of her voice, the man turned to greet her.

"Daniel," she gasped.

"Hello, Pamela," Daniel said as he took a step closer to the house. All the dogs followed close behind him.

She walked out to the porch and gazed down at him. He appeared to be a little leaner and his eyes had dark circles beneath them. His skin seemed paler and his warm features looked strained, as if all of the burdens in his life had finally come to etch their way across his face. This was a wearier version of the Daniel she had known before his disappearance from her life.

"How are you?" he asked as he climbed the steps to her porch.

She took in a deep breath and nodded. "I'm fine," she said. "How are you?" she inquired, trying to sound upbeat.

He came up to her and peered into her cool gray eyes. "I'm fine," he replied with a faint smile.

"Liar," she murmured. "You look like shit."

His smile widened. "Shit does not suit you, Pamela. Why don't you try crap, or even hell, but not shit." He took a step closer to her.

She laughed. "Well, you still look like shit to me."

"You look wonderful to me," he whispered.

An uncomfortable moment of silence filled the air between them. There were so many things to say, but neither said a word.

Seconds ticked by and Pamela could feel the strain building between them. The smell of his spicy cologne encircled her and instantly flashes of their night together invaded her thoughts. Her pulse quickened as her body yearned for his. Pamela fought to maintain control as their silence persisted. Unable to stand it any longer, she finally asked, "What happened to you, Daniel?"

He took in a deep breath and turned away. "The day after the party Bob came to see me."

"Your landlady told me about that," she confirmed. "I went to your place looking for you and she mentioned that Bob had been there."

Daniel walked to the porch railing. "Yeah, T.J. said you had stopped by. I dropped my bags off at my old place before I headed out here."

"So how long are you staying in New Orleans?"

He turned back to her and rested his hip against the railing. "Long enough to open a new office for my father. He wants to expand his import business, and he asked me to come down here and get it going."

"Is that where you went, back home to work with your father?"

He nodded.

"Why? I thought you said you and your father didn't get along."

"It was part of a deal I made with him." He paused and ran his hands through his hair. "When Bob came to my place, he told me he was going to stop giving you money unless I left town. He said he was going to have the loan called on your facility. He wanted me out of your life. I didn't want to leave, so I called my old man and asked him for the balance of my trust fund. I wanted to make sure Bob couldn't hurt you. My old man agreed to transfer the money from my trust fund over to you, but he had one condition; I had to come home and take over the business. I figured I had no choice but to go. It was the only way I could make sure you would always be safe from Bob." He slowly walked up to her.

"You could have said something to me," she argued. "You could have called and told me what was going on. Asked me what I wanted to do. We could have talked about it."

He rubbed his hand across his chin as he stopped in front of her. "You would have stubbornly refused my offer. And you probably would have gone back to Bob and kissed his ass until he was appeased."

Pamela looked down at the porch deck beneath her feet. "You don't know that," she whispered.

He raised her chin with his hand until her eyes met his. "I know you," he declared. "The only problem with my whole plan was that once you had the money I believed you wouldn't need me anymore. I figured you would forget about me and I hoped I would forget about you. But then my father returned from his recent business trip and told me that he had met you." Daniel removed his hand from beneath her chin. "Then he ordered me to pack my bags and move back to New Orleans."

"So why are you here?"

He placed his hands behind his back. "Because my father said I was an idiot to ever leave you and he was right." He inched closer to her. "I know what I did was wrong and I'm sorry I didn't call or tell you—"

"Look, Daniel," she said, cutting him off. "I'm not going to stand here and pretend your running off didn't hurt. It did, but things have changed and I really can't take your money." She turned and walked back into her house.

Daniel followed her inside. "What's changed? I want to be with you and I hoped you would want to be with me. I thought we could talk this through."

She went over to her desk and picked up the envelope Edward Phillips had given to her. She turned back to him, trying to keep the storm of emotions swirling inside of her hidden from view. "And then what, Daniel? Date? Spend a few more nights in bed and see how it goes?"

"Pamela, this is new territory for me," he said, impatiently. "I want us to have a chance together."

She walked across the living room to him and held out the large brown envelope. "When you left, you blew any chance we ever had. Here, I don't want your money. I don't need it."

He looked down at the envelope but did not reach for it. "What do you mean you don't need it?" he questioned, glaring at her. "When I left Bob was about to cut you off at the knees."

She avoided his eyes and focused instead on the envelope in her hand. "Bob and I have come to an understanding."

There was silence. She raised her eyes and caught sight of Daniel's face. His mouth was pulled tight in a painful grimace and the menacing darkness had returned to his eyes.

"I never thought you were the kind of woman to sell yourself to a man, even to save your facility," he growled.

"It's not like that," she refuted as she raised her head high. "I have had some medical problems lately, and Bob has been there for me."

Daniel cursed and threw his hands in the air. "You've been sick!" he shouted, sounding more hurt than angry. "Why didn't you say something to me?"

"Because you weren't here, Daniel. Bob was, and he has promised to continue to be there for me. I realized after you left that I do need someone to help me. I need someone I can count on."

"And you think Bob is going to be there for you? After what he did to you the first time round, how on earth can you trust him again?"

"Where in the hell were you, Daniel?! When things got tough, you ran. You showed me the kind of man you are and—"

"I left to protect you!" he shouted.

"Protect me! You ran off leaving me…" She shut her mouth and turned away from him.

"Yes, I left you," he said in a strained voice behind her. "I left, and I'm sorry. Don't throw away what we had because you think I can't make a go at a relationship. I want us to try again. I know I let you down, but I want you to give me a second chance. Can you give me that chance, Pamela?"

She felt a wave of nausea grip her insides. She struggled against the bout of morning sickness and prayed for Daniel not to see it. She took in a few deep breaths and turned around to face him.

"Please take your money and go," she pleaded as she held out the envelope to him.

Daniel backed away. "Keep the money. I don't want it. And you don't want Bob. You're just running back to something you know because you're afraid. But the safest choice is not always the right choice, Pamela. And sometimes a person has to run away to realize what they had." He paused and looked into her eyes. "I know I love you, and I came back hoping that you might love me, too." He turned away from her and walked over to the front door. "I hope one day you will learn that Bob can never make you happy. When you do, come and see me...I'll be waiting." He slammed the door shut behind him.

Pamela sank to her knees as she clutched the envelope to her chest. And for the first time since Daniel had left, she finally released all of the emotion she had kept safely locked away. She curled up on the floor and began to cry. As she lay on the floor, blinded by her tears, she felt a soft nudge against her hand. When she wiped the tears away, her eyes beheld Louis on the floor beside her, pressing his head against her hand. Shocked that the little squirrel had ventured so far from his cage, Pamela let go of the envelope and reached out to pick him up. She sat up and cradled Louis in her hands, feeling comforted by his concern. As she gently stroked the squirrel's back, she felt the tears, once more, fill her eyes. Not only had she lost her one chance at happiness with another, she realized she was about to walk away from the only contentment she had ever found. The loss of her animals, and the comfort they had always given her, enveloped her with an unfamiliar emptiness. Overwhelmed by her sorrow, Pamela began to gently rock back and forth as she sat on the floor, holding her dear little Louis against her chest.

* * * *

The following day Pamela returned to the city to meet the decorator, Linda, and go over design plans for the nursery. She was on edge as her white Ford pick-up maneuvered down the pothole-laden streets of uptown New Orleans, on her way to Bob's home. The interviews from the last few days had left her doubting that she could ever find anyone to run her facility. All the candidates she had met with were either too young, too inexperienced, too ignorant, or just did not have the right personality to work with wild animals. Bob had told her she was being too picky and felt anyone with a clear face and a high school education could do what she did. But what had really been bothering her was the visit from Daniel. She had tried to forget that he was back. She had even convinced herself that he was no longer a part of her life. But every time she looked down at her belly she realized that was a worthless rationalization. And from the moment she got out of bed until she fell asleep at night, the idea of him, the look in his eyes, the sound of his voice, even the smell of his cologne, haunted her.

As she pulled up into Bob's driveway, she could feel the stress mounting in her body. Her hands tightly gripped the steering wheel, and when she finally let go, her fingers were stiff. She tried to convince herself that it was just her emotions running in overdrive since she had so much to do between the facility and preparing for the baby. But as she got out of her beat-up truck, feeling more like a maid than a mistress of the mansion, she knew what the real problem was. Her only concern was how long she would be able to continue like this without erupting.

"Hey," Bob said as he opened the front door for her. "I thought I heard your piece of shit pulling into the driveway." He spied the dingy white Ford pick-up parked on his lavish red brick driveway. "Next thing on the list is to get you a new car," he told her as he ushered her inside. "Can't have you pulling up in that thing. What will the neighbors think? After all, you're my fiancée, not the gardener."

"I thought you would be at work," she remarked, ignoring his comment about her truck.

"No, I wanted to be here with you to pick out things for the nursery. And," he said, reaching into his pocket and pulling out a key, "this is for you. It's only for the front door, but I'll get copies of the back door made, and remind me before you leave to show you how the alarm works." He handed her the key.

Pamela took the key from him and a sickening feeling gripped her. She knew this feeling could not be attributed to morning sickness.

"And I wanted to show Linda the dining room," Bob added as he put a friendly arm about her waist. "I want to remove all traces of Clarissa from this house. I want you to make it over for me. Turn it into a sophisticated showplace that will be the envy of the entire city."

Pamela just smiled as she let Bob escort her up the stairs.

"Oh, and we received our first social invitation as a couple," Bob excitedly informed her. "Val Easterling invited us to a party she is having at her home in the French Quarter this weekend."

"Really?" Pamela hesitated for a moment. "How do you know Mrs. Easterling?"

"I've met her at a few parties, and she is the person to know for anyone who wants to get into politics in this town. I suspect she may have heard about my political aspirations and wants to talk to me. I think our getting back together is really going to pay off, P.A."

Pamela suspected Val Easterling had another motive entirely for inviting the two of them to her party.

Once they entered the room slated for the nursery, Pamela spotted a petite woman with thick glasses, dark brown hair, and big brown eyes. She had a long face, a hooked nose, sunken cheeks, and a sallow complexion that alluded to her Italian heritage. She instantly reminded Pamela of an opossum.

"Linda Oliveri, this is my former wife, and now my fiancée, Pamela Wells."

Linda extended her hand toward Pamela. "Congratulations on all of your good fortune." She looked Pamela over from head to toe.

The blue cotton dress and plain white flats Pamela had chosen to wear seemed almost gauche next to Linda's tailored suit and high-heeled designer shoes. Pamela wished she could escape to her sanctuary and be surrounded by her animals, but she pushed her regrets down deep inside of her and forced herself to stop thinking of her former life. This was her life now.

"Darlin', looking at you no one could ever tell you're pregnant," Linda said in a rather deep, almost masculine-sounding voice. "You're very petite. Oh well, enjoy it." Linda gave a warm, soulful laugh. "When I had my first boy, I gained damn near fifty pounds. My husband used to say I looked like a watermelon. I was much more careful for my second. Only gained twenty-five pounds with Mario." She walked to the corner of the room, opened her briefcase, and pulled out her notepad. "Now, Bob gave me a few ideas of what you needed in here, but I wanted to meet with you and go over some basic designs to get a rough idea of where we are going," she stated, moving into the center of the room.

"Linda is the best decorator in town," Bob declared as he patted Pamela's shoulder. "Does all the homes of the city's elite."

"How nice," Pamela softly replied, starting to feel like she wanted to blend into the beige walls and disappear.

"Now, since you don't know the sex yet, I figured we could hold off on the color scheme until your ultrasound," Linda began. "Any preference for a boy or girl?" she asked Pamela.

"Well, I want a girl," Bob jumped in. "I'm going to raise her to be a daddy's little girl. I'll buy her horses and send her to the best schools. Then we'll have to send her off to law school, so she can take over her father's law practice."

"How sweet," Linda cooed. "And if it's a boy?"

Bob laughed. "Then I guess he'll have to be a football star and we'll send him to the best schools. Then, we'll send him off to law school so he can one day take over my law practice," Bob admitted, grinning like he was already a doting father.

Pamela turned to him. "You never told me about your plans for law school."

"Does that matter?"

"It matters to me. I want our child to choose their own career path," Pamela insisted in a firm tone.

Bob waved off her suggestion. "Children need guidance, Pamela. My father was an absolute son of a bitch and pushed me from grade school all the way through college. He made me what I am today."

Pamela kept what she was thinking to herself. "But what if our daughter or son wants to go to art school or be a writer?" she asked as she folded her arms over her chest.

"Kids change their minds like you and I change clothes," Linda offered with a wave of her manicured hand. "My two boys talk about being fireman one day and plumbers the next. Bob is right. Children need to be molded into something."

"Thank you, Linda." Bob nodded his head. "But we've got a long time before we have to worry about that, Pamela. So let's get back to the nursery."

"I was thinking," Linda began as she gazed about the room. "You're going to need a bassinet, preferably an antique of polished oak or mahogany. Either one will match any pastel color you might choose to paint the walls. Depending on if you go with the…"

Pamela tuned out the rest of what Linda had to say. She spent the next hour nodding her head and agreeing with whatever Bob desired. She was too tired to argue about nursery décor. She was just too damn tired to argue about anything anymore.

* * * *

After Linda left, Bob escorted Pamela down the stairs, still gushing happily about decorating the nursery.

"And I think Linda was dead on about the oak bassinet, especially if we go with a nice pale yellow in the room. We can do it in yellow and white, like you did my office after we got married. Oh, and I'm especially interested in seeing what Linda will do—"

"Bob," Pamela said, interrupting his enthusiastic chatter. "What did you mean earlier about planning the baby's life? You know the horses if it's a girl and football if it's a boy thing." She stopped on the stairs and glanced over at him.

Bob shrugged and stuck his hands in his trouser pockets. "I didn't mean anything.

I'm just talking out loud about what I want for our child."

"And since when did you want this child to take over your law practice?"

"What's wrong with wanting that? Doesn't every father dream that their child will grow up and take over the family business?"

Pamela let out a slow and uneasy breath. "My father wanted the same thing for me. You remember, I told you about that. It was really tough growing up and listening to my father talk about the day I became a doctor and worked side by side with him. I know the kind of pressure that can place on a child."

"And look at you now!" Bob bellowed. "If you had taken your father's advice you wouldn't be in this position."

"And I wouldn't have been happy either," she countered.

He shook his head and furrowed his dark brows together. "Why are we even discussing this? The baby hasn't even been born and already you're arguing with me about how to raise it. Christ, Pamela, listen to yourself." He started back down the stairs.

"You don't get it, Bob. What if I'm not around to discuss this later? I have to know that this child will be raised according to my wishes and have the happy childhood I didn't have."

Bob reached the bottom of the stairs and looked back up at her. "All right," he said calmly. "I don't want to upset you. We can talk about all of this after the baby is born. We've got years to screw the kid up."

Pamela came alongside of Bob and stared into his intense eyes. "I just need to know we are on the same page."

He leaned over and kissed her cheek. "I'm sorry. The kid can grow up to be the next Monet if it makes you happy." He stepped back from her. "Don't forget the movers will be coming to your place on Monday to get your things. We can go over everything this weekend when I pick you up for Val's party. Make a list of what you want brought here and what the facility can keep."

Pamela just nodded, wanting to avoid any further discussion about leaving her beloved sanctuary.

"And go and get something nice to wear to Val's. Her parties are always black tie and I need you looking wonderful." He reached into his pocket and pulled out his wallet, then handed her a credit card. "Use this to buy whatever you want. The sky's the limit," he added with a smile.

Pamela took the credit card from him as a memory of Daniel taking her shopping flashed across her mind. She searched Bob's eyes and fought to find the words to tell him what she was really thinking.

"I have to get back," she said instead of clearing her conscience. "I have a few more interviews this afternoon," she lied.

CHAPTER 17

"I have it on good authority that Val wants to talk to me about my political aspirations," Bob reported as he pulled his silver Mercedes in front of an impressive gray Creole cottage located on the corner of Dumaine and Royal streets. "So don't distract her with your wildlife exploits. I know she's your patron, but this is my night to shine."

Pamela nodded just as a doorman, dressed in a black tux and tall black hat, opened her car door.

"Welcome," the well-dressed man said as he waved Pamela toward the front door.

The French Quarter home had a plaster exterior and large french windows on both the first and second story. Thick green painted wooden shutters were located next to each of the windows and surrounded the front door. Two gas lanterns flickered on each side of the entrance.

"Couldn't you have chosen something a little less revealing to wear?" Bob reprimanded as he took her hand and walked toward the entrance. "I'm trying to make a good impression tonight."

Pamela glanced down at the short, fitted black cocktail dress Carol had bought for her to wear. "What's wrong with this dress?"

"Pamela, you're almost three months pregnant. Pregnant women don't dress like that. Shouldn't you be covering up your body and not showing it off?" he whispered beneath his breath.

"I don't understand. It's a cocktail dress, Bob. I think you're making too much of it."

He worriedly played with his bow tie. "Just don't bend over in that thing; otherwise somebody is going to get a great view of your ass."

Once inside, Pamela took in the detailed plaster inlay in the ceiling and rich burgundy antique mahogany furniture as Bob shook hands with some people he knew. She noted the way he made a point of introducing Pamela as his fiancée. They had not even set foot out of the living room area when Pamela felt a gentle tug on her arm.

"There you are," a woman's deep voice said.

Pamela turned to see Val Easterling covered in a swirl of deep blue silk that accentuated her round hips and added a sparkle to her light blue eyes.

"Mrs. Easterling," Bob began as he reached for Val's hand. "I just want to say that I look forward to hearing your views on the current political situation in the city and I feel that—"

"Who are you?" Val demanded, turning her eyes to Bob.

Bob looked nervously from Val to Pamela. "I'm Robert Patrick. Pamela is my fiancée."

Val turned her attention back to Pamela and raised her gray eyebrows in surprise. "Is she? Weren't you already married to this ambulance chaser once before, Pamela?" Val asked, nodding to Bob.

Bob frowned. "Please, Mrs. Easterling, ambulance chaser is a bit—"

"Bob?" Val raised her voice to the man. "The bar is out in the courtyard." She pointed to the back door leading outside. "Go get a drink. I want to have a word with your fiancée."

Val and Pamela watched as Bob reluctantly made his way outside.

"I heard about your engagement," Val stated as her eyes inspected the diamond ring on Pamela's left hand.

"Bob and I plan on getting married as soon as his divorce is final," Pamela explained and cast her eyes to the red Oriental carpet beneath her feet.

"Pamela, when I saw you with my Daniel at that benefit, I thought you two looked pretty happy together." Pamela raised her eyes to Val. "Then Daniel left the city, without so much as a good-bye to me. The next thing I heard was that you had gone back to your ex-husband and are expecting." Val placed her hands on her hips. "I remember seeing you at a few parties when you were married to Bob. And I always wondered what you were doing there. You always looked so out of place. Not like you didn't belong, more like you didn't want to belong. You reminded me of another young woman I used to know. She was just as confused about her place in the world as you are now. And I watched her come close to making the same mistake that you're about to make."

Pamela smiled, trying to keep up her brave face. "And was this young woman you knew pregnant? I have someone other than myself to consider now."

Val shook her head. "The baby doesn't change anything." She paused and tenderly patted Pamela's arm. "I know a hell of a lot more than you think about what you're going through, so let me give you a bit of advice. Don't settle for someone you don't want when someone you do want is waiting just on the other side of that door," Val declared as she pointed to the door leading to the courtyard.

Pamela looked from the door and back to Val. "I don't understand."

Val took her elbow and urged her toward the back door. "You will," she whispered and then walked away.

Pamela started down the hallway, but stopped and looked back to see Val Easterling shaking hands with her other guests in the living room. Pamela sighed, faced the back door, and headed outside.

She stepped out into the cool evening air and took in the sweet smell of jasmine hovering about the courtyard. She was about to make her way across the bricked pavement toward the bar, when a familiar voice stopped her.

"I can't believe you're going to marry that asshole."

Pamela turned to her right and found Daniel leaning against the wall, holding a flute of champagne in his hand.

"When Val told me about your engagement tonight I almost punched out her front window," Daniel said as his eyes took in every inch of Pamela's body. He froze when he spotted the engagement ring on her left hand.

"What are you doing here?" she whispered to him.

"Val invited me. When she found out I was back in town, she called me. She told me she had invited you and Bob, and she figured this was my opportunity to win you back."

"Win me back?" Pamela almost laughed. "I was never yours to win back, Daniel."

Daniel downed the contents of his flute in one long sip. Then his eyes wandered about the courtyard.

"Please go," Pamela begged. "If Bob finds you here one thing will lead to another and someone will probably end up going to jail."

"Tell me something, Pamela," Daniel insisted as his eyes returned to her. "Did that night mean anything to you or was it all bullshit?"

Keeping her eyes on his, Pamela raised her chin slightly. "That night meant something, Daniel. I thought it meant something to you, as well. But then you disappeared."

"I can't change the past between us and I'm not about to stand here and—"

"What's he doing here?" Bob's angry voice cut in.

Pamela turned to see Bob's red face beside her. "Val invited him. It's her party after all. So don't make a scene, Bob," she whispered.

"I think you had better leave, Phillips," Bob growled. "You've hurt my fiancée enough with your lies and your manipulation."

"Lies and manipulation? This coming from a man who screws around on his wife and then dumps her when she gets sick," Daniel responded.

"Why you son of a bitch," Bob said, raising his voice as he made a move toward Daniel.

Pamela jumped in front of Bob. "Don't do this. There are too many people here tonight who could hurt your political aspirations if they witness you making a scene."

"Political aspirations?" Daniel laughed beside her. "You'll fit right in with all the other crooks in this town."

Bob lunged at Daniel. The two men slammed against the side of the house as Daniel's flute fell to the courtyard floor and smashed into a thousand shards.

"Stop it!" Pamela shouted as she tried to move in between the men.

Pamela felt a pair of strong hands pull her back.

"Let me handle this," a man's voice said.

A tall man with thick, wavy brown hair stepped in and pulled the two men apart. When Pamela caught sight of her rescuer's profile, she cringed.

"Care to take this discussion outside?" Lance Beauvoir calmly said as he looked from Bob to Daniel.

The buzz of conversation around their little party grew quiet. Pamela's eyes darted about the courtyard to see if any of the guests appeared distracted by the tussle.

Val came up to Pamela's side. "I had hoped Bob would show a bit more restraint tonight."

Pamela turned to Val. "You must have known what would happen if you invited Daniel."

Val shrugged. "I invited Daniel for you, not Bob. I know of Bob's reputation as a bully and I had heard about his little tussle with Daniel at Pat O'Brien's. But I figured he wouldn't be foolish enough to go after Daniel with this crowd watching." She nodded to the guests gathered in the courtyard.

"I can't believe this," Pamela whispered as she watched Lance pushing Daniel away toward the bar while ushering Bob inside of the house. "Why, Val? Why did you invite Daniel?" she asked in a low voice.

Val smiled at her. "I had to do something to make you come to your senses."

Daniel had moved across the patio to the bar while Bob had retreated into the house. Feeling that the situation was under control, Lance came up to Val's side.

"As always, you sure do put on one hell of a party, Valie," Lance commented as he wiped his hand across his forehead. "Remind me to bring a referee whistle with me next time I come to one of your shindigs." He nodded to Pamela. "You all right?"

"Yes, thank you," Pamela replied. "I'm sorry you had to get involved in all of that."

Val slapped Lance's shoulder. "Why do you think I invited Lance, anyway? Best bouncer this side of Rampart Street."

Lance shrugged. "Valie told me there might be fireworks, so I came prepared."

Pamela felt her cheeks go red. "So you were both in on this?"

Lance's green eyes twinkled with mischief. "Let's just say Valie and I are old hats at this sort of thing."

"What, starting fights?" Pamela asked.

"No, interfering," Lance clarified. "I think I'll just go over and join Daniel. I think we could both use a drink," he disclosed and made a hasty exit to the bar.

Val patted Pamela's shoulder as she motioned to the back door of her house. "You best be getting Bob out of here before he goes after Daniel's hide again. I think we have proved our point."

"Your point? What point, Val?"

Val gave her a frustrated sigh. "He may only be a bartender, Pamela, but he will make a better father than Robert Patrick can ever hope to be. Daniel doesn't know about the baby. I figured that is something he needs to hear from you."

Pamela was about to turn to go when Val reached out and held her arm.

"And one more thing," Val spoke up beside her. "You'll never make a good politician's wife. Bob may want a career in politics but you can tell him from me, he'll never have one if he marries you."

Pamela stared into Val's bright blue eyes. "Do you know what he will do if I tell him that?"

"Yes," Val replied with a cheeky grin. "He'll let you go."

* * * *

In the car on the ride home from Val's, Pamela watched as Bob's face waned in and out of different shades of red. His nostrils flared and his knuckles shone white against the walnut steering wheel of his Mercedes.

"Bob, you need to calm down. You're going to have a stroke," she said, observing the pulsating artery in his neck.

"Don't tell me to calm down. Did you see what that piece of shit did in front of Val Easterling? I'm never going to be able to get her backing now," he shouted.

"Don't worry about Val. I talked to her and everything is fine. She wants to help you. She understands what happened and she told me—"

"You talked to Val about me?" he shouted, silencing her. "What? You two are such good friends now that you can talk about me while I'm fighting off your ex-boyfriends?"

Pamela rolled her eyes. "Christ, I can't talk to you when you are like this," she whispered.

"Don't do that, Pamela. Don't start with that condescending gaze of yours. I'm not an idiot."

She looked out the window as they traveled down St. Charles Avenue. "Well, tonight you reminded me of the hot-headed idiot I was married to all those years ago. You haven't changed one bit."

"But I have changed. I have a reputation to consider now. There were important people at that party tonight who know me, who can help me. I'm not a poor drunk's son anymore, Pamela. So stop treating me like one," he yelled.

"I'm not treating you any different than I've always treated you, Bob. You're still the same insecure, selfish asshole you always were. You didn't have to go after Daniel like that. You could have just walked away. But no, you had to prove yourself just like you always—"

"Of course I had to prove myself!" he yelled, halting her rebuke. "Do you know what people would say if I had walked away from confronting that bartender? I'm a prominent attorney known all over town as a force to be reckoned with. I can't just roll over and let my reputation be destroyed."

"Reputation? Bob, you're a personal injury lawyer, with a short fuse, who settles everything with his fists. Everyone in the city knows what you are, except you."

"What I am is a well-connected and influential attorney, Pamela. I'm not some broke wildlife rehabber who has to beg people for donations to keep herself and her animals fed. You need me to keep that miserable little shit hole of a zoo going."

"I don't need you, Bob. I'm beginning to wonder if I ever really did."

"But you need my money. Let's not forget whose name is still on that mortgage of yours," he boasted in a loud voice.

"I've already paid off the mortgage on the facility, Bob. I don't need your money."

He looked over at her. "Where in the hell did you get that kind of money?"

"Daniel," she replied. "It seems the bartender that punched you is really a rich man's son, after all. Daniel signed over his trust fund to me. He wanted me to have the money so I could be free of you."

Bob watched her for a second and then turned his eyes back to the road. The tension in his body eased a little. "But your kid still needs a father," he reminded her. "You're not married and you're facing a tough pregnancy. You need me."

"Do I?" She hesitated as she took in his profile. "I don't know, Bob. Is having a father who pushes everyone around and starts fights with total strangers, more important than having no father at all?"

"Every kid needs a mother and father," he said, sounding like the last word on the subject.

Pamela played with the engagement ring on her finger. "No, Bob. Every kid needs love. Every wife needs love. And no one should marry for convenience or as a business arrangement."

"Pamela, don't do this, not now." He slapped his hand angrily against the steering wheel. "It's been a crappy night and I'm in no mood for your hormonal outbursts."

She stared at the road ahead of them. "Tell me something. Did you ever love me, Bob, or was I just a great catch?"

"Listen to yourself. You sound like some love-struck schoolgirl fishing for a compliment. This isn't you. You have more class than this."

"Pull over, Bob," she demanded.

Bob glared at her. "What is it? Are you going to be sick? Don't get sick in the car. I just had it detailed," he pleaded.

Bob pulled the car over to the side of St. Charles Avenue.

Pamela opened the car door and stepped onto the pavement. She took in a few quick deep breaths. Once she had calmed herself, she leaned over and looked back at Bob in the car.

"What's the problem?" he shrugged. "If you're not going to be sick then get back in the car, Pamela."

"You want to know what the problem is, Bob? You really don't know who I am, and you have no intention of ever trying to get to know me. The sad part is, I don't think you really know who you are either." She pulled the ring off her finger and tossed it on to the passenger seat.

Bob grabbed the ring. "What's this? Are you kidding me? You're just going to call the whole thing off, here, in the middle of St. Charles Avenue? You're not being rational. Get back in this car, right now!"

"Good bye, Bob," Pamela proclaimed and slammed the car door.

She quickly hurried over to the neutral ground in the middle of St. Charles Avenue to a waiting streetcar. She boarded the streetcar and watched as Bob's silver Mercedes sped away from the curb and down the street. She took a seat on one of the old wooden benches near a window and sighed with relief. As the streetcar headed down St. Charles Avenue to the French Quarter, Pamela could not help but smile. It was as if a weight had been lifted from her shoulders. She took in the bright full moon above and smelled the hint of magnolia in the air. She eased her body back against the bench and let the rocking motion of the long green car soothe her cares away.

CHAPTER 18

Pamela walked through the open green wooden door and down the dark entrance leading to Daniel's French Quarter carriage house. As she stepped into the moonlit courtyard, she heard the sound of water trickling down the three-tiered brick fountain. All around her shadows from the azalea bushes danced eerily along the high garden walls.

"I wondered how long it would be before you showed up," a woman's voice said off to Pamela's left.

She turned to see T.J. Powell kneeling over a flowerpot in a pair of dirty blue jean overalls.

"Hello, Ms. Powell," Pamela said, nodding to Daniel's landlady. "What are you doing out here so late at night?"

"It's T.J., sweetheart. No one calls me anythin' but T.J. around here." The woman stood up from her flowerpot and wiped her hands on her dirty overalls. "I sometimes come out here at night and work in my garden when I can't sleep." She grinned at Pamela. "What's your excuse?"

"I came to see Daniel," she admitted.

"I told him you had come a callin'. Said you had been inquirin' about where he had disappeared to." She paused as she noted the apprehension in Pamela's eyes. "He's home," she assured her. "He came back about an hour ago from some fancy party. Looked mad enough to spit nails. He barely said hello to me before he went inside his cottage and slammed the door."

"I think that may be my fault. There are things he needs to know. Things I haven't been able to..." she let her voice fade away.

"Then you best go and talk to him. Make him listen to you. That's a good man in there," T.J. said as she nodded toward Daniel's place. "In my experience, good men are like peanut butter. They stick to you no matter what." T.J. turned away and headed back into the main house.

Pamela went over to the carriage house, took a deep breath, and gently wrapped on the front door.

She counted down the seconds as she stood waiting for him to appear, but Daniel never arrived. She knocked again and again, but still there was no answer. Images of Daniel hiding away in his bedroom, wanting to avoid her, began to take hold in her mind.

She quickly turned away from the door, deciding that perhaps coming here had been a mistake after all. She was just about to walk away when she heard the click of the doorknob behind her.

"Pamela?"

She turned around to see Daniel, covered with only a towel and standing dripping wet at his front door.

"I thought at first you weren't home." She directed her gaze to the garden walls not wanting to see his dark eyes staring into hers. "And then I figured perhaps you were home and just didn't want to see me."

Unexpectedly, he reached out and pulled her inside the house. Once she was safely behind the front door, he shut it and secured the deadbolt.

He turned and looked her over for a moment. "I was in the shower and heard someone at the door, but I wasn't expecting it to be you." Daniel wiped his wet hair back from his face.

Her heart fell to the floor. "You're expecting someone else. I'm sorry. I should go," she mumbled as she turned to leave.

He grabbed her arm, stopping her. "No, that didn't come out the right way." He paused and let go of her arm. "I meant I was expecting it to be T.J., not you, standing at my door in the middle of the night. How did you get here?"

"Streetcar. I made Bob pull over on the way home from the party and I took a streetcar to Canal Street. I walked from there."

He scowled angrily at her. "You shouldn't have been walking around the French Quarter alone at night, Pamela. It's not safe."

She smiled at his concern. "I wasn't alone. I followed one of those ghost tours to your gate." She threw her purse on the couch.

He sighed. "So what happened? Did you and Bob have a fight?"

She nodded. "I'm sorry he went after you like that at the party."

"I'm sure you didn't come here in the middle of the night to apologize for Bob." He glanced down at the towel wrapped around his waist. "Look, why don't you let me get some clothes on and then I can take you home."

She took in his muscular chest and her body ached with desire. Suddenly regretting her visit, she turned away from him. "I shouldn't have come here," she stated, grabbing for her purse.

"No! You're not going anywhere alone in the middle of the night." He took her hand and stepped over to the couch. "Sit here while I get dressed."

With the touch of his hand, Pamela's resolve faded away. She put her purse down and made herself comfortable on his beige couch.

Daniel gave her one last going over with his eyes. "You all right?" he asked, thoroughly analyzing her features. "You're really pale."

"Go get dressed, Daniel," she ordered in a weary voice as she waved him away. "I'm fine."

Daniel trotted up the stairs. She smiled as she observed the taught muscles in his back flex as he made it to the top of the open stairway and turned to go into his room. She noticed he left the bedroom door open.

"Feel free to get something to drink," he called out from the bedroom.

Pamela got up from the couch and went into his efficiency kitchen to investigate his refrigerator. As she made her way around the kitchen she smiled to herself. She wondered how a tall man like Daniel was managing in such a cramped kitchen. She opened the refrigerator door and spotted only a carton of orange juice, eggs, a loaf of bread, and a bottle of white wine. She pulled out the orange juice and started searching the cabinets for a glass. The only ones she could find were on a high top shelf above the sink. She tried to stand on her toes and grab for a glass. Just as she was about to give up, she saw a man's hand reaching up from behind her and remove a glass from the top shelf.

Pamela turned around to see Daniel leaning over her. His face was inches from hers and she could smell his spicy cologne on his skin. His wet hair was neatly combed back and he was wearing a long-sleeved white shirt and a black pair of slacks. His shirt was not yet buttoned up and she caught sight of his muscular chest beneath the white fabric.

She swallowed hard and tried to remind herself to be business-like. "Thank you," she said as she took the glass from his hand.

Daniel smiled at her. "You're welcome." He placed his hands on the sink behind her, pinning her between his arms. "So tell me, why are you here?" he whispered.

"I came…" She turned her face away from his, trying to collect her thoughts without having to look into his disconcerting eyes. "I came to talk to you about something," she finally got out.

"Something? That doesn't sound very good." He leaned back from her and folded his arms over his chest. "And should I be expecting your fiancé to come flying through the door anytime soon?"

"I don't think Bob and I are going to work out. Conflict of interest, you could say."

Daniel frowned. "Conflict of interest?"

She placed the glass on the counter next to her. "My interests conflicted with his," she added coyly. "And ever since you showed up at my house the other day I haven't—"

"You haven't been able to stop thinking of me, eh?" he interrupted, grinning.

BROKEN WINGS

She pushed him away. "You're impossible." She eased herself around him in the tiny kitchen and then headed for the front door.

"Admit it, Pamela," he challenged as he followed her out of the kitchen. "You can't stop thinking about me just like I can't stop thinking about you. Tell me you want to be with me and then that's it. We will see where this goes."

She stopped by the couch in the living room and turned around to face him. "See where this goes? I need more than that, Daniel. I can't just see where it goes. I can't be so cavalier in my affections," she angrily replied.

"I'm not being cavalier. I want to be with you. I want to spend every free moment I have with you, but I need to know you want to be with me."

She shook her head. "You're talking about dating, and I'm talking about a relationship."

"What difference does it make as long as we're together?!" he countered, raising his voice.

"It matters to me!" she shouted. "I need to know you will be there no matter what."

He sighed and ran his hand through his wet hair. "You're talking about if you get sick." He threw his hand up. "Of course I will be there. I want to be there for you."

"That's not it." She picked up her purse from the couch. "You're not ready for this kind of commitment," she said over her shoulder as she moved toward the front door.

Daniel came up behind her and placed his hand against the door, halting her retreat. "Pamela, talk to me," he urged over her shoulder.

Pamela stood before the door and closed her eyes for a moment. She wanted to tell him, but reason told her not to say a word. Her heart, however, was arguing for a different approach. She took a deep breath and then turned to him.

"What I need from you, Daniel, is a promise that no matter what happens to me, you will take care of any unfinished business I might leave behind."

His eyes began frantically searching hers. "What's going on? You said you have been sick. How sick are you, Pamela? You're talking as if you are dying."

"I'm not dying, just…"

"Just what?" he demanded in a rushed tone.

Pamela took his hand in hers. "There is a reason I went to Bob, even after you sent me the money. It's the same reason that I'm here now. I wanted to give you the option to decide if you want us." She placed his hand against her abdomen. She looked up into his face and watched as his dark eyes filled with understanding. "I'm almost three months along and the doctors say—"

She never got to finish her words. Daniel pulled her into his arms and covered her mouth with his.

"Why didn't you just tell me other day?" he whispered against her cheek.

She sighed with relief. "I wasn't sure what you would say and I didn't think you would want to have anything to do with us."

"Are you kidding me!" he shouted, with a huge grin on his face. "This is the best news in the world." He paused and leaned back from her. His grin fell away and his mood darkened. "What did your doctor say?" he asked, apprehensively.

Pamela pulled away slightly from his embrace. "This isn't going to be an easy pregnancy. I'm already considered a high-risk patient because of my lupus, and my kidney function has the obstetrician Bob found for me a little concerned."

"Maybe I should find you a better doctor," he said, frowning.

"Dr. Holdford is considered one of the top high-risk OBs in the area. I like him and I want to stay with him."

"I'm going to go with you to every appointment from now on." He pulled her close to him again.

She let her forehead rest against his chest. "I wasn't sure what you would think. I mean, we didn't have enough time together and a baby is a big responsibility. I didn't know if you would even want this baby," she murmured against him.

"So that's why you were going to marry Bob, for the baby?"

She nodded. "If something happens to me, I need to know this child will have a father. You were gone and I didn't know where else to turn."

"I'm such an idiot. I should never have left. But I'll make it up to you. I promise."

"You don't owe me anything, Daniel," she declared, stepping back from him. "Maybe you should take some time and think about this."

"Pamela, there is nothing to think about. You're going to have my baby and I couldn't be happier."

"But we never really got an opportunity to be together. Perhaps this will be cramping your style."

Daniel laughed, a deep, resounding laugh that lifted Pamela's heart. "Not a chance. I told you before, I want some roots. With you, and the baby, I'm finally going to be able to settle down and have a real home."

All the years of pain and conflict instantly melted away inside of Pamela, leaving a strange sense of completeness in its wake. It was as if she had needed to live through the heartache to appreciate the joy she now felt.

She stroked her hand up and down the front of his white shirt. "I have to admit there is something awfully compelling about you."

"Just think of me as a large, fuzzy squirrel," he told her as he leaned forward. He kissed her tenderly on the lips.

Pamela pulled away from him as her thoughts became inundated with doubt. "Maybe I should call a cab and give you some time to mull all of this over."

"Oh, no." He laughed. "You're not leaving, not now. We have plans to make. We have to decide on our living arrangements and how we're going to manage traveling between your facility in Folsom and my new business in the city. Then there are plans we need to make for the baby." He pulled her back into his arms. He kissed her cheek and then he let his mouth hover over hers. "So first things first," he whispered. "What side of the bed do you prefer?"

* * * *

Pamela was naked beneath the sheets curled up against Daniel's chest. He lay next to her in the bed, his arm behind her head, stroking her body up and down with his hand. She listened to his steady heartbeat echoing beneath his broad chest as her mind reflected on their frenzied lovemaking.

"I don't think I've been that flexible since college," she mumbled.

Daniel laughed and she listened as the deep sound thundered through his chest. "I thought you were such an uptight prude when we first met. And here we lay, naked and pregnant." He laughed once more.

She sat up in the bed. "We do have a lot ahead of us." She looked down at her flat belly. "Sometimes I still can't believe it."

"Did you ever want children?" he asked.

She pondered his question for a moment. "It's not that I didn't want them, but I never really thought about it much." She shrugged. "When I met Bob I assuumed we would have children and then—"

"You got sick," he said, finishing her words for her.

"No," she replied as she shook her head. "I got scared. The Bob I married was not the Bob I ended up married to. In the beginning, he was kind and caring and I thought, yeah, this is a good guy. But then he started turning into the man he is today: ambitious, cold, and heartless. We could have adopted or even tried surrogacy after I got sick, but the truth was, I really didn't want a child with him. A woman wants a child with a man she respects, admires, and loves. Bob, never made me feel any of those things for him, so I backed away and made excuses to myself. I blamed it on the lupus, but Bob was the real reason I didn't want a child."

He sat up next to her and ran his finger along the outline of her jaw. "And how do you feel now?" He paused as a shadow of regret passed over his face. "I could never stop thinking about you after I left. I wanted to call you a thousand times, but instead…"

"Instead you sent repairmen, and plumbers, and electricians. I understand, Daniel. I think this is a big step for both of us. Planning a future is a lot harder than walking away from one. But I think as long as we are willing to work at this, we might just have a chance."

He wrapped his arms around her. "Do you think you could ever love a thug?"

She smiled into his face. "As long as that thug is you."

ALEXANDREA WEIS

CHAPTER 19

The next few weeks were a blur for Pamela. Daniel was with her every minute he could get away from setting up his new office in the Central Business District of the city. During the day she would tend to her wildlife facility and train new volunteers to take over a large portion of the responsibilities she had overseen in the past. At night, Daniel would drive up to her place and they would spend the evenings on the back porch, enjoying the warm nights of summer.

"When the baby comes, we're going to need to make a decision about where we're going to live," Daniel said as he sat beside her on the porch steps one evening, admiring her growing belly.

Pamela sighed as she thought of leaving her beloved sanctuary. "I know. We will have to get a place in the city, so you can be close to your business, and I can be close to the hospital." She glimpsed the dogs lying next to her on the porch and a sudden stab of guilt tore across her heart. She did not want to leave them, but she knew they would never be happy living in a small yard in the city.

He noted the sorrow in her face and put a consoling arm around her shoulders. "We could stay here," he suggested. "Dr. Holdford says you're doing well now that you are in the middle of your second trimester."

She nodded her head as she patted her slight bulge. "For now. But as the baby grows things will get harder for me, and being close to a hospital is probably a good idea. And you will need to be in the city more once they finish renovating your office building."

"How about some place in between, like Mandeville," he offered. "It's on the north shore of Lake Pontchartrain, has a few good hospitals, is not a bad commute for me, and it's away from the city. I don't think moving back to the city would be good for you."

Pamela gave him a wary glance. "What makes you say that?"

He removed his arm from about her shoulders and nonchalantly shrugged, as if trying to allay her concern. "I don't want you exposed to anything that reminds you of your former life with Bob. You weren't happy then and I want you to be happy now. Being someplace where we can make our own memories would be best, for both of us."

She contemplated his face for several seconds. "Nice speech," she finally said. "Why don't you want to move back to the city, Daniel?"

He sighed as he observed the sun setting on her facility. "What are you, psychic?"

"Not psychic. You're trying too hard to keep us out of the city. Why?" She frowned at him. "And don't sugarcoat it. I'm pregnant, not stupid."

He sat for a moment and collected his thoughts. When he turned to her, his eyes were filled with trepidation. "Bob found out that we got back together and has been spreading some nasty rumors around about me, you, and the baby," he told her in a calm voice.

She appeared surprised. "What kind of rumors?"

"That the baby isn't mine. He's telling everyone the child is his and that you left him because you saw dollar signs with me. He's trying to turn people against you." He hesitated for an instant. "And by people I mean patrons," he added.

"That son of a bitch!" She yelled. The dogs all jumped to their feet and stared anxiously at Pamela. "And how did you find this out?" she angrily questioned.

"Val called me after Bob had a chat with her at some political function. She said he basically ranted against the both of us and blamed my wealth for your final betrayal. She knows Bob is full of shit, but the Robillards don't. She saw him talking to the couple at the same party."

Pamela cursed under her breath. "That would explain why their accountant called me last week and said they would have to withdraw their funding for personal reasons." She shook her head. "Well, we don't need them. With your trust fund and some good business decisions, we'll be fine."

Daniel patted his hand on her knee. "I have a sneaking suspicion that Bob's antics have not been limited to just your wildlife facility, Pamela."

An uneasy knot nudged its way forward in her stomach. "What do you mean?" she anxiously asked.

Daniel rubbed his hands together and looked down at the porch steps. "I think he may be trying to put up a couple of roadblocks for my business. City inspectors have been out to my office building numerous times, claiming I didn't have the proper inspection stickers for the water heaters or the fire hydrants. They even said my business sign was not up to code. I've had problems with the landlord wanting to change the lease. He says a friend told him that I'm not good for the rent and is now demanding three months' advanced payment. My office staff keeps quitting for personal reasons, but the problems aren't limited to just my business. My landlady has even been threatened."

Pamela's jaw dropped. "T.J.? Why would anyone threaten her?"

"She got an unidentifiable phone call telling her to get rid of me as her tenant or else her safety, and the safety of her other tenants, would be in jeopardy. She came by and told me about it last week."

Pamela stood up on the porch step. "We have to do something. Confront him, or at the very least, have a lawyer contact him."

Daniel stood up next to her. "I don't think that would be a very good idea," he conceded. "Bob is angry and anything we do to address the situation might provoke him further."

She stared into Daniel's calm face. "I would have thought you would be the one who would suggest fighting Bob at this point. But you seem so relaxed and not bothered by the whole thing."

"He can't really hurt me, only aggravate me a little. My import business is very much removed from his sphere of influence and he may try to pull some antics in the beginning, but he will soon grow bored. And why should I let him bother me?" He pulled her into his arms. "I won. I got you and the baby."

"But what about the lies he is spreading about us. Doesn't that make you angry?" she asked.

He leaned back from her and nodded. "Before I met you, yes, that would have sent me on a tirade and I would have gone over there and confronted him. Probably gotten in another fight and gone back to jail." He paused and smiled at her. "But I'm not angry anymore. All the hate, hostility, and tension I always carried around have left me. I have a future to care about now. And that has changed my entire outlook."

She made a fist and lightly tapped it against his chest. "I wish I could be so calm. I want to go over there and kill the bastard."

Daniel chuckled. "Darling, you're pregnant. You're not thinking very clearly right now."

"Yes, I am thinking clearly," she argued.

"Pamela, last week you wanted to eat a steak for dinner and you're a vegetarian."

"Very funny." She stepped out of his embrace and walked over to the edge of the porch. "So what do you suggest we do?" she inquired as she took in the last vestiges of daylight.

"Let's just wait this one out. If it gets too out of hand, I will go over to his office and have a chat with him."

Pamela shook her head as she thought of her ex-husband. "It won't end peacefully, I can guarantee that," she insisted. "Bob has been fighting with the world as long as I can remember. When we were married he used to be known up and down St. Charles Avenue as the rampaging Robert Patrick."

He came up beside her. "And what's his excuse for being that way?"

"A past he's ashamed of, a drunken father who beat the hell out of him as a child, there are a number of reasons. He was good at keeping it under control when we were first together, but about six months after we were married, the real Bob suddenly appeared. We were out at a restaurant having dinner and he started a fight with the waiter. The kid was eighteen and was just being polite, but Bob went after him because he thought the poor guy was hitting on me."

Daniel took in her profile in the fading light. "Why didn't you leave him then?"

"I had watched my father go through four marriages and I swore I wasn't going to end up like him. So I stayed until Bob didn't want me anymore."

Daniel nudged her with his shoulder. "And when we are married, are you just going to take my crap, as well?" he asked softly. "Or are you going to remind me that I'm turning into Bob and threaten to leave me if I don't change."

She turned to him. "When we are married?" She tempered her excitement. "Are we getting married?" she calmly inquired.

He placed his hands about her waist. "I've wanted to bring it up, and while we're on the subject... I think we should make this legal before the baby comes."

She backed away from him. "Don't use the baby as an excuse for marriage. We could just live together and see how things go."

He moved closer to her, his dark eyes seemingly lit from within. "Then marry me because I love you and want to spend the rest of my days with you," he demanded.

A reluctant smile worked its way across Pamela's delicate face. "Are you sure?"

"Absolutely. I have never been so sure of anything before in my life. You make me happy."

Pamela shrugged, trying to appear unflustered as her heart quivered with happiness. "Then I guess we're engaged."

"Don't be so cavalier in your affections," he teased.

"I'm trying to be reserved, not cavalier," she informed him.

Daniel placed his arms about her. "Why don't you just tell me how you really feel," he suggested.

"How I really feel?" Pamela wrapped her arms about his neck. "Hungry!"

* * * *

Not long after the renovations to Daniel's business offices were completed, Pamela was putting the finishing touches on his private office. After she had hung the last picture on the wall, Pamela surveyed the room. She had decorated the pale yellow walls with framed photos of the animals that had passed through her facility. The pictures, and luxurious tan leather furniture, gave the office a peaceful ambience. Just as she was about to step down from the ladder, she felt the baby kick.

"Yeah, I like it too," she whispered, rubbing her protruding belly.

"Damn it, Pamela!" Daniel shouted as he came into the room. "What did I tell you about hanging pictures in here? I'm supposed to be going up and down on ladders, not you." He grabbed her hand and made sure both her feet were firmly planted on the floor before he reproached her with his eyes.

"You're being overprotective," she objected.

"You know me better than that. Dr. Holdford is the one who said you should be taking it easy. He told you not to stress your body in any way. No more exertion." He folded the ladder and moved it to the side.

"Do you like it?" she asked, waving around the room.

Daniel inspected the pictures of foxes, squirrels, skunks, Lester, as well as Rodney, covering his office walls. He pulled Pamela into his arms. "It's wonderful. It's like having a piece of your sanctuary here with me. And you put my little Pamela and her babies up there as well. Thank you."

BROKEN WINGS

Pamela nodded to the photograph of the flying squirrel family. "It was the last picture I took of her and the three babies before I released them. I figured if you're having a bad day, you can just look at the pictures and maybe it will help you to relax."

He felt the baby kick. "She's feisty today."

Pamela rolled her eyes. "Tell me about it."

Daniel gave her face a thorough going over with his eyes. "Are you all right? You look tired."

"I'm fine." She gingerly patted his cream dress shirt and red tie. "Where were you? You said you would meet me here half an hour ago. Were you held up in your meeting?"

"No, I had an errand to run after my meeting." Daniel reached into his pants pocket and pulled out a small blue velvet box. "I didn't want to tell you about it before because I wanted to pick this out myself." He handed her the box.

Inside Pamela found a diamond ring with three large round cut stones set side by side in white gold. She looked from the ring to Daniel.

"I figured we needed to get rolling on this wedding of ours." He pointed to the ring. "This is the first step."

"Daniel, it's beautiful," she said, admiring the ring.

He took the ring out of the box and placed it on the third finger of her left hand. "I don't know how you will feel about this but Val called me and I told her about our plans. She wants us to have our wedding at her place in the French Quarter. I said we wanted something small and she offered her house for the ceremony and reception." He searched her face for a reaction. "What do you think?" he anxiously asked.

"I'm stunned Val would want to do that for us," Pamela replied.

"She likes you. And she has always been a good friend to me."

"Well, if she wants to go to all of that trouble. It sounds like a wonderful idea."

"I told Val I would talk to you about it. She said she could take care of all the details but she needs to get together with you to find out what you want. It is your wedding after all."

Pamela shook her head. "I have no idea what I want, but definitely something simple and quick."

"Sounds great to me. I'll call Val and let her know," Daniel said.

Pamela gazed down at the ring on her hand. "When Bob gave me that ring after we had made our arrangement, I felt so empty inside. But now I feel like the world is filled with so much hope."

Daniel placed his hand over hers. "There is something else." He paused. "Val called me to give me some news about Bob. You remember you told me once that a patron owned the fifty acres next to your facility and that you would release animals there?"

Pamela felt all the happiness that had filled her heart suddenly melt away. "Bob owns that property," she mumbled.

"Well, not anymore. Val said Bob is going around telling everyone in the city that he sold the property to a developer. They want to put a posh subdivision there. And you know what will happen then."

She wrung her hands together and her eyes filled with dread. "My animals will be trapped and killed if they go into residential neighborhoods."

Daniel nodded in agreement. "And if enough neighbors complain, you could have problems with the zoning commission, animal control, and the Department of Wildlife and Fisheries."

"But where I live is surrounded by horse and cattle farms. They can't just rezone the whole area," Pamela reasoned.

"You know as well as I do how urban sprawl begins, Pamela. First, they take over the land and displace the animals. Then, with time, they force out the original residents until all that is left is concrete and manicured gardens."

A single tear trickled down Pamela's pale cheek. "That place is all I have, Daniel."

"It will be all right, Pamela," he whispered. He wiped the tear away and gave her an encouraging smile. "Val had an idea. She knows the developer. She suggested we make the guy a counter-offer for the property, or at the very least go in with him on the development. She says she knows for a fact that with the economy

BROKEN WINGS

being the way it is, the developer is going to have a tough time getting funding from any of the local banks. She proposed we go to him with our idea."

"What idea?" Pamela questioned as she felt her curiosity stir.

The heaviness in Daniel's heart lifted as he saw the tears retreating from her eyes. "If he doesn't want to sell the land, then we offer to fund the development on the condition that he will make it a nature friendly subdivision."

Pamela considered his words for a few moments, and then asked, "What exactly is a nature friendly subdivision?"

"I wrote down some thoughts on that." Daniel walked over to his dark oak desk and picked up a pad of paper. "You know how so many subdivisions have restrictions about keeping lots cut and cleared of debris, and even tell builders how and where to build? We could do the same thing, but make it less destructive for the woods and animals that will be displaced by the construction." He stepped back over to Pamela's side as he glanced down at the pad in his hand. "Maybe we could limit the amount of the land that is cleared and offer larger lots to potential residents. Put in non-trapping and no killing restrictions in the subdivision rules to protect animals that are not a threat. Encourage the use of green building materials that are environmentally friendly. Have an education center for people who want to aid in preserving the animal friendly environment." He raised his eyes to her. "You could offer wildlife rehabilitation and living with wildlife classes to all those who are interested. Design and develop a living area that is animal friendly instead of animal fearful. You know there are other animal nuts in the world, and I bet they would be willing to pay to live in a subdivision that tries to preserve nature instead of trying to conquer it."

Pamela shook her head, appearing doubtful. "That all sounds great in theory, Daniel, but has anyone ever done it before?"

He shrugged and he held up the pad of paper to her. "Every idea has growing pains, Pamela. But I think if we give this a try, we just might be setting a precedent for the way communities of the future are planned. You told me once that if the human race can't be kind to animals, then how in the hell are we going to be kind to each other? Maybe this is the first step."

She peered down at the diamond engagement ring on her finger. "All right, so what do we do next?"

"Val gave me the developer's name and number; let's give him a call and see what he says," Daniel said as he pulled a slip of paper from his front trouser pocket.

Pamela's happiness quickly returned. "Thank you, Daniel. Thank you for doing this."

"Don't thank me just yet. Let's see what happens first."

Pamela looked into Daniel's dark eyes and was amazed to realize that the brooding, almost sinister quality she had first noted there only a few months before had been an illusion. What she had originally taken to be a wild nature had turned out to be a kind and caring person wanting only to be understood and not mistreated. *Funny*, she thought to herself, *how much animals and people have in common.*

CHAPTER 20

One month later, Daniel and Pamela arrived at Emeril's Delmonico on St. Charles Avenue for their rehearsal dinner. Daniel escorted Pamela back to the private room Val had reserved for the small wedding party. When they stepped into the rectangular room, decorated with old pictures of St. Charles Avenue and streetcars, Pamela saw Carol and Ian, already seated and waiting for them. Ian was dressed in a fitted blue suit and Carol was wearing a pale pink dress with small white flowers on it. Her long, light brown hair was curled and framed her lovely face.

"Hey there," Carol called out as she rose from her chair and walked over to hug Pamela. "Ready to call the whole thing off yet?" she joked.

"Very funny, Carol," Daniel replied. "But Pamela has no intention of running out on me, right?" He glanced over at Pamela and raised his eyebrows inquisitively.

"Don't count your chickens before they hatch, buddy," Pamela remarked as she patted her hand against his gray suit jacket.

Daniel laughed and walked over to Ian. "Ian, make sure Carol doesn't get pregnant. A whole new side of them comes out when they are expecting. It's a side you do not want to know, trust me."

Carol pulled Pamela to the side, away from the men. "Are you feeling all right?" She asked as she examined Pamela's face. "You look kind of green."

Pamela waved off her concern "I think it's the dress," she said, nodding to the dark green print dress she had on. "Daniel said the same thing to me before we left his place."

"He still has his place? I thought he was going to move into your new house in Mandeville."

"In two weeks. We figured we would get the wedding out of the way first, then move in together. That will give me a month to get the nursery set up before I have to go in for my scheduled c-section."

"And how is my little girl?' Carol asked and lovingly placed her hands on Pamela's large belly.

"Kicking up a storm! You should see me, Carol. All the planning meetings I've had to attend for construction of the new educational facility, and I can barely sit still for ten minutes before I have to run to the bathroom. It's amazing we're getting anything done."

"Well, thank God that developer decided to sell you the land next door. Now you can have the kind of wildlife facility you always wanted. I think the new education center for children is a great idea. I can't wait for them to start construction."

Pamela nodded. "But Daniel hasn't completely given up on his animal friendly subdivision idea. We think maybe down the road we might try to develop part of the property to see if such a concept will work."

Carol laughed. "It will work, Pamie. Just don't take on too much. I think you'll have your hands pretty full after the baby comes."

Pamela looked down at her belly. "I never thought I would ever be this lucky, Carol."

Carol patted her arm and smiled. "You deserve it, Pamie."

"Hey, Pamela," Ian said as he came up and gave Pamela a kiss on the cheek. "Daniel was just tellin' me how difficult livin' with a pregnant woman is."

Pamela gave Daniel a dirty look. "Thanks," she grumbled.

"So are we the only ones comin' tonight?" Ian asked as he waved his hand across the long table next to them. "I see quite a few place settin's here. Do we even know this many people?"

"Val and Lance are coming, along with a few of the volunteers from the facility," Pamela announced. "Daniel's father is flying in as we speak so he should be here shortly, and then there is Daniel's landlord T.J." Pamela paused and counted the places set around the table. "That leaves two extra places. Who else did Val invite?" she asked Daniel.

Daniel cleared his throat. "I, ah, invited two extra people," he mumbled.

Pamela noted the glint of apprehension in his eyes. "Who?"

"Your father and your stepmother," he declared. "I called your father last week and told him about the baby and about us. I thought he might like to know that he was going to be a grandfather."

Pamela felt as if the wind had just been knocked out of her. She reached out for the back of a nearby chair. Carol instantly put a caring arm about her waist.

"And what did he say?" Pamela asked, trying to remain calm.

Daniel gave Pamela a heartfelt smile. "That he wanted to come. He wanted the opportunity to make things right between you two again."

"You should have said something. You should have warned me," she reprimanded, her voice tinged with frustration.

Daniel placed his hands behind his back and frowned. "I've learned over the past few weeks, Pamela, that warning you is as good as giving you the opportunity to change your plans. I figured it would be best if I just surprised you with this."

"Damn," Carol remarked to Daniel. "You're a brave man."

Pamela's gray eyes were roasting with fury. "Daniel Phillips, I can't believe you could do something so—"

A shadow crossed the entrance to the private room, stopping Pamela's rant in mid-sentence. When she turned and saw who was standing in the doorway, her heart rose to her throat.

"What a quaint little party," Bob sneered and then walked through the door.

He was dressed in a dark blue suit and holding a glass in his right hand filled with ice and a dark amber liquid that Pamela knew had to be his favorite drink, bourbon. She could tell by his bloodshot eyes and the slight sway of his body that this was not his first drink of the evening.

"Imagine my surprise when a little birdie told me about your pre-wedding party here tonight. I figured I would just come by and kiss the bride," he asserted, slurring his words slightly as he moved further into the private dining room.

"Oh, shit," Carol cursed under her breath.

"You need to leave, Bob," Daniel growled as he went up to him.

"No way," Bob cried out as he tried to push Daniel aside. "I deserve a kiss. After all, she was almost my bride until you came back in the picture." Bob took a step back from Daniel, carefully trying to keep his drink from spilling. "When you left her knocked up and alone, I thought I could make her want me again. I could get her to come back to me. I was going to be a father to her child and I was going to have the happy life I deserved. And now everyone is laughing at me behind my back. My political hopes are ruined because of her. My dreams are destroyed. She was mine first, not yours! I discovered her. I molded her into the refined ice princess she is today."

"Shut up, Bob." Pamela shouted. "You didn't mold me. You didn't do a damn thing but make me miserable for eight years. Everything was about status and money with you. What other people were thinking was always so important to you. But why in the hell did any of that matter? You could have risen above your upbringing and been a better person than your father, but instead you channeled all your anger into your fists. You intimidate and threaten everyone you meet and the only way you feel better about who you are is by hitting someone."

Bob snickered. "That's right, Pamela. I'm angry because I've had to work real damned hard for everything in my life. I didn't have a rich daddy. I didn't have the world handed to me on a silver platter like you." Bob looked over at Daniel. "She ever tell you how much she always hated me? She saw me as nothing more than a poor drunk's son. She never respected me or feared me. She was like a wild mare," he said, raising his voice. "I could never get the bitch to break."

"You bastard," Pamela hissed. She clenched her fists and her pale face filled with color. "I was your wife, not a piece of property."

"But you were my property. I owned you, just like I owned that little shit hole of a zoo you love so much. I had you under my control for all of those years and I relished it. You had to come to me, to beg money from me, and I loved every minute of it."

"Get that sick asshole out of here," Carol shouted as she took a protective step in front of Pamela.

"Get out, Bob!" Daniel yelled, pointing to the door.

"Not without my wife," Bob cried out and threw his drink to the ground. He lunged toward Pamela, grabbing at the sleeve of her dress and pulling her to the floor.

Daniel grabbed Bob by the back of his jacket collar and pulled him away from Pamela.

"Pamie!" Carol screamed as she went to the floor to help Pamela.

Daniel was struggling to get Bob to the door when two waiters arrived to see what all the commotion was about. They quickly went to Daniel's side and helped subdue Bob. The waiters carried Bob out of the private dining room.

When Daniel walked back into the room, Pamela was seated in a chair. Carol was frantically fanning her bright red face with a napkin.

"Pamela," Daniel whispered as he came to her side. He knelt down next to her chair and took her hand.

He saw the pink color spreading from her cheeks down her neck and underneath the low collar of her dress. Her gray eyes appeared glassy and her respirations were quick and shallow.

"What's wrong?" he asked, running his eyes over every inch of her face.

"I don't feel very good. Daniel, I think..." Her eyes fluttered. "I think..." She slumped over in the chair.

"Shit!" Daniel picked her up out of the chair. "Carol, call the emergency room and tell them I'm on my way."

"Wait," Carol cried out. "Maybe we shouldn't move her. I'll call 911," she said as tears began welling up in her pale blue eyes.

"No time!" Daniel yelled as he marched to the door. "Just call now! I can get her there faster than an ambulance." He went out of the room, carrying Pamela in his arms.

Carol grabbed a stunned Ian's hand next to her. "Come on!" she screamed at him. "We're going with them."

CHAPTER 21

"We don't have a lot of time to think here, Daniel," Dr. Holdford said in a private family waiting room outside of the emergency room entrance. "It's her kidneys. Her numbers have been getting steadily worse as the baby has developed. I was hoping we could get her to eight months, but we don't have a choice anymore. She has reached a critical point where the toxins in her blood are building too rapidly now. We could put her on dialysis and try to buy the baby more time, but I'm afraid if we don't take the baby now, we may lose Pamela and your child."

Daniel sat on a red couch across from Dr. Holdford's chair, his head in his hands.

"I can't lose her, and if she loses the baby, Christ, I don't know what she will do."

Dr. Holdford placed a reassuring hand on Daniel's shoulder. "The best thing to do is take the baby. It's early but the little girl is almost to the critical seven-month mark, and with today's technology she's got a real good shot."

Daniel looked up into the man's round face. "And what about Pamela? Will everything go back to normal once you deliver the baby?"

"I can't say. Her body has been through a hell of a lot. We'll just have to wait and see how she does after the baby is born," Dr. Holdford confided with a grave face.

Daniel said nothing and simply nodded his approval.

"I'll get her up to surgery right away for an emergency c-section, and you'll need to go to the desk and sign the consents." Dr. Holdford stood from his chair.

"Can I see her?" Daniel asked.

Dr. Holdford nodded. "They'll be taking her up to surgery in the next few minutes. I'm sorry, Daniel. I wish I could give you more encouraging news, but I promise we will do everything we can to save Pamela and the baby." He turned and slowly made his way out of the private room, limping as he went.

When Dr. Holdford reached the doorway, he stopped and turned to Daniel. "Don't give up on her. She's a tough woman, Daniel." He paused and gave him a reassuring smile. "I've been where she is, and when you have something to live for, you fight to live." He turned and exited the room, quietly shutting the door behind him.

Daniel sat back on the couch and for the first time since he had been shot in Iraq, he fought back tears. All the frustration, fear, anger, and hopelessness that had ricocheted throughout his body when the bullets ripped into him came clamoring back. He tried with every ounce of faith he had to hold it together. He rubbed his hands on his face and took in several deep breaths before he went to the door. As he placed his hand on the door handle, he pulled his shoulders back and willed himself to believe that everything was going to be all right.

* * * *

Pamela was lying on a gurney, being prepped for surgery by a petite nurse with a long ponytail of golden hair, when Daniel walked into the room. Pamela was still groggy, but she smiled when she saw him enter her little cubicle.

"I guess this is it," she said softly as she held her hand out to him.

He went over to her bedside and took her hand. "I talked to Dr. Holdford," Daniel told her, putting a reassuring smile on his face. "He says everything is going to be just fine."

"Daniel, I worked as an EMT for years. I know how to read laboratory results. So don't bullshit me." She paused and smiled for him. "I want you to do everything for our baby. I don't care about my life, just save our little girl."

"Pamela, don't talk like that," he gently scolded. "You're going to be just fine."

"Daniel, I have fought with my body for so long, I know when I'm losing the battle. You must promise me you will take care of Elizabeth."

He squeezed her hand. "We never agreed on the name Elizabeth."

"She is to be named after your mother. You're the one with the fond memories of your mother, not me. And I want you to teach her about animals. All the things I taught you. That's all I ask. The rest I will leave up to you." She paused and lovingly stared into his dark eyes. "You're going to be such a good father," she whispered.

"I'm sorry, Ms. Wells," the nurse said as she started to unlock the gurney wheels. "We have to take you up to surgery now." The nurse nodded to Daniel. "We've got to go, Mr. Phillips."

Two more women dressed in blue scrubs entered the room.

Pamela sighed as she closed her eyes. "I really would have liked to have become Mrs. Phillips."

Daniel leaned over and kissed her forehead. "You will be Mrs. Phillips one day, Pamela. I promise."

Daniel watched helplessly as the nurses quickly wheeled the gurney out of the room. He looked down to the array of debris covering the floor that had been tossed there when the emergency room team had gone to work on Pamela soon after they had arrived. He ran his hands through his hair and tried to suppress the sickening feeling of fear growing inside of him. He knew there was nothing else for him to do now, except wait and pray.

EPILOGUE

"Daddy," a little girl cried out as she came running up to Daniel carrying a clear plastic container in her hands.

Daniel was in the barn struggling to feed three rambunctious baby raccoons when he saw a bouncing mass of dirty blonde curls come running toward him.

She had Pamela's gray eyes, heart-shaped face, petite frame, and even her determined walk. But on the inside, Daniel felt she had inherited more of his impatience and boisterous temperament than her mother's cool demeanor.

"Bitsy," he called out to the child. "What are you doing out here? Isn't Uncle Ian supposed to be watching television with you?"

"He's no fun," the little girl complained as she turned her big gray eyes to him. "He fell asleep on the couch, again. Why does he always do that?"

Daniel struggled to put the baby raccoons in their cage. "I think being married to your Auntie Carol is wearing your Uncle Ian out."

"Huh?" Bitsy wrinkled up her face.

Daniel frowned. "I'll tell you about it when you're older."

"How come Maw Maw Val and Grandpa Ed never fall asleep when they come over to see me? Auntie Carol said they are old and that old people always sleep a lot and smell funny. Uncle Ian falls asleep a lot and he smells funny too. So is Uncle Ian old?"

"My father and your godmother are not old. Neither is Uncle Ian," he assured the little girl. "I think Daddy needs to have a talk with Auntie Carol," he mumbled.

The little girl held up the container in her hands to Daniel. "Look, Daddy. Mrs. Bird is much better today. Can I let her go now?"

Daniel kneeled down and looked at the fawn and white dove nesting in the straw covering the bottom of the container. He removed the lid, gently reached inside, and ran his fingers along the bird's damaged left wing. He felt for the small knot just along the line of flight feathers. The callus that had formed over the break seemed just about set.

"The break does appear to be almost healed," he told his daughter. "We can try and let her go today. See if she can fly with that wing."

"Can we take her to Mommy?" Bitsy asked. "I want to show Mommy how well Mrs. Bird is doing."

Daniel ran his hands over his daughter's silky blonde hair and sighed. "You do know Mommy is…" He nodded. "Sure, sweetheart. We can go and see Mommy."

The little girl grabbed her father's hand and they strolled out of the barn together.

* * * *

As they rode through the trail in the woods surrounding the little blue cottage, Daniel once again made sure the container with the bird was securely fastened to the ATV. Behind him, he could feel his daughter hugging her small arms around his waist as he very slowly made his way along the cleared path.

After five minutes, the ATV emerged in a large clearing. In the center of the clearing, a tall beige metal building stood with wide windows and a shiny tin roof. A sign above the door of the building read "Second Chance Wildlife Rehabilitation Education Center."

Just as Daniel pulled the four-wheeler up to the side of the building, two large metal doors flew open and a group of teenagers came barreling outside. They eventually made their way over to some picnic tables under a group of trees not far from the edge of the building.

"I guess Auntie Carol's class got out early," Daniel said as he grabbed his daughter from behind him and placed both her feet on the ground next to the ATV.

He handed her the container. "Here, hold Mrs. Bird while I take off your helmet," he instructed as he waited for the child to grab hold of the plastic box with both hands. Once he knew she had a firm grip on the container, he lifted the red helmet from her head.

"Hey, you two," Carol called out as she started down the steps from the building.

She came alongside the ATV. "What you got there, Bits?" Carol asked as she eyed the plastic box.

"Mrs. Bird. I wanted to show her to Mommy," Bitsy said as she looked up into Carol's face. "Oh, yeah." She rolled her big gray eyes. "Uncle Ian fell asleep on the couch again. Daddy says he's tired all the time because he married you. Is that true?"

Carol grinned at Daniel. "Well, honey, Uncle Ian is just catching up on his rest. Maybe he's still tired from the wedding. It was a really big wedding after all. You remember. You were my flower girl." Carol leaned over and tickled the little girl.

Bitsy started wiggling and giggling as she tried to get away from Carol's fingers.

Daniel grabbed the box holding the bird from his daughter before she dropped it.

After Carol stopped tickling her, Bitsy turned to her father. "Can I go see Mommy now?"

Daniel nodded. "Go on. Aunt Carol and I will be right behind you."

Daniel watched as his daughter took off around the side of the building.

"Do you think she understands?" Carol asked as she watched Bitsy running on ahead.

Daniel glanced down at the bird nestled comfortably in the container in his hands. "She knows something isn't right, but what do you tell her? She's only five, Carol. How do you explain death to a five-year-old?" He turned from Carol and headed after Bitsy.

Carol shrugged as she fell in step beside him. "Try starting with the truth," she suggested.

"The truth?" Daniel raised his dark brows at her. "Somehow I don't think the truth is going to help explain why Ian falls asleep every time he comes over to the house."

Carol laughed. "You're right. Let's just keep her in the dark for a few more years on that one, shall we?"

"Just give Ian a break; I think you're killing him."

"Hey, the fertility doctor said we need to do it as often as possible if we're going to get pregnant," Carol explained.

Daniel stopped and shook his head. "Carol, please. I have enough nightmares rolling around in my head without adding you and Ian to the mix."

Carol halted in front of him and looked up into his face. "Do those nightmares still include Bob? The other day when you were on the phone with Pamie's father, I overheard you telling him that you're going to make a statement at that Bar Association meeting against reinstating Bob Patrick's attorney privileges."

"Doc and I both feel the man should never be allowed to practice law again after what he did to her," he growled as he walked around her.

Carol turned and tried to catch up with him. "Bob paid his dues, Daniel. He lost his law practice, his house, his powerful friends, and eventually one year of his freedom. I don't think even Pamie would have wanted him to suffer that much for pushing her to the ground," she asserted as she came alongside of him.

As they rounded the corner of the building they came across a small graveyard. Set at the edge of the clearing against the green woods, hand made crosses and makeshift headstones of rocks with names carved into them were arranged in rows behind a black iron fence.

Daniel anxiously gazed about the small cemetery. "Where is she?"

BROKEN WINGS

Just as he was about to call out for his daughter, a slender, blond woman emerged from the brush next to the cemetery holding his daughter's hand. When she saw Daniel and Carol standing at the edge of the iron fence, she waved.

Daniel watched as Pamela walked hand in hand with Bitsy to a fresh grave. In Pamela's left hand were some wildflowers. As she kneeled before the grave and placed the flowers on top of it, a ray of sunlight reflected off the gold wedding band on her left hand.

Bitsy tilted her head to the side as she pondered the grave for a moment. "Is Rodney resting now, Mommy?" she eventually asked.

Pamela caressed her daughter's pink cheek. "Yes, baby. Rodney is happy now. He's free."

"Will we see him again?" Bitsy persisted.

"One day, most definitely," Pamela proclaimed. "Love never dies, Bits. It goes on forever."

"She wanted to show you Mrs. Bird," Daniel said as he walked up to Pamela and leaned over to kiss her cheek. "You all right, Mrs. Phillips?" He worriedly searched her gray eyes.

"I'm good, Mr. Phillips," she reassured him.

He handed her the plastic container.

"What's going on with Mrs. Bird?" Pamela queried as she cradled the box in her lap.

"She's ready to fly away, Mommy," Bitsy told her.

Pamela gazed up at Daniel. "Are you sure the broken wing is healed?"

He nodded at the container. "All healed. She's good to go."

"So can she fly now, Mommy?" Bitsy eagerly questioned.

Pamela looked from her daughter's angelic face to Daniel's dark brown eyes. "Yes, baby, she can fly now. It's time to let her have her chance to spread her wings and try to touch the sky."

The End

ABOUT THE AUTHOR

Alexandrea Weis is a registered nurse from New Orleans who has been writing novels and screenplays for over twenty years. Her first novel, To My Senses, was a finalist for commercial fiction in Eric Hofer Book Awards, a finalist for romance in the Foreword Magazine Book of the Year awards, and a finalist for romance in the USA Book Awards. Her second novel, Recovery, was ranked #1 on the Amazon top rated for romantic suspense in kindle books. Buyer Group International, an independent production company in Austin, has optioned the motion picture rights for Recovery.

Ms. Weis is also a permitted wildlife rehabber with the Louisiana Wildlife and Fisheries and when she is not writing, Ms. Weis is rescuing orphaned and injured wildlife. She lives outside of New Orleans with her husband and a menagerie of pets.

Made in the USA
Charleston, SC
07 February 2012